CHEYENNE

COMANCHEROS/WAR PARTY
JUDD COLE

LEISURE BOOKS NEW YORK CITY

A LEISURE BOOK®

April 1998

Published by

Dorchester Publishing Co., Inc.
276 Fifth Avenue
New York, NY 10001

ISBN 0-8439-4382-3

COMANCHEROS

Prologue

Twenty winters before the Bluecoats fought the Graycoats in the bloody war between the hair faces, a band of Northern Cheyenne warriors led by Chief Running Antelope was attacked by pony soldiers in a surprise pincer movement near the North Platte River. Running Antelope, his wife Lotus Petal, and 30 others were massacred.

The sole survivor was the squalling infant clutched in the dead chief's arms—Running Antelope's son, whose Cheyenne name was now lost forever. The baby was returned to the Wyoming Territory settlement of Bighorn Falls. Adopted by John Hanchon and his barren wife Sarah, the child was named Matthew and raised as their own son.

Matthew worked in his parents' mercantile store and, at first, felt accepted in his limited world despite occasional hostile stares and remarks from strangers. But during his sixteenth year he fell in love with Kristen Steele. Kristen's bitter, Indian-hating father, Hiram, had the youth savagely beaten for meeting secretly with his daughter. Steele also warned Matthew that another attempt to meet with Kristen would get him killed.

But soon the threats widened to include his white parents. A young cavalry officer named Seth Carlson, who had staked a claim to Kristen's hand, was humiliated when Matthew's hard-hitting fists sent him sprawling into the mud. Carlson delivered an ultimatum: Either Matthew pointed his bridle out of the territory forever, or Carlson would make sure his parents lost their valuable contract to supply nearby Fort Bates.

His heart saddened but determined, Matthew left his home forever and rode north toward the Powder River and Cheyenne country. Captured by braves from Chief Yellow Bear's tribe, he was declared a spy for the Bluecoats and sentenced to torture and death. But at the moment when a youth named Wolf Who Hunts Smiling was about to execute the prisoner, old Arrow Keeper intervened.

The tribal medicine man and the keeper of the four sacred Medicine Arrows, Arrow Keeper had recently experienced a great vision at Medicine Lake. His vision centered around a mysterious young Cheyenne stranger who would eventually lead the Shaiyena people in one last, great victory against the white men. And the warrior of that medicine vision bore the same mark on his scalp that this young prisoner bore: a mulberry-colored birthmark in the shape of a perfect arrowhead, the traditional symbol of the Cheyenne warrior.

But Arrow Keeper's vision also foretold extreme suffering and many bloody battles before the youth could ever raise high the lance of leadership. Given the Cheyenne name Touch the Sky, Matthew was ordered to join the warriors in training. But his ignorance—and his many enemies within the tribe—combined at first to ensure his failure and lack of acceptance.

Then Touch the Sky, assisted by his boyhood friend Corey Robinson, saved Yellow Bear's tribe from a Pawnee attack. He was honored by the Council of Forty for his bravery and cunning. But now his enemies hated him more than ever— especially Black Elk, the fierce young war leader who was enraged by the growing love between Touch the Sky and Honey Eater, Chief Yellow Bear's daughter. And Black Elk's young but hateful and ambitious cousin, Wolf Who Hunts Smiling, walked between Touch the Sky and the camp fire—a Cheyenne's way of announcing his intention of killing a man.

When Touch the Sky rescued Honey Eater from Henri Lagace's camp of ruthless whiskey traders, the two swore their love for each other. But soon after, Touch the Sky was forced to desert the tribe and return to Bighorn Falls to help his adopted parents. Hiram Steele and Lt. Seth Carlson had already driven them out of the mercantile business. Now they threatened the Hanchons' new mustang spread.

Assisted by his new friend Little Horse and the sympathetic cavalry officer Tom Riley, Touch the Sky helped defeat his parents' enemies. But deserting his tribe caused a twofold tragedy: Cheyenne spies saw him conferring with Tom Riley, and they reported to the headmen that Touch the Sky was a spy for the Long Knives. Honey Eater, in turn, believing he had deserted her *and* the tribe, was pressured into marrying Black Elk after her ailing father crossed over to the Land of Ghosts.

Touch the Sky was heartbroken, discouraged, sick of the constant struggle now that he had returned to discover his loss of Honey Eater. But his hopes once again faced east after he too experienced the important medicine vision which foretold his future greatness—and promised him a wife and child. Determined now to join the tribe at any cost, he braved assassination attempts by his tribal enemies, defeated white land-grabbers, and suffered unjust punishments for supposed violations of the strict Cheyenne Hunt Law.

His constant courage and warrior's skill eventually earned the respect of more and more members of the tribe, now led by their new chief, Gray Thunder. But everyone in the tribe knew of the great and forbidden love between Touch the Sky and Honey Eater. Touch the Sky locked horns with Black Elk more than once because of the latter's jealousy.

While with the tribe on a hunt to the south, Honey Eater and other Cheyenne women and children were abducted by a combined band of Kiowas and Comanches. They intend to sell them to the Comanchero slave traders in the New Mexico territory. Once again Touch the Sky and his enemy Black Elk were on a collision course: Each brave claimed a husband's right and swore to save Honey Eater and the others. And each brave knew one of them must die.

Chapter One

"Brothers, you have listened to River of Winds. Now have ears for my words!"

Chief Gray Thunder folded his arms and immediately silence fell over the clearing where the Cheyenne headmen and warriors had gathered for this emergency council. Beside him, his buckskin leggings still covered with pale alkali dust from his hard journey across barren country, stood the scout named River of Winds. He had just returned from the dangerous mission of following the combined band of Kiowas and Comanches as they fled to the southwest with their Cheyenne captives.

"We are trapped between the sap and the bark," Gray Thunder said. "No one here wants to get our women and children back more than I. But we are intruders in a hostile land, surrounded by enemy tribes and unscouted country. You heard

River of Winds report that he also saw Bluecoat soldiers with their big-talking guns mounted on wagons. If we move as one people, we will surely attract unwanted attention. And in this desolate, open territory, the screaming steel from those guns would be impossible to avoid. Our horses would be shredded to stew meat."

His words prodded nods and murmurs of approval from many. Gray Thunder was a still-vigorous chief in his early forties, a veteran of several skirmishes with blue-bloused soldiers.

"Yet have we not learned just recently," he continued, "about the dangers of leaving the noncombatants alone? While the hunters were out, the Kiowas and Comanches killed six of our elders, wounded twelve elders and children, and stole twenty of our women and children! This thing would be examined carefully.

"Brothers! Yes, we must save our captured women and young ones! What else are warriors for if not to protect their tribe? But we must not destroy the bush to save the berries! Our carelessness during the hunt has already cost us dearly. Now we must act like men and not endanger the others still left to us."

The tall, broad-shouldered youth named Touch the Sky felt heat rise into his face at the mention of carelessness. Though Gray Thunder did not point him out for blame, Touch the Sky knew his terrible mistake in judgment had allowed the abduction of Honey Eater and the others. Believing his band had routed the small force of Comanches and Kiowas sent to kidnap prisoners, Touch the Sky had ordered his band to join the main battle well away from the camp.

But he had only ridden into a decoy—another enemy force was hidden near camp, ready to pounce on the women and children in a lightning raid.

This council was being held outdoors. Normally, back at their permanent summer camp on the Powder River far to the north, they would meet in the huge, hide-covered council lodge in the center of the camp clearing. But now the tipis were gathered into their defensive clan circles in a temporary hunt camp in the valley of the Red River—far south of their usual hunting grounds in the Wyoming and Montana Territories. Thin strips of buffalo meat were still stretched tight on the wooden drying racks. Everywhere, travois were loaded with the spoils of the hunt: hides for clothing and sleeping robes, horns for cups and bowls, sinews for thread and bowstrings, bones for awls, bladders for water bags, hair for ropes and belts—nothing would be wasted.

It was old Arrow Keeper who spoke next.

"Brothers! I feared this hunt, even though a medicine dream told me the kill would be good. We have an abundance of meat now, but at what price? True it is we had no choice but to come here. Our ancient Hunt Law requires us to hunt as a tribe. Yet the paleface crews working on the roads for their iron horses, the crews stringing their talking wires, the buffalo-hiders and soldiers—all these have sent up the white stink and driven the herds south.

"Brothers! We had no choice. But now we must act carefully so that no more of our women and children are stolen. These Kiowas and Comanches are no tribes to fool with."

Touch the Sky nodded with the others. He kept his eyes on the braves named Spotted Tail, leader of the military society known as the Bowstrings, and Lone Bear, leader of the feared and despised Bull Whips. Though Chief Gray Thunder was presiding, the tribe was still officially engaged in the hunt expedition. Thus, normal tribal law gave way to the Hunt Law. And since this hunt was being policed by the Bowstrings and the Bull Whips, Spotted Tail and Lone Bear would be the law-givers and decision-makers until the tribe was back in permanent camp.

But the young man's attention shifted to Black Elk when that fierce young war chief rose to speak. The coup feathers in his war bonnet trailed nearly to the ground. It was Honey Eater who had made that war bonnet, Touch the Sky reminded himself. And now she was gone, stolen by enemies thanks, in part, to his mistake.

"Fathers and brothers!" Black Elk said. "You know me. You have followed me into battle and smoked the common pipe with me. I am no brave to hide in my tipi when my brothers are on the warpath. Nor am I one to speak merely for the sake of noise, as the whites do."

His eyes met Touch the Sky's, and for the space of several heartbeats everyone present felt the hatred between the two bucks. Again Touch the Sky felt an involuntary inner shudder when he saw the dead, leathery flap of skin where Black Elk's ear had been severed in battle, then sewn back on crudely with buckskin thread.

"So I will speak words you may place in your sashes and take away with you," Black Elk continued. "After hearing River of Winds, I say our chief speaks wisely when he tells us a large war party would not do. We are northern Plainsmen, used to meeting our enemy in open battle. But these drunken, murdering dogs to the south prefer nighttime raids and swift attacks from hidden positions.

"Therefore, I will lead a small band of our best warriors, just as I did when I led the defeat at the whiskey traders' camp. Not only am I your war leader and a Bull Whip trooper, but these Kiowa and Comanche dogs have stolen my squaw! *I* have a husband's right and will rescue Honey Eater and the rest. I will ride with my cousin Wolf Who Hunts Smiling, Swift Canoe, and a few of my fellow Bull Whips.

"Kiowa guts will string our next bows! Comanche hair will dangle from our coup sticks! We are the fighting Cheyenne! We have defeated the Pawnee, the Ute, the Crow, and our battle cry is feared throughout the plains. I will defeat this new enemy too, and get Honey Eater and the rest back."

Again his eyes met Touch the Sky's.

"Any man who blocks my path," Black Elk said, "will be dead before he hits the ground. My squaw has been stolen, and I swear by the earth I live on, I *will* get her back!"

Touch the Sky had heard enough. Honey Eater loved him, not Black Elk, and would be his wife today if she had not been convinced that Touch the Sky had deserted the tribe to be with his white family and Kristen Steele. Since Black Elk had taken to humiliating and beating Honey Eater, Touch the Sky had served warning—it was *he* who had a husband's right, not Black Elk. And

Touch the Sky could see now that Black Elk's pride and jealousy would make him a dangerous choice to rescue the others. Now he rose to speak.

"Yes, a large war party is a bad idea. I too am no stranger to you, fathers and brothers. You honored me in council when I helped save our tribe from Pawnees, and many of you saw me count first coup against the white militia at the Tongue River Battle. So listen now to my words, for you know I speak only one way and never in a wolf bark." Touch the Sky boldly met the stare of Black Elk's wily young cousin, Wolf Who Hunts Smiling. He too had recently joined the Bull Whip Society, using his new authority to arrest Touch the Sky during the hunt.

"You know," Touch the Sky said, "that no matter how much blood I shed for my tribe, I am marked as an outsider by my enemies. So now I will act like one. I always obey the laws of the Cheyenne way. But in this matter of the rescue, I will follow no one.

"During the hunt, I was beaten by the Bull Whips after Wolf Who Hunts Smiling claimed I ran the herd over a cliff. Then these two *braves*"—scorn poison-tipped his words as he looked at Wolf Who Hunts Smiling and Swift Canoe—"bribed an old squaw of the Root Eaters Clan and convinced her addled brain that she had had a 'vision,' one which said I must set up a pole to atone for my violation of Hunt Law or the tribe was doomed."

Many braves nodded sympathetically. "Setting up a pole" was a grueling voluntary penance which required the penitent to hang suspended for hours from bone hooks driven through his breasts. Arrow Keeper had learned of the deception and announced it at council. Wolf Who Hunts Smiling and Swift Canoe would be punished for their hand in it, but not until this emergency was settled.

"After this and many other injustices done to me, I speak now in straight words. Yes, I will obey Cheyenne law. But remember, I belong to no clan, no military society, and have been accused of having the white man's stink on me. Other than Chief Gray Thunder and our shaman, Arrow Keeper, I *have* no masters! I have spoken to my friends Little Horse and Tangle Hair, and they have agreed to ride with me. Now that we have heard River of Winds give his report, I ask Spotted Tail, as the Bowstring leader, to grant his permission that these two may accompany me."

All eyes turned to the brave who led the Bowstrings. Spotted Tail was known as a fair man, and his Bowstring troopers were respected for their habit of preferring peaceful negotiations to settle disputes. This was in direct contrast to Lone Bear's Bull Whips, a collection of arrogant, mean-spirited braves who resorted all too often to their feared whips of knotted rawhide.

"Tangle Hair is one of my soldiers," Spotted Tail said. "One of my best. And Little Horse fights like five braves. And you, Touch the Sky—I have seen you grease your enemy's bones with war paint! But what can three men do against this huge force, and in the heart of their territory? I too am sickened by the loss of so many women and little ones. But we are warriors and must not let our hearts overrule our heads."

"We will show you what three Cheyennes can do," Touch the Sky replied. "I ask you again, will you grant these two your permission so that they will not be violating Hunt Law? I ask nothing for myself."

"Do not worry about me," Little Horse suddenly said. "I ride with my brother whether or not it has the tribal sanction on it! Tangle Hair is your trooper, Spotted Tail. Authorize him alone."

This was followed by a long silence. More and more of the tribe, in their hearts if not publicly, had grown to respect this tall young Cheyenne who came in among them four winters ago dressed in white man's clothing and ignorant of the Cheyenne way. Not only had they come to admire his battlefield heroics, they had also watched him suffer unjustly in silence during the whipping and the pole torture.

But still, there was doubt about his loyalty. Had he not drunk whiskey with murdering white dogs at the trading post? Had he not been seen conferring with a Bluecoat officer, holding a sun-haired white girl in his arms? Many at the council today had lost loved ones to the bullets of white men. This Touch the Sky, truly he was one to fight like a she-grizzly with cubs; but deep in his heart he still loved the worst enemy of the red man, the paleface intruders arriving in hordes to exterminate the Indian.

Finally, Spotted Tail shook his head. This thing was awkward. But a decision had to be made, action must be taken. The camp was in no immediate danger. Well-armed sentries ringed this hunt camp and were in constant communication. But time was their enemy. The longer they remained, the greater their risk.

"I not only authorize Tangle Hair to go," he said, "but Little Horse and Touch the Sky also."

Black Elk and Wolf Who Hunts Smiling both spoke up at the same moment, protesting this decision.

"Spotted Tail is a troop leader," Chief Gray Thunder said. "If the Bull Whips may send out a band, so too may the Bowstrings."

"She is *my* wife," Black Elk protested. "This pretend Cheyenne wants to put on the old moccasin by marrying my squaw. Only loin heat makes him so eager to ride after her!"

"Even now," Touch the Sky said, "he cheapens his good wife with this low talk. She has always behaved as what she is, the daughter of a great chief. Yet this mighty war leader has lately taken to cutting off her braid and beating her!"

Rage turned Black Elk's face scarlet. But before he could reply, Gray Thunder spoke up again.

"I have no more ears for this clash of jealous bulls! Unless we act quickly and well, it hardly matters about Honey Eater's braid. This is no time for bickering amongst ourselves. We must stand shoulder to shoulder. I do not agree with this thing, this sending out of two separate bands. But the troop leaders have spoken, and Hunt Law is clear on the point of their authority."

Soon after the council disbanded. Touch the Sky watched Black Elk, Wolf Who Hunts Smiling, and Swift Canoe quickly form a little group on the far side of the clearing. They were joined by two of the Bull Whip soldiers. Now and then one of them would cast a malevolent glance toward him.

Old Arrow Keeper too watched Black Elk's little band. Clearly Touch the Sky's enemies were once again plotting against him. Pulling his red Hudson's Bay blanket tighter around his shoulders, the medicine man crossed the clearing to speak with his young apprentice.

"Carry these words away with you, little brother," he said. "Black Elk is baiting you for a fight to the death. I know you hate him, and I understand why. I also understand why he hates you. Things are the way they are, and if forced to it, you must defend yourself. But I am not teaching you the shaman arts so that you will freely shed Cheyenne blood and stain the Sacred Arrows. Do you understand this thing?"

Slowly, reluctantly, Touch the Sky nodded. The old man had the most important responsibility in the tribe: protecting with his life the four sacred Medicine Arrows which symbolized the fate of the entire Shaiyena people. For this sacred task was he named Keeper of the Arrows. They must stay forever sweet and clean. Any Cheyenne blood shed by another Cheyenne would stain the Arrows— and thus the entire tribe, ruining the buffalo hunts, bringing the red-speckled cough and other misfortunes.

"This mission will be among the most dangerous of your life," Arrow Keeper added. "You are learning to be a shaman. You must rely on the language of your senses and strong medicine too, not just the warrior way."

Abruptly the old man turned and walked off.

"Clearly, brother," Little Horse said as he and Tangle Hair prepared to ride out with Touch the

Sky, "Black Elk plans to leave first."

Touch the Sky nodded. "He is eager once again to play the big Indian. He is more concerned about his reputation than his wife and the others."

"Should we hurry and leave first?" Tangle Hair said.

"Not at all," Touch the Sky replied. "If we race them, we will only put the prisoners at more risk by forcing Black Elk to his hotheaded foolishness. I see that his band are taking no lead lines with them. This means that in their hurry they are not bothering to take remounts. Against Comanches and Kiowas, with their powerful ponies, this is a mistake. We will cut extra mounts from the herd before we leave."

"Not one buck in Black Elk's band would mind seeing carrion birds pluck out your eyes," Little Horse said, his voice troubled. "I fear they are planning more than the rescue of our women and children. They also plan to send you under."

Touch the Sky nodded. But that thought was less important than the menacing refrain of Chief Gray Thunder's words, which had struck Touch the Sky like lance points: *Unless we act quickly and well, it hardly matters about Honey Eater's braid.*

Chapter Two

A rifle bolt clicked in the chilly darkness just outside the cave, and Victorio Grayeyes woke instantly.

Moonlight as pale as ice slanted in past giant boulders which formed a natural rampart at the cave entrance. The dry bunchgrass mat under his blankets rustled when the young Apache brave sat up. The sound was exaggeratedly loud and called attention to itself in the cold stillness of the limestone cavern.

A full moon outside limned much of the interior in a soft glow. He could just make out dim mounds where the others huddled together for warmth. There was a creaking like stiff saddle leather as one of the infants moved in its wicker cradle.

Victorio's pulse slowly stopped throbbing so

hard in his palms. The sound he'd heard was nothing, he assured himself. Just a memory from the hard days spent fighting and running from the bloodthirsty Spaniards. Now the Apache-hating Mexicans were taking over where the Spaniards left off, and the Americans were no better. But his clan was safe here, high in the mountains of the New Mexico Territory. Victorio's father and uncles had selected this stronghold because they knew Mexican Federales and Anglo bluecoats alike were too lazy to search it out. *Only with the help of a turncoat Apache,* his father had said over and over, *will anyone find us here.*

Just then Victorio smelled the bitter smell of the cactus liquor known as *pulque.* No one here had drunk any for days now. But he knew someone who liked to drink it all the time—someone who had fled from this place after stealing everything of value.

A cold tickle of fear moved up his spine. A moment later he spotted a Mexican soldier.

Everything happened fast after that, though to Victorio it felt like he was trying to run in thigh-deep water. It was a Federale officer. Victorio glimpsed the familiar kepi and crossed bandoliers. He made out the coarse-grained face, eyes far too small for the huge skull, a weak chin stubbled with beard. Victorio opened his mouth to shout a warning to the others. But the first gunshot beat him to it.

At night Victorio always tucked his rifle into his blankets to protect it from dew. He drew it out now, his fingers struggling in dream-time clumsiness, his index finger groping to find the trigger guard.

Comancheros

We're all going to die, Victorio thought as he struggled with the weapon. Again he heard his father's voice: *Only with the help of a turncoat Apache!*

A moment later he saw his clan cousin, Juan Aragon, step inside, followed by more Federales. Juan brought the strong smell of *pulque* with him. He had stolen all of it when he left.

Victorio finally found the trigger even as another Apache discharged his weapon at the intruders. But when he aimed it into the middle of Juan's body and squeezed the trigger, the hammer clicked on a damp primer cap.

Victorio's grandfather, Atoka, had been asleep about 15 feet to the youth's right. Now Victorio watched Juan move as swiftly and smoothly as a wraith. Victorio glimpsed Juan's empty shoulder scabbard, glimpsed moonlight glinting cruelly off the curved blade of his upraised machete.

Atoka struggled to free himself of his tightly wrapped blanket. There was a swishing whisper as the machete sliced through air, then a sound like a hoe digging into flinty dirt. Victorio heard his grandfather grunt in death, heard the blood splashing heavily onto the stone floor of the cave.

White-hot rage replaced the numbing fear in his veins. He could hear his cousin's little babies crying, his younger brother and sister wailing. More guns, mostly the intruders', spat fire into the night, and there were more curses in Spanish. Victorio grasped his sturdy trade rifle like a club and rose even as one of the soldiers fired his pistols point-blank into the wicker cradles, killing the infants one by one.

Victorio swung hard at a shadowy figure, heard a surprised grunt as a soldier slumped to the floor. He moved forward amidst a hell-spawned clamor of shouts, screams, and gunfire. He was forced to watch, unable to move fast enough in the confusion of flashing weapons, as his mother and father rose together, still naked, and lunged toward the outcropping where Victorio's six-year-old brother Delshay and nine-year-old sister Josefa slept. Victorio knew they hoped to grab the children and escape through the hidden tunnel behind the limestone outcropping.

It all happened too quickly for Victorio to stop it. His *mestizo* cousin Juan drew his famous Anglo pistol, the heavy-bore Smith & Wesson cavalry gun with its huge muzzle. Victorio could see his mother's bare back in the stark moonlight, slim and muscle-ridged. Then Juan fired, and Victorio saw his mother collapse like a rag puppet as the huge-caliber slug punched into her. Another percussion cap cracked, and his father tumbled dead to the rock floor.

The acrid smell of spent cordite was thick in the air. Victorio swung on another Federale, felt the satisfying thud of solid contact with his skull.

Suddenly Victorio's bare feet hit a smooth patch of water-covered shale, and he went down hard on the rock, cracking his head.

For some time he lay balanced on the feather edge of awareness, drifting between cold, dark sleep and a blurry confusion like a waking dream. He was unable to move, had fallen half wedged into a fissure. Each time he even attempted to move, pain exploded inside his skull and sent him reeling under hot, red waves.

"Maldita sea!" he heard one of the Mexicans curse. "Someone has laid Jorge out like a corpse!"

"Never mind that," said another. "Make sure all the Apaches are dead."

"Not all of them. Kill the babies and the adults. But you gave your word. The boy and the girl are mine." Victorio recognized this last voice as Juan Aragon's.

"Madre de Dios, do you believe this Comanchero half-breed?" one of the soldiers exclaimed, laughing. "Shoots his own uncle and aunt in the back, then reminds us we gave our word! Our word that he might sell his own cousins to the whoremongers!"

"Basta ya! Shut up! I said to make sure they are all dead before you start crowing like a rooster! Check that one over there. I thought he moved."

Victorio heard steps coming closer to him, braced for the bullet which would surely be put in his brain to make sure he was dead. But now the pain was sucking the breath out of him, and he slipped into unconsciousness even as his dead father's voice still repeated its accusing litany: *Only with the help of a turncoat Apache could they find us here.*

Chapter Three

"So much for the tall Cheyenne 'shaman' who strikes fear into the Pawnees!" Hairy Wolf said scornfully. "He may conjure up grizzly bears and insane white men, as the Pawnee claim. But his big medicine could not stop us! Ahead only one sleep lies Blanco Canyon, brother! We are safe! Even the blue-dressed soldiers know better than to attack us here."

The Comanche leader named Iron Eyes nodded in agreement with his Kiowa ally. The two braves had halted their bands in the midst of the vast, sterile wasteland known as the Llano Estacado or Staked Plain. This remote wilderness, covering much of the Texas Panhandle and eastern New Mexico Territory, was an unsettled, almost treeless expanse seldom visited by the hair faces.

It was divided, near its center, by Blanco Canyon, home to Iron Eyes and his Quohada or Antelope Eater band of Comanches. Hairy Wolf had led his Kiowa warriors from Medicine Lodge Creek in Oklahoma to join their longtime battle allies for this important raid against their joint enemy, the Cheyenne.

"Soon," Iron Eyes said, "we will be rich in whiskey and new rifles. Aragon tells me he cannot find enough good women and children to supply those who wish to pay handsomely for them. He will take every one of these Cheyennes."

All around them stretched the endless, barren desert plains broken up only by sterile mountains and bone-dry arroyos. The setting sun was a huge, dull-orange ball on the western horizon. Its dying light turned the chalky alkali dust into a strange yellow fog. By day, that sun burned with a merciless intensity that kept even the jackrabbits and rattlesnakes in hiding.

Hairy Wolf rode a huge sorrel with a fine, hand-tooled saddle stolen from the Mexicans. The Kiowa leader was a member of the elite Kaitsenko—the ten best warriors of the entire Kiowa tribe. He wore captured Bluecoat trousers and boots. He was bare from the waist up except for a bone breastplate. Like most Kiowa men he was tall and broad-shouldered, and wore his flowing black hair well below his waist unbraided.

He turned in his saddle to glance back toward the rear of the column.

"Aragon will not buy every one of them," he said. "Our men will want to celebrate their victory. We have one or two prisoners who will not be worth much. There is blood to atone for. Do not forget those who may no longer be mentioned."

Iron Eyes nodded, understanding his meaning. Though the recent raid had been successful, several Kiowas and Comanches had been picked off by the sharp-shooting Cheyennes. Their bodies had not been recovered. Thus, by custom, their names could never again be mentioned.

Physically, Iron Eyes was a stark contrast to his companion. Unlike the handsome Kiowas, the Comanches were small and bandy-legged and considered homely by most other Indians. Yet in fierce temper and love of battle the two tribes were one. They were also one in their love of inflicting torture on captives—an entertainment that ranked above even pony races and gambling.

He too turned around to glance back. His eyes landed on the beautiful Cheyenne girl with the jagged crop where her braid had been cut off. Even without her long hair she was clearly a beauty: skin the color of wild honey, huge, wing-shaped eyes, delicately carved cheekbones.

Iron Eyes lifted one hand to touch the ragged laceration on his left cheek. The girl had fought like a she-bear when he snatched her up, cutting his face open with the suicide knife Cheyenne women wore on thongs around their necks.

"Yes," Iron Eyes agreed, "the men will want to celebrate. We will give them one of the children. And perhaps there is one more Aragon will not get—though surely he would love to have her for she will bring the most money."

Hairy Wolf narrowed his eyes, studying his friend's face. His eyes too looked where Iron Eyes was looking. Then he smiled, understanding. He too had been thinking that *this* one should be kept back when the sale was made. There still remained the problem of deciding which one of them would own her as his personal slave. But this thing could be worked out. Women were like horses—arrangements could be made.

"We will ride a little further, then camp. We will keep a guard out on our back trail," Hairy Wolf said. "In one more sleep we will reach the Blanco Canyon. Not even carrion birds will follow us into that stronghold."

"No," Iron Eyes said. "But Cheyenne warriors are braver than carrion birds. They must be respected. We will need to hold the prisoners there until we are convinced their tribe is not on the warpath against us."

Hairy Wolf nodded, his long hair whipping out behind him as the dust-laden wind picked up. "Then we can send a word-bringer to Aragon."

As the two men spoke, they shifted fluently from Kiowa to Comanche to Spanish. Both tribes spoke all three languages and used them interchangeably, especially to fool their enemies. It was the Spaniards who had taught them the pleasures of torture. It was also the Spaniards who had taught them the value of slave trading. Now both tribes were active in the Comanchero trade conducted with New Mexicans and Mexicans, supplying various Indian captives as slaves in exchange for firearms and alcohol and rich white man's tobacco. Slavery was technically illegal in both Old Mexico and the New Mexico Territory. But a constant market for cheap labor and prostitutes, combined with a lack of lawmen, made it very profitable—much more so than selling hides or even fine horses.

Behind them, one of the captured children raised his voice in a pathetic wail. A moment later, the sound was lost in the fierce shrieking of the wind.

Hairy Wolf lifted his streamered lance high overhead. The long column moved forward into the dying sun.

The Comanche warrior named Big Tree spoke some Cheyenne, a language he had learned several winters ago when the mountain men known as the Taos Trappers still hired Indian scouts to lead them into the north country. Now he led a small chestnut pony by a rawhide lead line. Honey Eater rode the chestnut, her ankles lashed together under the pony's belly.

Occasionally, in the dying light, the Comanche turned around to stare at her. He was big for a Comanche, though he had the characteristic bowed legs which were only at home on horseback. Of all the tribes to the north which had driven his people to this desolate land, he hated the Cheyennes the most. They had killed his father in the famous battle at Wolf Creek, a Cheyenne throwing ax opening his skull like a melon.

But Big Tree was a Quohada and knew that revenge was a dish best served cold. Patiently, over the many years since Wolf Creek, he had honed the warrior's skills until he had become the deadliest and most feared Comanche in the Southwest. In the time that it took a blue-blouse soldier to load and fire a carbine twice, Big Tree could ride a horse 300 yards while stringing and firing 20 arrows with deadly accuracy.

"Your Cheyenne bucks have already had a taste of my skill as a warrior," he told Honey Eater in her own tongue. "They will taste much more if they are foolish enough to pursue us. And perhaps you will learn one of my skills too, haughty Cheyenne she-bitch!"

Once he had ridden back and shoved one calloused hand into her doeskin dress, fondling her breasts. Too weak to pull his hand away, she had bent quickly forward and gripped his forearm between her teeth. With a harsh yowl he had pulled his hand back out. But the glint in his eyes had hinted that he would be back for more—much more.

Honey Eater was numb with shock and fear, as were all of the prisoners. For days they had been forced to ride hard, existing only on alkali-tainted water and the hard, unleavened bread the whites called hardtack. She had been unable to sleep, to bathe. Now her pretty face was streaked where sweat had mixed with the chalky alkali dust.

Adding to her misery were the constant cries of the children. They did not understand what was happening, why they had been wrenched away from their parents. Nor were the women captives allowed to console them.

Riding nearest to Honey Eater, likewise lashed to a pony, was a young girl named Singing Bird. She was the sister of Two Twists, the young junior warrior who had helped Touch the Sky ward off a Kiowa-Comanche attack on the women and children during the recent hunt.

Though all the prisoners were suffering, Honey Eater was especially worried about her. Singing

Bird was pretty but in delicate health. The shock of capture and the hard pace of flight had taken their toll. She was conscious, but had not responded to any of Honey Eater's anxious attempts to engage her in some kind of talk. It was important to rally Singing Bird, to keep her from giving up—Honey Eater knew full well what these tribes would do to any who could not finish the journey.

Finally, as the shimmering orange sun went to its resting place, the leaders signaled a halt for the night. But soon Honey Eater realized there would be no rest this night—not for the prisoners.

The Kiowa and Comanche braves were worked up to a frenzied mood by their successful raid. Now and then one of them would let loose a yipping war cry. Others engaged in a favorite source of amusement, holding their pistols right next to a prisoner's skull while they fired them. Not only did this damage the ears, but it caused severe burns and bruises from powder flash and flying cartridges.

But tonight, Honey Eater saw, the suffering would be far worse.

She sent a silent prayer to Maiyun, the Good Supernatural, when she saw the two leaders slowly walking among the prisoners. They stopped here and there, looking, poking, before moving on. Then they paused in front of the place where she sat on the ground, her ankles and wrists lashed together.

Accompanied by Big Tree as their translator, they had been lifting the women's dresses as they went, looking to see which ones were still virgins wearing the knotted-rope chastity belts of the unmarried maidens. Now, as the smaller

Comanche gripped her skirt, Honey Eater tried to pull back. But a moment later both men were staring at her exposed nakedness.

The huge Kiowa grinned and said something to Big Tree. He too grinned as he translated for Honey Eater.

"Hairy Wolf sees that you have no rope over your belly mouth. He says, '*Now* I know who cut off her braid—it was a jealous husband. But no one misses a slice off a cut roast.'"

As she had from the beginning, Honey Eater refused to say anything. A moment later the warriors were gone, moving among the children now. Honey Eater felt her heart sink when they selected a scrawny young boy with only four winters behind him, Little Sun of the Panther Clan. The child was taken, kicking and screaming, to the center of the camp.

There was no available wood for fires, but the Kiowa-Comanche band had lashed plenty of good drift cottonwood to packhorses. Now they built a huge central fire.

The braves were out of whiskey. But they had learned from the Navajos how to brew corn beer, and now they were getting crazy drunk on it. Two of them used stakes and rawhide thongs to tie Little Sun spread-eagle beside the fire. The child's wails of fear infected the other children and set them to crying. Now the Cheyenne women were pleading with their captors to spare the child, but the frenzied warriors ignored them.

At least Honey Eater was far enough away that she wasn't forced to look. But some of the others, including Singing Bird and Blue Feather of the Sky Walker Clan, were not so fortunate. Honey

Eater saw Kiowa and Comanche warriors grabbing their heads and holding them so they could not look away. Their screams were as pitiful as Little Sun's.

Even though she could close her eyes, Honey Eater could not close her ears. They told her more than she needed to know. At first the torture was the usual fare: pistols were fired right next to Little Sun's skull, terrorizing him, evoking pitiful shrieks.

But as the moon crept toward his zenith, and the corn beer flowed, the scene got even uglier.

She could not see Little Sun. But she saw the warriors dancing in a circle, now and then stepping close to kick or strike out with their bows. His shrieks of pain rose above the commotion and sent tears of pity and helpless frustration springing into Honey Eater's eyes.

Honey Eater was past screaming now. For a moment the horrible nightmare reminded her of the time when she had been held prisoner by Henri Lagace and his ruthless whiskey traders. She had been forced to listen then too as Touch the Sky was similarly tortured. Yet in spite of his pain, he had sworn his love for her.

But this now was even more hopeless. At least then Black Elk and a few others had been in hiding nearby, waiting to strike. There could be no hope now. In the vast openness of the Llano, not even a prairie dog could sneak up on them unnoticed.

She wasn't quite sure when Little Sun finally died. He had suddenly quit screaming in a way that could only mean death.

Evidently the two leaders agreed that this was too abrupt an end to all the fun—now they walked among the women prisoners, thrusting a flaming torch in their faces to inspect them where they sat upon the ground. The one who had been holding up Singing Bird called them over. The two leaders glanced at the unconscious girl and nodded.

Clearly, their manner said, this one would probably not even survive the journey, much less earn a decent price as a slave. The Comancheros wanted strong young women, not sickly runts of the litter like this one.

Blue Feather was closest to her. When their captors started dragging Singing Bird toward the middle of the circle, she tried to lunge forward at them. A Comanche shoved her back down hard, being careful not to inflict any marks that might lower her price.

Despite everything she had seen and endured already, Honey Eater felt hot tears welling up in her eyes as they dragged Singing Bird forward. She had only 14 winters behind her. Honey Eater had helped her make a beaded shawl for the girl's first Sun Dance ceremony. Now she was forced to watch as her dress was ripped off. A Kiowa used his bone-handled knife to slice through her knotted-rope chastity belt. She too was tied down spread-eagle, tied tight at the ankles so she couldn't close her legs.

Whooping, shrieking, firing their pistols in the air, the braves lined up behind her.

Big Tree stood within hearing of her. "No!" Honey Eater shouted, the first word they had heard her utter.

All of the braves turned to stare at her.

"You," she said to Big Tree, "tell your leaders I beg them not to do this thing. It will kill her. And even if it does not kill her now, she will have to kill herself when she can. Our law demands this."

"You Cheyennes have many foolish laws," Big Tree told her before he translated for Iron Eyes and Hairy Wolf.

Both war leaders were surprised to hear the girl finally speak. Her request was foolish, of course. The girl would be killed anyway when the braves were finished with her—she would be "stoned into silence" about the deed, as were all rape victims.

But both braves were also thinking something else. This Cheyenne girl was extraordinarily beautiful. Taken as a wife, she would be a source of much pleasure. And a grateful woman gave far more pleasure. Each man already harbored secret hopes of owning her.

"Truly," Iron Eyes said now, looking at Singing Bird. "We have already given the men a child for their entertainment. It is foolish to waste another prisoner. This one is sickly, yes, but note the fine face and flawless skin. She will earn her keep in Over the River."

"Well spoken, Quohada," Hairy Wolf said. "I will give another gift to the men."

The braves watched, some curious, some impatient to begin the fun, as Hairy Wolf crossed to a packhorse and drew a large parfleche out of a pannier. Honey Eater saw the men crowd around him when they realized it was his highly guarded store of fine, rich tobacco, the kind white men smoked. Each man received a ration. Some of them, however, began to complain when a brave, instructed by Iron Eyes, started untying the still-unconscious Singing Bird.

All complaints ceased, however, when Big Tree stepped forward to confront the disgruntled few. Later, when Singing Bird had been returned close to her side, Honey Eater felt a small nubbin of relief beneath the thick layer of numbness.

It turned to cold fear, however, when Big Tree again squatted beside her and spoke in Cheyenne.

"Do not think that you moved their hearts with your plea. Their blood is hot to rut on you. Like two dogs, they circle the meat and wait for their chance to grab it. Count upon it, little proud one: As soon as they puzzle out how to divide you up, you will learn firsthand what the sickly one was just spared."

Chapter Four

The combined band of Kiowa and Comanche warriors, their Cheyenne prisoners lashed to ponies on lead lines behind them, rode past the last in a series of round sandstone shoulders. The first sight to greet them in the Blanco Canyon was their magnificent pony herds.

A herd guard below raised his skull-cracker—the stone war clubs so deadly in the hands of a mounted Comanche—in greeting.

Hairy Wolf and Iron Eyes lifted their streamered lances to return the greeting. Then they led their men and the prisoners down the narrow and rock-strewn trail which descended into the canyon.

Despite her utter exhaustion, Honey Eater also noticed plenty of bleached-white bones littering the trail—most of them human. As they drew closer to the bottom, she watched the well-disguised camp began to emerge from its natural camouflage. Unlike the tipis preferred by her northern Plains tribe, the Comanches who inhabited this canyon lived in one-room, mesquite-branch huts called jacals and in even cruder wickiups—curved-brush shelters which withstood the strong wind and dust storms of the Llano better than tipis. The visiting Kiowas had stolen Army tents.

For the last part of the grueling journey, Honey Eater had slipped in and out of consciousness, exhausted and faint from hunger. The ordeal of Little Sun's death and Singing Bird's near-tragedy had drained the Cheyennes as much as the rapid escape across the burning inferno of the Llano. Honey Eater's lips had parched so badly they were cracked like old clay, and despite her copper skin that rarely burned, she was burning and feverish from dehydration and sun exposure.

The reception below in the camp was no friendlier than the journey had been. A group of Comanche wives had gathered to stare at and taunt the prisoners. The prettiest girls—Honey Eater standing out by far despite her wretched condition—were singled out for the worst treatment. Several women spat on her, and another threw a rock which barely missed her face.

Iron Eyes barked a sharp command in Comanche and the women scattered. Hairy Wolf nudged his pony up beside his companion's. The Kiowa's long, black hair was matted under a thick white layer of alkali dust. Rivulets of sweat poured out from under the extra heat of his bone breastplate.

"Send a guard out in addition to the herd

guards," he said. "And since your men know Silverton best, send one of them as a word-bringer to Aragon. You know he is keen for laborers and whores."

Iron Eyes nodded. "Don't worry about a war party crossing the Llano unobserved. There, from the rim of the canyon? One man can easily spot the dust of any large movement, one full sleep before enemies can attack. It matters nothing if they choose another direction of attack. The Llano completely surrounds us, and it is the same everywhere."

"Just like the place called 'hell' which the Spanish priests live in fear of," Hairy Wolf said. "The white men made up this place for their fairy tales, now they find living Kiowas and Comanches for their devils! Let Cheyenne warriors taste what long knives have tasted when they tried to attack this place—bloody death. We are safe here."

As if by silent agreement, they had both stopped beside Honey Eater's pony. Though the knot of wives had obediently scattered, the women noticed this and passed jealous looks and comments among themselves. It was bad enough, said those looks, that their men took more than one wife, killing any they chose to kill without having to answer to Comanche law. But to bring Cheyenne whores into the camp for their filthy pleasures! This haughty Cheyenne she-bitch, their looks seemed to agree, would soon be doing the hurt dance along with her sisters.

"We have enough jacals if the children are packed in tight," Iron Eyes said, his gaze resting steadily on Honey Eater as she slumped on her pony. "Don't trust the women, though. These

Cheyenne girls are taught to fight and scheme like their warriors. We should keep them in separate wickiups."

"Except for her." Hairy Wolf nodded toward Honey Eater. Though they had said little about it to each other directly, both braves had been longtime battle allies and could read each other's thoughts like sign on a trail. Both knew they had no intention of trading this one to Juan Aragon.

"Except for her," Iron Eyes agreed. "She goes in a separate jacal of her own—one where we might be free to visit her."

Hairy Wolf liked this suggestion. Iron Eyes was offering the best solution. Until they found some amicable way of deciding which one of them would own her, they would put her where they could share her. This was especially convenient for Iron Eyes, as he had three jealous wives in camp with prying eyes. They were wily, patient men in certain matters. Arrangements could be made.

"We must be careful that Aragon doesn't see her," Hairy Wolf said. "Out of spite, when he learns she is not for sale, he will lower his offer on the rest. They will bring plenty, even without this bob-tailed beauty."

"Surely, brother, Aragon must not see her," Iron Eyes agreed. "That Aragon, he has the mind of a distempered dog. He is loyal to no one and gold-crazy like the white men. And though I would put Big Tree up against any man, I swear by the skin of a roadrunner that I fear Aragon's machete! His blade sings only one tune—the death song."

While Iron Eyes spoke, Hairy Wolf had noticed

41

several of the men staring at Honey Eater and the other girls. Many of them still felt they had been robbed of their manly right when the rape had been prevented. Nor were they happy to see their battle leaders hoarding such a prize. Both tribes were marauding raiders, and it was understood that raiders shared the wealth. Only the nearby presence of Big Tree held them in check. Extra rations of tobacco and coffee kept him loyal to his leaders, and not one man in the Blanco would ensure his own death by challenging Big Tree.

"We will place a sentry in front of each jacal and wickiup," Hairy Wolf said. "How much we receive for them in goods will be determined by their condition when Aragon inspects them. I see some of our bucks are randy for Cheyenne flesh."

A wide grin split Iron Eyes' dusty, sweat-streaked face. "Good. After Aragon sells them in Over the River, our randy bucks can visit them all they want. For now, let us make sure that Big Tree guards this one here."

Touch the Sky's little band rode out well behind Black Elk and his group, bearing southwest across the Staked Plain. The trail, as River of Winds had assured them, was as easy to follow as a herd of buffalo. No one bothered to cover their sign on the Llano.

Touch the Sky did not want to pressure Black Elk into revealing their presence to their enemy any sooner than was necessary. As he had already learned from experience, in a contest against superior numbers the element of surprise was the key to victory. Unfortunately, the Kiowas and

Comanches had perfected the surprise attack and the art of stealth. Like a hawk or an eagle, they liked to attack out of the sun and strike before they were seen.

As if reading his troubled thoughts, Little Horse said, "Brother, I see you shedding much brain sweat. Do you have a plan?"

Miserable, Touch the Sky shook his head. Little Horse rode on his left, Tangle Hair on his right. Touch the Sky's percussion-action Sharps protruded from the scabbard sewn to his blanket. Little Horse had wrapped his four-barrel flintlock shotgun in doeskin to protect the hand-rotated barrels from dust. Both weapons were gifts from John Hanchon, who had been Touch the Sky's white father in the days when he was named Matthew. Tangle Hair, a young Bowstring soldier who had befriended Touch the Sky during the recent hunt, carried a sturdy but small-caliber British trade rifle.

"No," Touch the Sky admitted. "My only plan right now is to keep Black Elk on his leash while we get a map in our minds of this canyon River of Winds spoke of."

It was the height of the afternoon, the sun's heat so searing that none of them could look ahead and keep his eyes open. The horses could only reluctantly be pushed to a long trot, despite a generous watering before they departed. Buffalo bladders lashed to the remounts carried extra water, but it was being quickly depleted in this bone-dry heat.

The suffocating dust sometimes made conversation impossible and cut visibility to a few feet in front of them. The horses balked and had to be forcibly driven on. There was no shelter even if they had wanted to stop. What little water they found was tainted, and the bones of men and animals were found as frequently as any vegetation.

"They will have sent scouts to watch their back trail," Touch the Sky said when the three bucks had stopped in the lee of a small mesa to get a breather from the relentless dust. "We should ride single file now, and move farther away from the trail. If we keep our eyes keen, we can spot them before they spot us."

They rode on, fighting wind and dust and reluctant horses. Despite the desperate conditions and the persistent image of Honey Eater plaguing him, Touch the Sky remembered Arrow Keeper's urgent warning. He also tried to keep his "shaman eye" open too, attending to the clues of all his senses.

Toward late afternoon the wind died down, the pale white dust settled, and the going was easier. For some time they had been riding parallel to a long redrock spine which formed a ridge to their left.

Suddenly Touch the Sky, who was leading the three, tugged on his pony's hair bridle, halting the sturdy little chestnut.

"What is it, buck?" Little Horse asked him anxiously, seeing his friend stare toward the redrock spine.

Touch the Sky said nothing at first, still staring. For the past few minutes, a prickling sensation in his scalp had warned him of something. Now he felt he knew what it was: Somebody was watching them from the other side of that spine.

"Perhaps it is only *odjib*," he finally replied.

"Only a thing of smoke. But as soon as it grows a little darker, brothers, I am taking a look behind that ridge. Meantime, live close to your weapons. I fear trouble is only a stone's throw away."

Chapter Five

As dusk descended, grainy twilight replacing the dust haze, Touch the Sky halted his companions in a jagged arroyo which followed the course of the redrock spine.

"Hobble your ponies and eat something," he told them. "But we will not make a camp. The horses grazed well before we left, but River of Winds reports there is no grass until we reach Disappointment Creek, a full sleep's ride from here. The longer we wait, the harder it will be on our horses. Give them a little of the water."

While he spoke, Touch the Sky was wetting his body with small handfuls of water, then smearing himself with the dark sand of the arroyo's bottom.

"Hold, brother," Little Horse said. "Take me with you."

46

Touch the Sky shook his head as he made sure his throwing tomahawk was secure in his legging sash. He laid his rifle and bow and quiver aside, opting only for his obsidian-bladed knife and the tomahawk Arrow Keeper had made for him. The latter was the same weapon which he had used to split open the skull of the Pawnee leader War Thunder when he tried to kill Chief Yellow Bear—Touch the Sky's first kill in battle.

"One person only should go. In open country, even one person is too easy to spot."

"But tell me, brother," Tangle Hair said. "Have you seen something, or heard a noise? I have watched that spine closely for some time. If anything larger than a tarantula is moving behind it, my pony would have shied."

"I have heard or seen nothing. But count upon it, someone is back there watching us."

"But if you have heard or seen nothing," Tangle Hair said, "how can you know this thing?"

It was Little Horse who spoke next.

"Tangle Hair, do you recall what Arrow Keeper told the Council of Forty when he announced that Touch the Sky was to be his apprentice?"

"That he has the gift of visions. But he has had no vision here today."

Little Horse was hobbling the remounts. Touch the Sky noticed that his friend still limped from the shattered kneecap he had suffered while a prisoner aboard the land-grabber's keelboat.

"No vision, perhaps," Little Horse said. "But those who have the gift of visions can also learn to notice things the rest of us miss."

This talk embarrassed Touch the Sky. But Little Horse had seen the mulberry-colored birthmark hidden in the hair over his right temple—a perfect arrowhead, the mark of the warrior. It was the same mark carried by the great warrior of Arrow Keeper's Medicine Lake vision: the warrior who would someday gather the far-flung Cheyenne bands for one last, great victory against their enemies. Nor could Little Horse forget what Touch the Sky had finally announced for the first time during the recent hunt: that he was the son of a great Cheyenne chief and like his father, destined for greatness. Many had scoffed openly at this, demanding proof which the youth could not provide. But Little Horse had learned long ago that Touch the Sky always spoke straight-arrow.

Tangle Hair knew it was bad luck to talk about such things, so he let it go. By the time Touch the Sky had covered the lightest parts of his body with wet sand, the sky had grown dark enough to let him move up out of the arroyo. First he moved forward a few dozen yards, and then pulled himself carefully over the edge and up onto the still-warm alkali dust of the level plain.

His friend Old Knobby, the hostler from Bighorn Falls, had taught him never to move at night without first fixing on a point in advance. Getting his bearing, he fixed his eyes on the shadowy form of a spiked jolla cactus halfway between his present position and the redrock spine. Then, moving low and silently on his elbows and knees, sometimes even slithering in the sand like a snake, he moved out.

As he drew nearer the dark ridge, fear make his scalp sweat. But he moved steady and slow, stopping now and then to listen.

He reached the cactus, paused to check his bearing, and began low-crawling again. Sweat beaded in his thick black locks and rolled down into his eyes, sand fleas bit at him, and his elbows were chaffing in the rough sand. But finally he felt the rough, porous texture of the redrock under his fingers.

Slowly he rose, pulled himself over the redrock. The moon chose that moment to scuttle out from behind a huge rock pile of clouds. Just downridge to his right, crouched low to spy on the Cheyennes in the arroyo, was a shadowy figure.

Now Touch the Sky spotted the shape of the lone intruder's horse, picketed well back from the ridge and out of sight from the other side. A Kiowa or Comanche scout, he guessed. Or maybe even an Apache or Bluecoat scout. Either way, it was no friend.

He slid his knife out of its beaded sheath and placed it handy between his teeth. Now he did move like a snake, inch by inch, until he was almost close enough to spit on the crouched spy.

He rose, transferred the knife to his right hand, leaped.

The spy was surprisingly light. Touch the Sky hit him hard, knocking the wind out of him as they tumbled down the back slope of the ridge.

The Cheyenne way forbade killing except in self-defense, and this one had not yet fired on the Cheyenne. Touch the Sky raised his knife hand, turned the blade up so the bone handle was his weapon, and started to plunge it toward his opponent's temple in a crippling blow.

"Touch the Sky!"

His knife was halfway to its target before the mystery figure shocked him by saying his name. With a supreme effort, he managed to avert his thrust. The handle thucked into the sand only inches from the spy's face.

Touch the Sky grabbed him by the hair and jerked his head up so his face was exposed to the moonlight.

"Two Twists! Have you eaten strong mushrooms, little brother? What are you doing spying on us?"

Two Twists was the brave young junior warrior who had led the warriors in training, under Touch the Sky's direction, in narrowly averting the first Kiowa-Comanche raid on the women and children during the recent hunt. He was named after his old-fashioned style of wearing his hair in two braids, instead of the single braid or loose locks preferred by most Cheyenne men.

Two Twists sat up, still gasping for breath.

"I want to join you," he said. "But I was waiting until you had traveled farther from our hunt camp before I made my presence known, so you might not send me back."

"Join us? Little brother, I am proud of the way you stood and held during the attack on our women and little ones. You will someday be a warrior to be reckoned with. But you have yet to count your first coup, yet to be blooded for your tribe. Pups are quick to bark like dogs, but barking and biting are two different things."

"I can bite," Two Twists said with confidence. "As deep as a rattlesnake! Please, Touch the Sky, do not send me back. My sister, Singing Bird, is among the prisoners! My father was killed by

Utes in the Wolf Mountains, my mother by Blue-coats at Washita Creek. Singing Bird is my only family, the soul of my medicine bag. She is not strong, Touch the Sky, she must be rescued soon or she will surely die. Please let me lift my battle lance beside yours and help to save her!"

"I *do* plan to save her, if she is still alive. And that is why I ride with two of the finest warriors on the plains. You heard River of Winds describe this fierce Comanche called Big Tree, the one who makes his brothers cower in fear. Are you ready to ride against such as him? Your feeling for Singing Bird is strong and good, little brother, and I admire you for it. But the heart should not rule the head in combat."

"But Touch the Sky, I—"

"I have spoken, buck. Point your bridle east and return to the hunt camp. If your sister can possibly be saved, we will do it or die trying."

Touch the Sky rose and stepped up onto the ridge, signaling to the others that he was all right. He had started to descend back toward the arroyo when Two Twists cried out bitterly behind him.

"All right, *play* the big Indian! If you have a right to die saving my sister, then so do I. You treat me like a child still sucking his mother's dug! I am not so young that I cannot remember what it was like for *you* when you joined our tribe! You were not much older than I am now. You were called a spy, a white man's dog, a woman face, and the others refused to use their names in front of you, as if you were a paleface. During all of this, I felt sorry for you. I was sure you were better than your enemies who tormented you. Now you too turn on a less-experienced buck and tell him he is not a man!"

These words, and Two Twists's angry tone, irritated Touch the Sky. Yet something plaintive in the youth's speech also touched his heart. There were some nuggets of truth mixed up with the childish spite of his words. Right now Two Twists felt like an outsider who belonged in neither world, the child's or the man's—and hadn't Touch the Sky chaffed under that same feeling?

"Is the calf bellowing to the bull?" he demanded.

"No," Two Twists said. "Only crying to be heard."

That settled it. Touch the Sky had watched this youth stand tall before enemy fire, firing one bullet for one enemy. Now he had listened to him state his case boldly like a man, not fawning to those in power as Swift Canoe liked to do. The injustices and scorn heaped on Touch the Sky made him reluctant to heap them on others.

"Are you willing to die?" he demanded. "For surely this is a suicide mission if ever I have seen one. We are vastly outnumbered in a hostile land."

"If I must die, then it will be the glorious death my father died!"

"Some call it glorious, but there is little glory in watching Comanches feed your guts to their dogs while you are still breathing. Bring your pony, then, and join us. But I tell you now, Two Twists, and you had better place my words close to your heart. My mission is to save our women and children. At the first sign that you are endangering that mission, I will *order* you back to the hunt camp. If you disobey me then, sassy words will not sway me again. Now quit smiling and show a war face, for soon you will need it."

Something was troubling Juan Aragon.

Whatever it was nagged at him like a toothache, but he couldn't spell the thought out plain.

He slipped into the shanty-and-sod no man's land, known as Over the River to soldiers and Indians alike, through a series of cutbanks which led down from the Comanchero camp in the nearby hills. The son of an Apache father and a Mexican mother, Aragon wore his hair cut short in contrast to most Indians—this because he knew from experience that long hair was convenient to grasp when cutting a man's throat, and he was the last man to help his enemies kill him.

He was smaller than most full-blood Apaches. But his legendary skill with the machete in his shoulder scabbard, and the long-muzzled cavalry pistol in his holster, added much to his stature.

Himself a former slave who had escaped from forced labor in Old Mexico, he had grown up as hard and ruthless as the hacienda *jefes* who controlled the slaves. He had also seen firsthand the inner workings of the illegal slave trade. Now he led his band of Comanchero slave traders, all half-breeds like himself except for one full-blooded Comanche, toward the one place which could buy all the young Indian women he chose to supply.

Over the River had sprung up in the days when water still flowed in the now-dry tributary ditch which separated this isolated hovel from the more respectable town of Silverton. The Silverton side was strictly limited to white settlers and the soldiers stationed at nearby Fort Union, which sat on the northern boundary of the Llano Estacado. The other side was their solution to the problem of providing entertainment for the Indian scouts and interpreters, as well as the reservation Indians who frequently visited the fort to receive their ration allotments and sometimes ended up waiting for days. Officially, no one from Silverton ever crossed the "river" and it was forbidden to Army personnel—though Aragon knew for a fact that a new shipment of pretty Arapaho or Cheyenne girls could lure even the paleface soldiers over while the girls were still fresh.

But he also knew that girls didn't last long here. The lucky ones, the strongest ones, might still be sold for hacienda labor in Chihuahua once they ceased to lure money here. The others would join the many rows of shallow, unmarked graves behind Over the River, stones piled on them to keep the animals off.

Tonight he had an Arapaho girl to show to the old Mexican named Valdez, who sold whiskey from a clapboard shanty and kept women out back in a row of dark brown adobe huts. So far the soldiers and white settlers had ignored the Indian-slave trade. Nonetheless, Juan Aragon and his men entered the squalid village with one hand on their weapons—they had made many enemies over the years, and after dark very few lights burned in the treacherous, narrow alleys of Over the River.

They passed a few adobe buildings, unmarked by signs and poorly lit inside. Aragon carefully studied each open doorway, making sure no rifles protruded. Loud voices spilled from each, and he knew that men were getting drunk and gambling inside all of them. Money was flowing, white man's gold, but what of that? Aragon had seen the wealth and power of the hacienda owners, and white man's gold could help him achieve that.

A figure stepped outside one of the clapboard shanties and, in the space of an eyeblink, Aragon's machete was in his hand. The wide, curved blade glinted cruelly in the light of a three-quarter moon. The figure froze, recognizing Aragon immediately.

"It's only that half-wit Comanche thief they call Sticks Everything in His Belt," Benito, one of Aragon's men, said. "He has slipped outside to steal something lashed to the ponies."

"Steal what you will," Aragon said in his voice which was like a dry husk. "But touch these ponies, hombre, and you sleep with the worms."

Finally they reached the last and biggest shanty, one which even boasted a crude awning: a ragged flap of canvas mounted on old corral poles. Valdez lived in the slope-roof partition off to one side of the saloon. While Benito went into the saloon side to get Valdez, Aragon led the girl into the one-room living quarters.

As always, his men stood watch outside. Aragon lit a coal-oil lamp, then ordered the girl to sit on the crude shuck-mattress bed in the back corner. The room had a rammed-earth floor and was furnished only with the bed, two kegs for chairs, and a crude deal table. A firepit in one corner also served as an oven.

"What is it tonight?" Valdez said in Spanish as he stepped inside. "Another skinny Apache with buck teeth?"

"They're all skinny to you, fat brown one. You eat too much of your profits. No, my friend, tonight I have a fine young Arapaho virgin for you."

"They're all skinny to me, they're all virgin to you, no? Take her clothes off," Valdez said impatiently. "My help is robbing me blind while we talk."

The girl cowered when Aragon reached for her buckskin dress. He said something to her sharply and she submitted as he pulled the garment over her head and dropped it on the mattress. Valdez picked up the lamp from the table and stepped closer, inspecting her as if she were a side of beef.

Tears of shame and humiliation welled in her eyes as Valdez reached out and roughly pinched her various parts.

"She'll do," he finally said, "but I'd swear by the two balls of Christ she's no virgin. She has at least twenty years on her, and no twenty-year-old Indian woman is still virgin."

"So what? She'll pass for one once they've got your panther piss inside them."

"Fifty dollars," Valdez said.

"In a pig's ass, old man! Two hundred."

"You thieving bastard! I'll give you one hundred."

"You'll make that on her in one week, you old fart. One hundred and seventy-five."

"I can buy white women for those prices! One hundred and twenty-five, and that's my last offer."

They finally agreed on a price of $150. Aragon knew the old Mexican was desperate for women right now, and wisely he seldom brought him more than one or two at a time, to keep the prices up. Valdez wanted Cheyenne women, of course, as everyone knew they were called the Beautiful People throughout the plains. But they were far north of here and difficult to come by.

Now he thought of his young cousins, being held back in the Comanchero camp. Delshay was a boy and would go with the next delivery to Old Mexico. But Josefa, though only 11, would come here. Many of the drunks asked for young girls.

"*'Stá bien*, old man," Aragon said as he pocketed the double-eagle gold coins Valdez drew from the rawhide pouch on his belt. "Next time I come, I'll have a fresh young Apache for you."

Outside, Aragon found the Comanche brave named War Song waiting with his men.

"I bring word from Iron Eyes and Hairy Wolf," he told Aragon in Spanish. "They are waiting in the Blanco with a load of about twenty Cheyenne prisoners, all young women and small children."

Safe in the darkness, Aragon permitted himself a wide smile. This was indeed a stroke of fine fortune. "Tell them," he replied, "I'll be there soon."

But even as he slipped back out of Over the River and toward the safety of the remote hills, Aragon finally realized what had been bothering him every since the raid on his Apache clan's cave. It was Victorio Grayeyes, his cousin. He had seen him sprawled, apparently dead, half in and half out of a fissure. But in the confusion of that night, had anyone verified that he was dead?

Chapter Six

Black Elk pushed his band hard, five riders in all: he, his cousin Wolf Who Hunts Smiling, Swift Canoe, and two of Black Elk's troop brothers from the Bull Whip soldier society.

Unencumbered by remounts or many supplies, they made good time across the Llano in spite of the conditions. But as they drew nearer and nearer to the huge canyon River of Winds spoke of, not slackening their rapid pace, some of the others began to talk among themselves.

"Brother," Swift Canoe said to Wolf Who Hunts Smiling late in the afternoon as their shadows lengthened behind them in the dust haze, "you have seen me count coup and kill my enemies. But look out there, nothing covers the land! Your cousin trained us, and Black Elk is no warrior to fool with. But I fear he is leading us into certain death. He has no plan. In his jealous rage to keep Touch the Sky from Honey Eater, he is leading us straight into the belly of the beast. We will soon be spotted, if we have not been already."

Swift Canoe was not known for always grasping truth firmly by the tail. But Wolf Who Hunts Smiling nodded at these words, knowing he was right. They had paused to wait, resting their ponies, while Black Elk climbed atop a jumble of rocks to scout the terrain.

"There was a time," he told Swift Canoe, "when I considered Black Elk the best warrior in our tribe. But he has spent too much time thinking about Touch the Sky rutting with his squaw, and now jealousy has tangled him. A war leader can not lead his men in the red heat of emotion against these southern tribes. They are cool killers who smile as they slice an enemy's throat in his sleep."

"What can we do?"

Wolf Who Hunts Smiling's furtive eyes cut to Black Elk, still carefully studying the terrain between their present position and the huge, gaping maw of the Blanco.

"I will speak words with him. But remember, buck. Jealous or not, Black Elk can rise up on his hind legs and make the he-bear roar with the best of them. And he can read signs we cannot even find. I will speak to him, but I will speak carefully. He is in no mood for trifling."

Wolf Who Hunts Smiling untethered his pure black pony and rode across the dust flat to counsel with Black Elk. Each step his pony took sent up a pale white cloud. His cousin was just then climbing down from the rocks as he rode up.

"Black Elk, I would speak with you."

"And so you will," his older cousin said, "but not right now."

Black Elk nodded off to the right, toward the northeast. "There is a deep arroyo in that direction. And right now there is a Comanche hiding in it, hoping we do not spot him! I am keen for him, cousin. We are the fighting Cheyenne! Ride like the wind! These ugly, bowlegged cricket-eaters love to torture their captives—now we will play turnabout. We will put him over the fire and get information from him about their plans for the captives."

Black Elk leaped on his pony. In a moment his rifle was out of its scabbard, his black locks streaming out straight behind him.

"*Hi-ya!*" he screamed. "*Hi-ya hii-ya!*"

Wolf Who Hunts Smiling too took up the war cry, raising his streamered lance high and digging his knees into his pony's flanks. The others, seeing and hearing the commotion, also leaped on their ponies and fell in behind them.

Hooves thundered across the plain as they drew closer to the arroyo.

"He is mine, cousin!" Black Elk shouted. "I want him alive!"

The hidden Comanche had decided to run for it. In a flying leap, his magnificent buckskin pony rose from the arroyo. The Comanche broke for the southwest and the Blanco Canyon, cutting away from them diagonally.

"There he goes!" Black Elk shouted triumphantly. "Now he is ours!"

Black Elk raised his rifle and settled it in the hollow of his shoulder, planning to fire a quick snap-shot and knock the Comanche's horse out from under him. But what happened next caught all of the Cheyenne pursuers by complete surprise and shocked them into disbelief.

They already knew that the Comanches were the undisputed champions of the plains horse-men. But the display this brave now put on made their jaws drop in slack amazement. While he fled, bouncing with effortless ease atop his pony, not even seeming to hang on, he spun easily around to face them. Then he unleashed a deadly volley of arrows, all while riding back-wards.

One after the other they came, as if ten men were firing. He drew new fire-hardened arrows from his quiver and strung them, then fired them, in one smooth, continuous movement. At least ten arrows were launched before Black Elk fired his first shot, missing by a wide margin as he was forced to duck for his life. An arrow thwapped into Black Elk's bone breastplate, and another suddenly caught Wolf Who Hunts Smiling's horse a glancing blow that nonetheless spooked her out of control.

Screaming at the fiery agony, the Bull Whip named Hawk Feather clutched at his belly, try-ing to dislodge the Comanche arrow that had just pierced it. Another dropped out of the chase when an arrow punched into his thigh.

Incredibly, the flurry did not cease. Wolf Who Hunts Smiling was still trying to regain control of his frightened horse. Black Elk had halted and now actually reversed, fleeing back out of range. It had all happened so quickly the Cheyennes had not even had time to swing down into their classic defensive riding posture, hugging the pony's neck to present a small target.

Hawk Feather lay on the ground now, writhing in agony. While Battle Sash, his troop brother, tended to him, Black Elk grimly watched the trailing dust cloud as the Comanche fled to safety.

"It is useless to follow him," he said bitterly. "We will never get close enough for a shot. This is no time to have a pony killed. I wish now that we had cut extras from the herd before we left."

"That is the brave whom River of Winds spoke of," Wolf Who Hunts Smiling said. "And I remember him now from the final attack during the hunt, when they lured us away from camp so the rest could steal our women and children. Did you see the roadrunner skin tied to his pony's tail? The Comanches believe this bird brings them luck. That is how I remember him. That, and did you see that he carries two quivers, he needs so many arrows?"

"All I see," Black Elk said, "is that he will soon return safely to the canyon. And now the Kiowas and Comanches will know we are out here, if they do not already. What about Hawk Feather—can he ride?"

Battle Sash, who had broken the arrow shaft and pushed the point through, nodded. "If he goes easy, he can make it back to camp."

Black Elk said, "Then we are four instead of five. But brothers, hear me well. Now that we are found out, it is useless to stay cowered out here in this dead waste, making clear targets for all who would shoot. Now I think we would do better to make for the canyon—now, while they expect us to flee back toward our camp. River of Winds said there are trees, boulders, natural hiding places. True it is we will be in our enemy's teeth. But sometimes that is the safest place to be."

Black Elk was also thinking something else: Touch the Sky and his small band could not be far behind them. If the Kiowas and Comanches did send a war party out, they might very well mistake Touch the Sky's group for this one the lone warrior had just given the slip. Not only would that take Black Elk's worst enemy out of the picture, it would lull the Kiowa-Comanche bands into a false sense of security.

"Look!" Swift Canoe said.

Black Elk stared where he pointed. A spiral dust cloud approached from the south, the direction of the hunt camp.

"Here comes the mighty shaman now," Black Elk said. "Say nothing to his group about what just happened here. We will say that we were attacked by renegade Apaches. Let the haughty pretend Cheyenne approach the canyon and ride into a deathtrap!"

About the time that Touch the Sky's band came in sight of Black Elk's, Victorio Grayeyes suddenly woke up from a long sleep like death.

Pain exploded in bright orange star wheels when the Apache tried to sit up. Groaning, he lifted one hand slowly and felt the huge, hard, swollen lump covering the back of his skull.

Then the cobwebs of sleep cleared, and memory returned in all its brutal force.

With it came the first, faint traces of the

decaying smell of death. He didn't know how long he had lain there, dead to the world. But it must have been at least several days, judging from the sickly-sweet stink.

Why was he even still alive? He remembered now that one of the soldiers had been ordered to check his body. Then, touching the dry, matted blood covering the back of his skull, he realized what must have happened. The soldier had mistaken all the blood, caused when Victorio slipped on wet shale and struck his head hard, for a bullet to the brain.

With a supreme effort that made dark lines dance across his vision, he managed to sit up and pull himself out of the fissure. Though it was unlikely, he must check to see if anyone else had miraculously survived the surprise raid on the cave. Then there were graves to be dug.

His mother and father and others in his clan lay dead, killed in their blankets. Despite the pain of loss inside, so great it felt like a hot knife twisting into his guts, Victorio bore his suffering as Apaches always did: in stoic silence. But the determined set of his jaw hinted at another truth about Apaches: that they held a grudge until it screamed.

After he dug the graves, he told himself, when he had eaten and rested, it would be time to go in search of Delshay and Josefa—and of course his turncoat cousin who had led the soldiers here, Juan Aragon.

"Brother," Little Horse said, "this thing bothers me. It is not your fault that Honey Eater and the others were taken. Even your enemies, who accuse you of everything from spying for the whites to scaring away the buffalo with your stink, have not made this charge against you."

"It happened while I was in command. That is enough. When we routed that first band of Comanches and Kiowas, and the herd forced several of them over a cliff, I was sure that we had stopped the rear attack on the camp."

"So was I, buck! So were the others present. Like you, we were keen to join the battle, thinking the noncombatants safe. If you were wrong, then so were we all."

Touch the Sky nodded. "I have ears for that. We all *were* wrong. They lured us into a running battle, and the second force we should have routed attacked the camp at will. There can be no excuses, we were wrong, and those we *should* have protected are now doing the hurt dance."

The others listened respectfully. This was spoken by a leader who did not single out warriors to blame—they were a tribe, and as a group the tribe's warriors had failed in their most important function. They had been too intent on covering themselves in glory and adding scalps to their coup sticks, and should have kept calmer heads and thought more like their stealthy enemy.

"But *this* fox has learned to recognize poisoned bait," Touch the Sky said. "Let Black Elk worry about his pride. We are concerned only with the safety of our women and children who are still alive. You have sworn to follow me for this battle. Good. Then place these words in your sashes. There will be no scalps taken, no race to count first coup. We move in shadows and let the wind cover our noise. We strike out of the sun. When all seems lost, we must become our enemy."

Touch the Sky startled himself with these last words, words spoken by the spirit of Chief Yellow Bear during the youth's vision at Medicine Lake. But a bigger surprise lay ahead: Tangle Hair was riding scout and turned around to report that Black Elk's band was apparently waiting for them.

"Draw your weapons," Touch the Sky said, "and watch their eyes, especially Wolf Who Hunts Smiling. They have the numbers over us and may go for us. Let them know we will fall on their bones."

"A man is down!" Tangle Hair called back now. "It's Hawk Feather. And Battle Sash has a wounded thigh."

Touch the Sky immediately felt hot blood rising into his face. "It is as I feared. Black Elk, who once led men into battle with the wisdom of a cunning fox, now shows less brains than a rabbit! He has alerted the enemy! Keep your weapons to hand, and watch their eyes."

Touch the Sky rode up first, Tangle Hair, Little Horse, and Two Twists riding abreast just behind him, covering him. But their tribal enemies did not seem bent on another fight, apparently having just lost one.

"Are you content now?" Touch the Sky demanded of Black Elk. "You swore to save Honey Eater, and this is a fine start. Now we have lost the element of surprise."

"You have been visiting with the mushroom soldiers," Black Elk retorted. "We were jumped by Apaches hiding in that arroyo. No Kiowas or Comanches have seen us."

Touch the Sky, never letting his eyes leave his enemies too long, glanced at the piece of broken arrow lying in the dust beside the supine brave Hawk Feather. It was lighter than the green pine of the Cheyenne arrows—osage, he guessed, or maybe dogwood. Comanches used osage, but so did Apaches.

"Apaches, you say?" He stared at Wolf Who Hunts Smiling. "They rode off, and this hot-blooded warrior did not pursue them?"

"Our mission is to save our women and children," Wolf Who Hunts Smiling said, his dark eyes snapping sparks. "I will kill Apaches some other time."

"I welcome this newfound dedication to the tribe. But know this, even as we speak we might be under observation from enemy scouts. We *certainly* will be if either of our bands proceeds much closer in daylight. I ask you—I *beg* you, for the sake of the prisoners—do not advance further until nightfall."

Wolf Who Hunts Smiling and Swift Canoe exchanged secret glances, amused by Touch the Sky's urgent need to believe the enemy had not been alerted. Clearly, a surprise lay in store for him and his little ragtag band, which included a boy still on mother's milk! Wolf Who Hunts Smiling's keen, furtive eyes missed nothing—they also noticed the jealousy raging in Black Elk's eyes as he too understood the reason for Touch the Sky's concern: Honey Eater.

"Begging should come naturally to a white man's dog," Black Elk said. "But rest easy, Woman Face. We will wait until night."

"Insult me freely," Touch the Sky said before he whirled his chestnut back around. "Call me what you will. One of us will kill the other yet,

Black Elk. But for now we both want the same thing. Do we forget our hatred long enough to join forces and save the others?"

Black Elk did not hesitate the space of a heartbeat. "No! As I said, I will wait until dark to move. But all of them, buck, including Honey Eater, will die a dog's death before I team up with you! You are a squaw-stealing dog who openly pants to put on the old moccasin with my wife. But I swear I will eat your warm liver before you bull my squaw!"

Chapter Seven

Tom Riley secured his horse in the post stables, rubbing her down and slipping a nose bag of oats on her before stalling her for the night. Then he crossed the parade square, heading toward his quarters in a long row of single-story adobe huts behind the headquarters building.

"Captain."

He turned around in the darkness to confront the Papago Indian scout named Rain Dancer. Riley, who was in charge of a platoon of cavalry soldiers, had sent Rain Dancer out for a routine scout of the nearby Llano Estacado. There had been recent reports of large movements of Comanche and Kiowa, the two tribes Riley and his men had been ordered to prevent from raiding supply trains bound for Fort Union near Silverton.

"You're back," Riley said. "How do things look out there?"

"No large war party. The Comanches under Iron Eyes are back in the Blanco Canyon camp. The Kiowa Hairy Wolf and his men are with them. They have prisoners. A word-bringer has been sent to Over the River."

"That means they have prisoners to sell the Comancheros," said Riley. The young officer did not approve of the illegal slave trading. But so long as it involved only Indians, his orders were to ignore it.

"Arapaho prisoners?" he asked.

Rain Dancer shook his head. He was plump and short, and twin braids trailed down from under his Army hat. "Cheyennes."

"Cheyennes? This far south?"

Riley looked thoughtful for a moment. He had originally been stationed farther north at Fort Bates near Bighorn Falls in the Wyoming Territory, near the heart of the Cheyenne hunting grounds. If Cheyennes had come this far south, they must be on a buffalo hunt.

"Not just Cheyenne prisoners," Rain Dancer said. "I have also seen two small bands of Cheyenne warriors. They are moving separately across the Llano. Clearly they mean to rescue the prisoners."

Again Riley looked thoughtful. The young officer was in his twenties, a towhead with a perpetual sunburn that stopped at the brim of his hat. A former enlisted man, he had been breveted to his present rank as the result of superior performance.

"What do the leaders of these two bands look like?" he asked.

"I could not get too close on the Llano. But one is taller and broader in the shoulders than any Cheyenne I have ever seen. At first I was sure he must be an Apache."

Now Riley's thoughtful look had grown sharply curious. "Tall? A young buck?"

Rain Dancer nodded.

Now Riley was silent a long time, thinking. He thought about the youth, once named Matthew Hanchon, who had returned to his white parents to help them fight Hiram Steele, the greedy rancher who was trying to drive the Hanchons from their new mustang spread. Riley had met the youth and respected him. When the officer learned that his colleague, Lt. Seth Carlson, was in cahoots with Steele, he had decided to secretly help the Hanchon boy. Together they had defeated Steele and Carlson.

Could this be the same youth? The tall Cheyenne now called Touch the Sky?

Riley made up his mind. Lately he and his men had been patrolling north of the Llano. Now it was time to swing closer and keep an eye on things.

"Prepare to ride out with me in the morning," he told Rain Dancer. "I want to take a look at things on the Llano."

"By now," Black Elk told the others in his band, "the Comanche brave we chased off will have reached the Blanco Canyon and alerted the rest. If they are not riding out to meet us, they will be poised for our arrival. Only, it will not be us they

71

encounter— we will let Touch the Sky ride into the teeth of the enemy."

Full dark had descended over the Llano Estacado. Black Elk and his band had sheltered in the same arroyo from which they had routed the Comanche spy. Touch the Sky and his group had taken cover behind the jumble of rocks which Black Elk had climbed earlier to scout the terrain. The wind howled in steady shrieks which forced the braves to raise their voices to be heard. Hawk Feather's wound had been packed in moist tobacco and wrapped with doeskin. Then he had been sent back to camp. Now there were four in the band.

"But cousin, what about us?" Wolf Who Hunts Smiling said. "How do we get into that canyon without being spotted?"

"A herd divided weakens itself, cousin. Under cover of this darkness, the others will soon advance closer to the canyon unaware that their arrival is expected. Using night's cloak to cover us, we follow them. When the enemy attacks them, count upon it, they will put up a good fight. I hate Touch the Sky, but he is a warrior, and Little Horse and Tangle Hair can fight like ten men.

"This bloody fight will keep the enemy engaged. It is then, when their attention is elsewhere, that we will move into the cover of the canyon. But we must avoid the fight or even being seen."

Suddenly, above the mating-wolf howl of the wind, they heard the Bull Whip named Battle Sash loose a whistle. He was on sentry duty between their position and the jumble of rocks.

"There is the signal," Black Elk said. "They are moving out. Prepare to ride, brothers, and remember. Glide like a shadow. We will stay well behind them until they meet the enemy, then we make our move."

All through the night Touch the Sky pushed his band across the treacherous Llano, orienting himself by the Grandmother Star to the north.

More than ever before Touch the Sky now realized the importance of not being observed before they reached the safety of that canyon. There was simply no place to run if they were attacked, nor were their numbers enough to stand and hold. But something had to be done. Every day that passed was one more day that Honey Eater and the rest spent in misery and terror—and brought them one day closer to being sold, perhaps to disappear in unknown lands where Touch the Sky could never find them again.

They rode fast under cover of a clouded sky that gave off little moonlight. He no longer worried about where Black Elk was. His only goal now was to reach that canyon under cover of night, elude the sentries and herd guards, and get into position close enough to obtain some information on the prisoners and their whereabouts.

Finally, as the eastern sky began to take on the first roseate hues of morning, they topped a long rise and Touch the Sky halted his band. A slight difference in the darkness out ahead of them told his night-trained eye that a vast opening lay before them—the Blanco Canyon.

As the moon began to peek out from behind a scud of clouds, Touch the Sky warned his men to move further down off the ridge so they would not be skylined.

"Now we are in the belly of the beast," he warned

the others. "From here, wrap the ponies' hooves in rawhide to muffle them. And lead the ponies, do not ride them. Secure any gear on your pony which might give off a noise. And whatever you do, do not let the wind get behind you or the horse herds will alert our enemy. Even now this area must be ringed with sentries. If we are seen, count upon it, be prepared to sing the death song."

He thought of something else. "Before we move out, transfer your rigging and gear to the remounts. If we must run for it, at least we will have the freshest ponies."

They made their final preparations, then fanned out. Step by slow step Touch the Sky advanced toward the rim of the canyon, trying to use whatever depressions and hummocks he could find for cover. It seemed ominously quiet, as if not a soul stirred below in the wide canyon.

The wind had fallen silent. In the stillness, Touch the Sky winced when his chestnut pony, smelling the herds and the river below, nickered.

They moved steadily closer. Now the edge was so near that Touch the Sky could feel the subtle change in temperature that always marked a deep canyon. Elation began to hum in his blood. Only a few more paces and they would be on their way down. Cheyennes were excellent at taking cover and could operate for days unseen in the shelter of thickets and shrubs.

Abruptly, he heard the loud, fast clicking of a lizard. He thought nothing of it until another lizard answered the signal. What happened only a few heartbeats later shocked all the Cheyenne braves into frightened immobility.

The Comanches and Kiowas loved to mock their

enemies in battle. One of them had captured a bugle during a skirmish with Bluecoats. Alerted by Big Tree's report, they had been fully aware when Touch the Sky's band approached so quietly. Now the Comanche bugler suddenly blasted the rousing cavalry charge known as "Boots and Saddles," the bugle notes frighteningly amplified against the stillness of the night.

Yipping their battle cries, the enemy poured up from the canyon and leaped out onto the plains, racing straight at the startled Cheyennes.

"Fly like the wind!" Touch the Sky shouted to his companions.

Now he gave silent thanks to Maiyun for granting him the foresight to insist on remounts. All four Cheyennes mounted their ponies in running leaps and turned them away from the attack, heading back in the direction they had just come.

Fortunately, though their enemies had sufficient handguns, they were short on rifles and ammunition for them. Now a deadly hail of arrows filled the air all around them as they began a desperate running battle—the style of fighting which the Cheyennes had originally developed.

An arrow flew past Touch the Sky's head so close he felt a hot wire of pain crease his ear. He glimpsed Little Horse on his left and Two Twists and Tangle Hair on his right, all bent low over the necks of their ponies as they drove them on. Behind them, rolling thunder welled closer as their enemy gained on them.

"Hi-ya!" Touch the Sky urged his mount, lashing her with the buffalo-hair reins. "Hi-ya hii-ya!"

Behind him, the bugle notes mocked them,

bringing the promise of an agonizing death closer
and closer.

Black Elk's band had tracked Touch the Sky's
all night, staying well back and far to the right
of them. Now they too sprang into action at the
sound of the bugle notes. Only they ran in the
opposite direction—right toward the Blanco.

As Black Elk had predicted, the enemy's attention was focused on the other Cheyennes. And a
good thing, he realized. Their own mounts were
nearly exhausted and dehydrated. Had they been
forced to flee like Touch the Sky's group, they
would have been sent under by now.

But as things worked out, they reached the brim
of the canyon unchallenged and unobserved.

"Quickly!" Black Elk said triumphantly. "Make
for cover."

He was elated. Not only had they finally slipped
into the formidable Blanco Canyon, considered an
impregnable fortress—but soon his worst enemy
would be roasting over a blazing fire, and with
luck Black Elk could even watch him die.

As the sun burst forth from her birthplace
in the east, Touch the Sky's little group were
grimly living up to their nickname, the fighting
Cheyenne.

Thanks to their reasonably fresh ponies, they
were able to execute the classic Cheyenne fighting strategy: They fled hard until their pursuers'
horses started to falter, then suddenly whirled
and fired on them. In this they were also aided
by the range of their long arms, which easily
dropped the enemy ponies.

Time after time, when death was apparently about to envelope them, Touch the Sky screamed the command and they whirled, firing another volley.

"One bullet, one enemy!" he screamed repeatedly, calming the less-experienced Two Twists and reminding the youth that each shot had to count. At one point, when several enemy riders were about to converge on Two Twists, Little Horse suddenly rode into their midst with all four barrels of his flintlock shotgun loaded. He fired and rotated, fired and rotated, blasting horses and Indians into eternity.

Slowly, as they advanced across the plains, a trail of dead ponies, Kiowas, and Comanches gave silent testimony to the skill of these northern warriors. But the more that dropped, the more determined the rest became to seize these hated enemies.

The Cheyenne ponies were beginning to falter, and the warriors' gun barrels were smoking hot, ammunition was low. Worst of all, the new day's light showed no hope of shelter in any direction. Soon their horses would play out and they would have to sing the death song, killing each other to avoid certain torture.

Then, amazingly, the enemy abruptly halted behind them. Even more amazingly, moments later they reversed course and began riding hard back toward the Blanco. Touch the Sky realized why when Little Horse suddenly shouted his name.

"Look!"

The sturdy little warrior pointed to the east. There, flying over the horizon, was a detachment of Bluecoat pony soldiers, an American flag snapping and fluttering in the wind. The soldiers ignored the smaller band of Cheyennes, giving chase to the larger battle party. They would stop before actually entering the canyon, of course. But their presence above would keep the Kiowas and Comanches below.

"Never," Touch the Sky told the others, "did I think I would be relieved to see Bluecoats!"

He was too far away to recognize the officer leading them as his old friend Tom Riley. Nor was this any time for rejoicing. They were still stuck in the middle of hostile territory, unable to penetrate that canyon. Honey Eater and the others were no closer to freedom. And where was Black Elk's band?

They had eluded death this time only by a miracle. And miracles never happened twice in a row. Nor was there any proof those blue-bloused pony soldiers might not soon ride against his band.

"Brothers," Little Horse said as they veered west from the direction of the attack, "did any of you spot the fleet-shooting Comanche called Big Tree? I could not."

"Count upon it," Touch the Sky said. "He was not in the attack. When trouble threatens this close to the hive, Big Tree is kept in the canyon. But be patient, you shall meet him soon, brother, because the canyon is where we are headed!"

Chapter Eight

"It was their own hotheaded foolishness which warned us," said Hairy Wolf, leader of the Kiowas from Medicine Lodge Creek. "Now I think the Cheyenne warriors who dashed at us like summer-drunk colts will be lurking about in the darkness. We should give them something to listen to. Something to remind them of what they have brought upon their own people."

"Well said, Kaitsenko warrior," Iron Eyes said. "We cannot afford to waste another Cheyenne. But Stone Mountain was scouting the north rim of the Blanco and captured a Caddoe woman. Though she is young, she is fat and has been scarred by pox and is worth nothing to Aragon. We will put her to the coals and let her screams accompany our Cheyennes into sleep. If we cut out her tongue first, she will not be able to speak her language and they will never know she is not one of theirs."

Iron Eyes paused before adding, "This one thing troubles me. When Big Tree rode in to tell us a Cheyenne band was on the way, he did not say the tall young bear-caller was among them. I asked him when we returned, and he said the youthful shaman was not one of them. Yet you saw him too! Could it be that these northern dogs, who foolishly treat their women better than their horses, have played our own trick upon us?"

Hairy Wolf did not have to ask what trick he meant. By dividing into two bands and letting one serve as a lure, the Kiowas and Comanches had made off with their valuable prize of many women and children. Now Iron Eyes was suggesting the Cheyenne too might have just tricked them—meaning that instead of only lurking up on the plains, Cheyennes might be within the Blanco Canyon walls right now.

Iron Eyes stepped outside of the mesquite hut and stared out at the canyon with the deep-brown eyes characteristic of the Quohada Comanche. He had a sun-darkened, oval face. His hair was shorter than Hairy Wolf's, parted exactly in the center and worn just long enough to brush behind his ears.

His eyes again studied the single trail into the canyon, a narrow and rock-strewn path which descended by a series of sharp cutbanks. Blanco Canyon was the largest single break dividing the Staked Plain, so of course it could be entered elsewhere on horseback. But that would mean many more hard miles across treeless, bone-dry wasteland. And although the fertile canyon, divided by the Rio de Lagrimas or River of Tears, provided much cover, it was also heavily patrolled by mounted guards for the magnificent pony herds, the best on all the plains.

Hairy Wolf saw where he looked and nodded at his smaller companion. "We are tipping lances with Cheyennes, so anything is possible. I will speak to Big Tree and the other guards, warning them. Aragon will be here soon. With luck, the prisoners will be gone soon."

Iron Eyes said, "Speaking of Big Tree. Have you noticed how he watches the Cheyenne girl? How he taunts her in her own tongue, making her face flame red?"

"I have noticed this thing, Quohada. But he is your man. You know him better. Will he go for her?"

"Perhaps," Iron Eyes said, "perhaps not. Thanks to us he lives better than the rest. But when he looks at the bob-tailed beauty, his loins burst into flame. He knows that you and I have set her off until an arrangement can be made between us. We are war leaders, he respects that. But you understand, Big Tree has done much for us and has a certain right."

"If he must demand his rights," Hairy Wolf said, "let it be with another of the girls. There are several fine ones besides her."

Iron Eyes nodded. "I will tell him this."

"Brother," Hairy Wolf said, meeting his companion firmly in the eye, "I have not yet visited her."

Iron Eyes did not look away. "Nor have I. Do you hint that I have?"

"Of course not, brother. But any man would want to."

"Yes," Iron Eyes agreed, watching his friend shrewdly. "Any man would."

"However," Hairy Wolf said, "we have raised our lances together in battle many times. A mere thing worth less than a good horse would not make us fight like dogs over a scrap of meat."

"Well spoken, Kaitsenko. Besides, if the men see us going to her, we will never keep them from the rest of them."

"Good. We think as one. But I warn you, speak to Big Tree. I fear we may have asked the cat to guard the bird."

Honey Eater's misery was complete.

She had been isolated in a mesquite-branch jacal with a fierce warrior—usually the Comanche called Big Tree, who spoke Cheyenne—always just outside the single entrance. She was completely cut off from Singing Bird and the rest. The only sign of them was an occasional cry from the jacal where the children were gathered together. Her eyes were swollen and red, now almost tearless, from so much crying.

She told herself, again, that she must stop this useless sobbing and look for a plan of action.

Was she not a Cheyenne woman? Was her tribe not known throughout the Great Plains as the Fighting Cheyenne? In her heart she knew that her tribe would not desert them. But neither would Chief Gray Thunder or the soldier troop leaders be willing to risk the entire tribe to save these prisoners. She could not merely wait and wring her hands, hoping for rescue. If she saw even the slightest chance of escaping and aiding the others, she must take it.

She told herself again that she must use every possible weapon. And she had already noticed how the two war leaders jealously watched each other when near her. Honey Eater would never disgrace herself, but she would risk much for her tribe.

The two war leaders made her shudder in fearful disgust. The Comanche had a hard, pinched face and eyes made mean from witnessing too much killing and brutality. The Kiowa, though much more handsome, was even more repugnant to her—perhaps because when his eyes went over her, they felt like brutal fingers inspecting meat.

But though both of them frightened and disgusted her, she was even more fearful of Big Tree. In his eyes was the same mad glint of those who had gone Wendigo.

She glanced warily toward the open doorway again. His legs were visible, as was part of his highly feared osage bow. Honey Eater turned away, but without meaning to, once again she found herself staring at a clump of scalps which had been cured, then dyed bright green, vermillion, and yellow and hung from the ceiling with a roadrunner skin.

Big Tree's voice abruptly startled her.

"I wonder which will be the first one to come visit with our pretty prisoner?" he said in slow but clear Cheyenne. "Hairy Wolf or Iron Eyes?"

As always she said nothing. But he did not expect her to speak. He knew she could understand him.

"The Mexicans down in the south country, they say, 'Give the land to those who work it!' I have

83

ears for this. And I say, give the women to those who guard them."

He laughed, but still she held her silence.

"You know, bob-tailed one, I have wondered a thing. These bucks who ride to save you. I wonder if the one I killed, the tall brave with the broad shoulders, was your husband?"

He had glanced inside as he said these words. A sly smile split his face when he saw her face drain white. Then he had guessed correctly! He decided to keep up the lie a bit, just for sport.

"He died hard, little one! My lance punched into him so hard that pink froth blew from his mouth. I carved out his eyes, and—"

"I have no ears for this!" she cried out, the first words she had spoken since begging for Singing Bird's life.

Big Tree laughed again, watching a Comanche buck lead the Caddoe woman toward the half-circle of grass before Iron Eyes' jacal, where firepits had been dug and stakes driven into the ground to facilitate torture sessions. His prisoner could not see her.

"You have no ears?" Big Tree said. "Good. Your god has smiled on you, then. Because once the sun goes to her resting place, one of your Cheyenne sisters will be making much noise."

The Bluecoats had continued north, around the rim of the Blanco and toward Fort Union, after their enemy retreated into the safety of the canyon. Clearly, thought Touch the Sky, they had been concerned only with discouraging a large war party. Still, he was curious—he had seen Indian scouts with the palefaces, and they had probably identified the Cheyennes for their superiors. Why didn't the soldiers investigate armed Cheyennes so far from their legal hunting grounds?

But he had little time to worry over such things. With the darkness they made straight for the Blanco Canyon, determined to either make it or die in the attempt. River of Winds had told them about the single entrance trail. But it would be too heavily guarded. Instead, Touch the Sky planned to enter the canyon well to the east of this trail, on foot leading the sure-footed ponies. It would be risky, but by now every move was.

"Brother," Little Horse said just before Touch the Sky gave the order for total silence, "what happened to Black Elk's band? Are you thinking what I am?"

"You too? Yes, I think Black Elk cleverly lured us into a trap meant for him."

"And that he is already in the canyon?"

Touch the Sky nodded. "If he can save our women and children, then let him. I am not locked in a contest to play the hero. But I no longer trust his judgment. And do not forget, Wolf Who Hunts Smiling and Swift Canoe are there to goad him on in his spiteful foolishness. I will proceed with this rescue as if the others were not here."

Strict silence was ordered now as they once again neared the rim of the vast canyon, this time bearing further away from the entrance. Their only hope now was to get to cover and learn what they could. When they reached the canyon rim, they dismounted and ran their weapons and equipment through one final check.

The descent here would be steep and treacherous, threading their way down a rocky slope and through dangerous piles of talus or loose rock. Each Cheyenne made sure his equipment was securely tied to the horses. Moonlight occasionally leaked through openings in the clouded sky, showing the edge of a huge horse herd below. Using hand signals, Touch the Sky reminded the rest: If they were surprised by herd guards, they must kill them silently.

They soon realized, however, that silence was hardly necessary.

They had made their way about one-third of the distance down the canyon wall, the going rough all the way. The horses, tired and hungry and thirsty, were reluctant to advance toward the unfamiliar smell of so many new horses and men. Handholds were few, a scrub tree here and there, and it was difficult to avoid rock slides. Touch the Sky had already lined his moccasins with handfuls of wiry bunchgrass. Still, sharp pieces of flint cut through the elkskin and into his soles.

Even as they advanced, they had watched a huge fire spring up well to their left, following the curve of the Rio de Lagrimas. The warriors who were not on guard had gathered, drinking corn beer and talking and laughing. Touch the Sky was grateful for the distraction—until a woman's scream of unimaginable pain suddenly rent the dark fabric of the night.

Before any other words entered his mind, Touch the Sky thought: *Honey Eater!*

Again the woman screamed, again, and cheers and shouts and pistol shots rose from the gathered Kiowas and Comanches. As much as he hated the sound, Touch the Sky strained to hear each scream. *Was* it Honey Eater? Pain had so distorted them there was no way to tell.

It hardly mattered, he reminded himself sternly, if it was Honey Eater. That they were torturing a Cheyenne woman was enough. Something had to be done, and immediately.

More screams from below as he huddled down with Tangle Hair, Little Horse, and Two Twists.

"As I said, we must become our enemy! They take pride in their stealth on foot. I need one man to go below with me. There must be herd guards around. We are going to get one ourselves and pay them back in their own goods."

All three volunteered, but he selected Little Horse. They hobbled their ponies and left their long arms with their companions, taking only their knives and tomahawks. Thus unencumbered, they made good time gaining the canyon bottom. The wind was in their faces, and so far they had avoided spooking the herd.

More screams punctuated the stillness of the night and urged them to even greater speed. Touch the Sky had guessed correctly. Plenty of guards were out. Using clumps of grazing ponies for cover, moving quietly to keep from shying them, they crossed closer to the trail where the guards rode.

When the next brave rode by, Touch the Sky suddenly leaped out behind him, took a running jump, and sailed up onto his pony behind him. Even before he landed the flat edge of his tomahawk was arcing toward the Comanche's skull. The man went limp as death when the weapon clubbed him over the right ear. But Touch the Sky held him up on his pony while Little Horse grabbed the reins and led the animal back up to join their companions.

Quickly, before the brave could recover consciousness, Touch the Sky bound him at wrists and ankles with lengths of rawhide. Below, the girl again unleashed a hideous scream.

"Brothers," Touch the Sky said, "unlike them we cannot build a fire. Nor is there time for anything but what must be done. One of our own is being tormented. They know we are here. Let us now let them know they will also pay for their sport.

"As your leader, I cannot order any man to do what I would not be willing to do. Yet I confess, I have been under the knife, over the coals, too often myself to inflict torture. Will someone else do it? If not, I will."

This time the volunteers were not so quick. But finally Tangle Hair said, "Torture sickens me also. But what must be done must be done. I am a Bowstring soldier. Turn your backs, brothers, for it must be fast and hardly pretty!"

The brave had already come to and was staring up defiantly at them. Tangle Hair drew the knife from his beaded sheath.

"Beg," Touch the Sky told him in English, knowing a Comanche was more likely to speak it than Touch the Sky's language. "Beg loudly. It is your only hope."

He turned his back. Below, more screams from the canyon bottom. But suddenly a piercing scream from behind him made Touch the Sky wince. Tangle Hair was indeed doing a good job of inflicting pain with his blade.

More screams, and shouts for mercy in Spanish

and Comanche. Now all the commotion in the canyon had quieted.

"Give him more," Touch the Sky said grimly. "We only have their attention."

Whatever Tangle Hair did next evoked a cry that echoed long out over the canyon.

"Perhaps they will understand our terms," Touch the Sky said. "Let us see if they have lost their appetite for this sport."

Indeed, the entertainment was apparently over. Now the braves, angered that one of their own had been captured, were scattering to search the canyon.

But even as the Cheyenne warriors moved to a more secure position in a thicket of scrub oak, Touch the Sky agonized: Had the victim below been Honey Eater? And did her sudden silence signify release—or death?

Chapter Nine

Juan Aragon decided to travel alone when he went to inspect the Cheyenne prisoners.

The word-bringer from Iron Eyes' camp had warned him that Cheyenne braves were in the area. So he knew that, even if the deal were concluded quickly, he would not be herding the prisoners back. His Comanchero band were experienced fighters and killers, but they were only six strong. Instead, the Kiowa-Comanche band would bring the prisoners to Over the River, assuming a price was agreed upon.

Aragon selected his best blood bay for the ride, a big mare trained for speed and endurance. As always, his shoulder scabbard and machete were strapped over his shirt and the long-barreled cavalry pistol rode low in its stitched-leather holster.

He hoped there were plenty of young women. Valdez and a few others in Over the River would pay well for good woman flesh. Young boys were easy enough to sell also. But they required a longer trip, to Old Mexico and the haciendas of Chihuahua. There they would be put to work in the fields and orchards and mines. Because of the constant threat of rebellion, only young boys were used—when they reached young manhood, "accidents" happened to them or many became "lost." No one really cared what became of Indians.

Aragon trusted no one, but he had little fear of treachery from the Kiowas or Comanches. They were both crafty tribes who recognized the difference between personal feelings and profit—unlike these proud, hotheaded tribes from the lands of the short white days in winter. He had no way of knowing if the Cheyenne tribe knew about him and the local Comanchero slave trading. So he played it safe and assumed they did.

He let his bay set her own pace along a seldom-used trail which wound down from the northern edge of the Blanco. It ran through Comanche burial grounds, and thus was avoided by all area Indians—just as the Blanco Canyon was avoided by all whites. Even Aragon, who though a *mestizo* was raised like most Apaches and thus was not very superstitious, avoided glancing at the heaps of rock which marked the graves.

But other things troubled him more than fear of ghosts. He had been drunk on cactus liquor during the night of the raid on the cave of his Apache clan. He remembered now. The Mexican soldier named Alvarez had called over to him and told him that Victorio was as dead as last summer thanks to a bullet in the head. But Alvarez was a soft-brained fool whom the Mexican Army employed for dirtwork no one else would do. Aragon chastized himself yet again. He should have personally made sure that his cousin was dead.

Any Apache was sweet on revenge. But a Grayeyes of the Jicarilla? Victorio's father had actually infiltrated a Mexican fort to kill the officer who had murdered his first wife. Aragon knew their clan well. The blood of the father flowed in Victorio. Now Aragon regretted getting so drunk and making the offer to help the soldiers. But he felt a little better when he reminded himself that, after all, Victorio was probably dead.

Still, as his horse picked her way along the rough trail, Aragon's slitted eyes scoured the terrain carefully. The small river, its water tainted by salt springs but drinkable, wound along on his right, separated from the trail by cottonwoods and hawthorn bushes. To his left, tall, lush grass was dotted with trees and huge boulders which had fallen from the canyon walls. There were plenty of places to seek cover—whether you were a Cheyenne *or* Victorio Grayeyes, Aragon told himself.

It was small comfort, but an old habit, when his right hand went to the ivory haft of the machete and gripped it.

"Take her clothes off."

Hairy Wolf was happy to comply with Aragon's request. Singing Bird said nothing, only trying to cover her nakedness after the Kiowa war leader pulled her doeskin dress off.

"See?" Iron Eyes said. "She has her rope. Still a virgin."

"I can rub mud on my horse and call her a claybank," Aragon said. "Besides, I can call any girl a virgin yet lose money when she's as sickly and sad as this one. Yes, her face is pleasant to look at, but look how weak she is. Count her ribs!"

"Some bucks like this," Iron Eyes said. Like the other two, he spoke in Spanish. "It makes them pay for a second time with her perhaps."

"The men who buy these women cannot think about this. Their worry is to at least break even— a sickly girl, on a rough night in Over the River, can die before she has earned back her owner's price. Turn her around and slap her hands away so I can see her better."

Aragon looked at her for a long time, circling her, examining her from every angle.

"Well, both of you have brought me steady business. So I will be generous and include her in the lot."

He nodded toward the corner, where Blue Feather sat, still naked though she had huddled into a tight ball to conceal herself. Both girls wore a glazed, battle-shocked look and had given up protesting long ago when they saw it was useless.

"One more like her," he said, "and that old fart Valdez would throw his gold teeth into the bargain. She has meat on her bones, yet plenty of curves and soft places. Just one more like her."

Iron Eyes and Hairy Wolf exchanged a quick glance, but said nothing.

The children Aragon had inspected outside, pronouncing them a fit lot. Girls over 11 or so were lumped with the women; the younger ones would be transported with the boys to be sold in Mexico. Down there, they would face greater indignities than forced labor, but that was not Aragon's problem—to him, human beings were commodities, and Mexican gold spent as easily as American.

"This is the last one, then?" Aragon said.

The two war leaders nodded.

"It is a good group, you are right. I agree to your terms, if you agree to mine. I will supply you and each of your men with a new carbine, ammunition, and rations of tobacco and liquor. You will inspect the merchandise first and approve it before you surrender the prisoners to me.

"In exchange, you two agree to oversee the safe passage of the women prisoners to the outskirts of Over the River, where I and my men will take over for the actual delivery. You will also take the children to my camp."

"I agree," Hairy Wolf said.

"I too," Iron Eyes said.

"I see from all the guards you have out that you are worried about these Cheyennes. Have you had trouble?"

"Just slapping at gnats," Hairy Wolf assured him. "They grabbed one of our herd guards and slit his belly to pull his intestines out. But they cannot strike in any force. We know this canyon like a fox knows its favorite hole. Soon our dogs will eat their livers."

*   *   *

Honey Eater had lost the last of her will to resist when Big Tree announced that he had killed Touch the Sky.

He could be lying, but why? He could not possibly know she loved Touch the Sky. And certainly Big Tree was a brave capable of killing many men.

She knew that something ominous was going on today. She could hear the signs of it: the children crying as they were herded together, men's voices speaking in Spanish, occasional sobs from one of the Cheyenne women. But a buffalo hide had been draped over the entrance to her jacal, hiding her from view. By now she could guess her fate. The two war leaders had their eyes on her. So she was to remain behind while the rest of her tribe was sold into slavery elsewhere.

She knew, of course, that she would commit suicide at the earliest opportunity. Though they had taken her knife, there were certainly other ways. With Touch the Sky dead, she had nothing to live for even if she were rescued. Life as Black Elk's wife was intolerable. He had always been a hard man, but at least he had once been fair. Now jealousy and hatred had bent him.

Suddenly it occured to her: She did not have to stay quiet in here, helping her tormentors to hide her so they could separate her from her tribe. And at the same time, she could rally the others.

There was a prayer song she used to sing at the annual Sun Dance ceremony. She sang it now, her voice rising sweet and pure and clean and carrying the notes outside of her jacal:

Oh, Great Spirit,
Whose voice I hear in the winds,
And whose breath gives life to all the world,
Hear me! I am small and weak, I need your
strength and wisdom.

Aragon was about to swing up onto his blood bay when he heard the lilting voice singing in a language he recognized as Cheyenne. Several children who had been crying inside their jacal now quieted, listening to the comforting words:

Let me walk in beauty, and make my eyes
ever behold the red and purple sunset.
Make my hands respect the things you have
made and my ears sharp to hear your voice.

Make me always ready to come to you with
clean hands and straight eyes.
So when life fades, as the fading sunset,
my spirit may come to you
without shame.

To avoid making Aragon suspicious, Big Tree had been ordered to watch Honey Eater's jacal from a distance. So he was unable to get to her in time to stop her from singing her prayer song. Aragon had been standing near her when she broke into song. Before the two war leaders could make a move to stop him, he had stepped up to the jacal and flung the buffalo hide aside.

His dead-as-stone eyes met Honey Eater's, and the singing stopped.

For a long time Aragon stared, his eyes feasting on beauty the likes of which he could not recall seeing before. He took in the perfectly sculpted, high cheekbones, the flawless skin like wild honey, huge, almond-shaped eyes. Even the ragged crop where her braid had been cut off could not detract from her beauty.

Finally he turned to Hairy Wolf and Iron Eyes.

"So," he said. "No explanations are necessary. You are saving her for yourselves."

Neither man said a word. Honey Eater noticed how the Kiowa and Comanche jealously watched each other around her, watched to see which of them she was looking at. She tried to make each man think she was glancing only at him. She could not understand the Spanish they spoke in, but their meaning was clear enough in the burning eyes they turned on her.

"I cannot blame you for wanting to add her to your own string," Aragon said. "But are you fools? For this one alone I can get as much as I will for the other girls put together. When I get more, you get more."

Still both braves held their silence. This thing was awkward. Their men had still not been told of this decision to keep the Cheyenne girl—nor had Iron Eyes' wives.

"How will you decide which of you gets her?" Aragon persisted. "A man does not willingly share a beauty like this. Will you cut her into two lengths like firewood? She will only cause trouble between two old friends."

Hairy Wolf again glanced at the girl. Her eyes seemed to meet his with secret cunning.

Iron Eyes too found her eyes with his, and was convinced she was telling him she secretly favored him.

"Throw her in with the rest of the lot," Aragon said, "and I will be generous."

Both braves shook their heads.

"She stays here," Hairy Wolf said.

"Right here," Iron Eyes agreed. "We are long-time friends. We can decide this matter."

Aragon laughed, a harsh bark that made Honey Eater wince. "There are no friends where women are involved, compadres! You are both wading into deep waters here. Give her to me with the others. You will avoid much trouble and profit handsomely."

But still the Kiowa and Comanche war leaders refused.

"*Stá bien*," Aragon said, still staring at Honey Eater. Secretly, the Comanchero leader had already decided he *would* sell this sweet little morsel. Valdez was a tight old bastard, but the lecherous old Mexican would buy her for his own regular night woman, and he would pay handsomely.

Honey Eater stared into those eyes like two chips of obsidian, took in the machete in its shoulder scabbard, the cavalry pistol so huge its muzzle ended nearly at his knee. And in that moment a cold shudder moved up her spine as she realized: This half-breed with the short-cropped hair and reptile eyes was more cold and dangerous and murderous than both Indians put together.

Touch the Sky felt his desperation increasing with every heartbeat.

He was ensconced below the rimrock of Blanco Canyon, evenly spaced from the other three in his band. All four Cheyennes had watched, the bitter gall of anger rising in their throats, as the Mexican-Apache half-breed below had inspected their women as if they were meat.

But Touch the Sky, who had been nearly sick with worry ever since the unknown Cheyenne woman had been tortured, had not spotted Honey Eater below. Nor was he close enough to hear her singing. Now the question plagued him in a litany that would not stop: *Was Honey Eater dead?*

Clearly this half-breed was a slave trader. So why wasn't Honey Eater among the others if she were still alive? But on the other hand, why would their enemies kill the one woman who would bring in the best price? Perhaps they meant to keep her for themselves—or even worse, perhaps they had already defiled her with rape, and Honey Eater had found some way to kill herself rather than live with such shame. Not seeing her below gave rise to various possibilities, all harrrowing.

Even in the midst of all these troubling speculations, Touch the Sky became aware of it: an odd tingling in his scalp.

Arrow Keeper's words drifted back to him now from the hinterland of memory:

This mission will be among the most dangerous of your life. You are learning to be a shaman. You must rely on the language of your senses and strong medicine too, not just the warrior way.

Following a hidden impulse, Touch the Sky suddenly shifted his attention from the canyon floor below to the scrub brush just beneath his position.

He stared, stared harder, squinted. Finally he realized what he was looking at, and his face broke out in cold sweat.

Hidden just below him, nearly naked and cleverly camouflaged with mud and brush, was an Apache brave!

Chapter Ten

"You're sure Aragon was by himself?" Tom Riley said.

The Papago Indian scout named Rain Dancer nodded.

"That means he won't be transporting any prisoners soon, then," Riley said. "He must know there are Cheyennes somewhere in the area."

Again Rain Dancer nodded. "This is why he rides alone."

"I don't want to push my luck," Riley said, speculating out loud. His platoon was patrolling the wagon road just north of the Llano, a vital commerce link between the St. Louis settlements and Santa Fe. He had ordered his men to picket their horses and make a nooning. "By treaty, the Blanco Canyon is Comanche territory. If we ride too close too often, we're pushing their hand for a retaliation raid against the settlers."

But Riley was determined now to keep a close eye on this situation. For one thing, the Comanchero slave trading was getting out of hand. Some argued that what the Indians did to their own was no business of the white man's. But Riley had learned it wasn't as simple as the newspaper editorials made it sound. Sometimes, in a desperate bid to buy their loved ones back, Indians would kidnap whites and ransom them. Then the angry citizens lashed out at the Army for being "soft" on Indians.

Besides, recently, when his men had chased the Kiowa-Comanche band back into the Blanco, Riley had recognized Matthew Hanchon through his field glasses—the tall, broad-shouldered Cheyenne called Touch the Sky, who led the small band Riley's men had saved. Riley liked the youth, respected his courage and fighting ability. Accompanied only by his friend Little Horse, Touch the Sky had ridden into a mare's nest of trouble in Bighorn Falls; to save the white parents who had raised him, he had risked death and rejection by his tribe.

Now Riley knew the brave Cheyenne youth was under the gun once again. Only this time, the situation was even more desperate. He was no longer on his home ground or fighting on his own terms. Riley would do what he could, but he was far from having a free hand in this matter. He could not put settlers and soldiers at risk to save a friend—particularly an Indian friend, which U.S. Army officers were not supposed to have.

But it wasn't his men Riley was worried

about. Though bloody contact with Kiowas and Comanches and Pawnees had left many of them keen to kill Indians, they were loyal to their platoon commander. Riley was the type of leader who made sure every last man had eaten before he broke out his own rations. And he never gave an order he himself wouldn't be willing to carry out. As a result, his men would follow him into hell carrying empty carbines.

"Pull up pickets and prepare to mount!" he ordered now, and the squad leaders repeated the order to their troopers. To Rain Dancer he said:

"I want you to stick to the Blanco like ugly on a buzzard. Keep me informed. Odds are, Juan Aragon has arranged to have those prisoners delivered. I want to know at the first sign that they're being moved."

Touch the Sky's first shock of surprise, upon spotting the lone Apache, gave way to rapid action.

He knew the Apache must be overpowered before the element of surprise was lost. Whatever he was doing here, he was surely a risk to the Cheyennes. The two tribes were not at war, but they were longtime enemies. The Cheyennes respected horses so much they made an annual ritual out of their Gift to the Ponies Dance; the Apaches, in barbaric contrast, ate horses as casually as the northern tribes boiled young dogs. The Apaches placed little importance on tribal unity or their gods, and even less on the northern style of horse-mounted warfare on an open battlefield. Such deep-rooted differences kept both tribes suspicious of the other.

Touch the Sky knew he already had enough enemies surrounding his band. They didn't need an Apache drawing a bead on them too. He had to find out what was going on. Perhaps this was a scout preparing the way for a raid—in which case Honey Eater, if she was still alive, and the others faced a new danger.

He made a soft lizard-clicking sound in the back of his throat, signaling to the others. Then, cautiously, he slipped out from behind the shelter of the rimrock and began to make his way slowly down the hard slope of the canyon.

He slithered from shrub to shrub, boulder to boulder, hanging on and moving closer. Still the Apache was intently watching the activity below in camp. Now Touch the Sky was close enough to see the nasty, blood-encrusted gash on the back of the young brave's head.

His foot dislodged a stone and sent it tumbling. The Apache turned quickly around, but Touch the Sky managed to duck behind a rock.

The Apache turned back toward the canyon. Clammy sweat coated the Cheyenne's back as he resumed his downward climb. He slid his knife from its sheath, crouched deep, leaped hard.

He hit the unsuspecting Apache hard and sent him crashing to the ground. For a moment Touch the Sky had him completely pinned. Then, with a mighty twist of his muscle-corded back and shoulders, the strong Apache squirmed out from under him.

They wrestled violently but silently, first one on top, then the other. They were both about the same size, though the mountain-climbing Apache had the advantage in his iron-muscled legs. Now he used those leg muscles to suddenly and violently flip his opponent off him.

Touch the Sky felt himself being lifted, then he landed with a hard *"Whumpf!"* and a bright-orange blossom of pain exploded inside his skull. The blow packed enough force to stun him so that his arms and legs felt like lead weights he couldn't move. But the pain wasn't quite severe enough to knock him out.

He was forced to watch, helpless, as the Apache drew a long Spanish bayonet from his sash. Deep blood gutters had been carved into both sides of the blade.

Their eyes met, the Cheyenne's a deep, fierce black, the Apache's a bottomless, nimbus gray. His flowing black mane of hair was held in place with a strip of red flannel.

The paralyzing blow had stunned Touch the Sky's speech muscles too. Now all he could do was stare defiantly at his enemy, his lips set in their straight, determined line.

The Apache tensed his muscles, preparing to seek warm vitals with cold steel. But at the last moment, impressed by the defiant lack of fear in the Cheyenne's eyes, he relented. Instead, he dropped to his knees and pressed the lethally honed edge of the bayonet to the supine man's throat.

The Apache said something in an unintelligible language which Touch the Sky assumed must be his own tongue.

The Apache spoke again. *"Qué haces aquí?"*

Touch the Sky thought he recognized the language as Spanish, but he didn't know the words.

A third time the Apache spoke, though clearly

his face showed that he held little hope of being understood. "What are you doing here?" he said in stiff but adequate English.

Still Touch the Sky couldn't speak. But the shock of again hearing his native language showed in his eyes.

"You understand?" the Apache said.

Touch the Sky blinked rapidly, indicating a "yes" answer. Now a prickling tingle up his spine hinted that power was returning to his dead limbs.

"Understand," he gasped.

"What are you doing here?" the Apache repeated.

For a few moments longer Touch the Sky lay helpless. But now he could twitch his legs, his arms.

"Take the blade away from my throat," he said. "Right now I couldn't attack a fly."

The Apache watched him a moment, calculating. Then he slid the bayonet back into his sash.

"You speak good English," he said. "Too good for an Indian. My name is Victorio Grayeyes. Who are you?"

"I am called Touch the Sky. I am with Gray Thunder's tribe. Our permanent summer camp is at the fork of the Powder and the Little Powder Rivers."

"You have strayed far from your hunting grounds, Cheyenne."

Touch the Sky nodded. "That's because the white man's stink has driven the buffalo herds far south. My tribe came down here for the hunt."

"The hunt? Surely you are not searching for buffalos in *this* canyon?"

"Not for buffalos," Touch the Sky replied grimly. "For my people. These Kiowa and Comanche dogs raided our camp while the hunters were out. They have stolen many of our women and children."

It was Victorio's turn to nod. He had already learned, from runners, that Aragon was coming here from Over the River. He had hoped to follow him and learn where his brother and sister were being held.

"Yes, I understand. And that short-haired dog below is making arrangements to sell them."

"Clearly. Do you know him?"

Victorio's face hardened, his gray eyes narrowing to slits as he glanced below. "Know him? Cheyenne, his name is Juan Aragon and he is my clan cousin. Only, he is like a cat who eats her own young. This gold-hungry soldiers' dog led Mexicans to our cave. They killed my mother and father and others in my clan. But that treachery was not enough. He also took Delshay and Josefa, my younger brother and sister, planning to sell them. However, he made one drunken, stupid mistake."

Victorio pointed to his blood-matted hair. "He failed to make sure that I was dead. Now I plan to make sure *he* soon will be."

Touch the Sky nodded. "So that's the way it is."

"Are you by yourself?"

"No," Touch the Sky said. "Three others are hidden up near the rim. We could not send a large war party and desert the rest of the tribe. Besides, a large group of warriors could never enter this canyon without being picked off like birds on the ground."

"True words, buck. Even the blue-bloused soldiers with their big-thundering guns will not attack the Blanco."

But Victorio was thinking. By himself he was virtually helpless. However, with a few Cheyennes on his side, the odds might look a little better. Victorio, like most Apaches, considered the Cheyennes an hereditary enemy. But no one had ever called them cowards or poor fighters. And like him, they were motivated by the need to rescue their own.

Touch the Sky too was thinking much the same thing. He knew nothing about this area, where this half-breed Comanchero dog named Juan Aragon had his camp. It would be valuable to have a local on their side, especially one who hated the Comanchero as this Apache did.

"Have ears for my words, Victorio. You know that our tribes are no friends to each other. But shall we put our bitter feelings aside this once and join forces? Shall we kill this dog Aragon and get our loved ones back?"

Victorio nodded. Touch the Sky was startled when he offered his hand to shake on it—a white man's custom which northern Plains Indians found hilarious.

"Agreed, Cheyenne. We have a common enemy in Aragon. But have you heard yet of a place called Over the River?"

Touch the Sky shook his head.

"Believe me, it is a human snake pit. This is where Aragon sells his women. And this, I fear, is where we will end up fighting before this is over."

"I will take the fight wherever it must go," Touch the Sky said. He didn't add what he was thinking: that he hoped to Maiyun it wasn't already too late for Honey Eater.

Chapter Eleven

From where he was hidden, Black Elk had a far different angle of vision into the Blanco Canyon.

Black Elk, his cousin Wolf Who Hunts Smiling, Swift Canoe, and the Bull Whip soldier named Battle Sash were hidden at intervals in the thickets bordering the Rio de Lagrimas River. Thanks to their trick of luring the enemy out of the canyon to chase Touch the Sky's band, they had been able to penetrate further into the Blanco than the other Cheyennes had been able to get before being forced to find concealment.

Black Elk and the others with him realized Touch the Sky's band had escaped and made it to the canyon—there could be no doubt of it when, last night, that captured herd guard had cried out, clearly the victim of Cheyennes. But the location of that scream also told Black Elk his tribal enemy was not nearly as close to the camp as his band was.

When the short-haired half-breed with the long knife dangling from his shoulder had whipped aside the buffalo robe of that lone jacal below, Black Elk had glimpsed Honey Eater. Thus he now knew not only that she was alive, but exactly where she was being kept.

But so far, Black Elk thought, the advantage had proven useless. Like Touch the Sky and the others, they had been so far helpless to act. The camp was crawling with armed warriors, as were the outlying meadows and groves of the fertile canyon. It was risky enough simply trying to keep their ponies grazing without being spotted.

But even worse, he told himself, watching the slave trader's big blood bay return toward the northern entrance of the Blanco, arrangements had clearly been made, terms agreed upon. Preparations for a journey were under way. The Cheyenne prisoners would soon be transported out of here—protected by a guard so strong that at least 40 warriors would be required to mount a good battle against them.

Either he acted soon, or the opportunity was lost.

Black Elk was nearly wild with frustration and impatience. It was not just a question of rescuing Honey Eater and the others. The Cheyenne war leader also knew that his reputation with the other braves was on the line. Every one in the tribe knew of the love between Honey Eater and Touch the Sky. It had become a great unspoken thing of tribal life, an unofficial legend. Indeed, Black Elk had even heard the young girls singing about it in their sewing lodge—falling silent when they saw him walking past.

Every one also knew that Black Elk had not yet planted a baby in Honey Eater's belly. Some hinted that perhaps he could not sire a whelp. It would only humiliate him further and add to the talk if Touch the Sky saved Honey Eater and the others.

As he did often lately, Black Elk cast his thoughts back to the early days of Touch the Sky's life with the tribe. After the raid on the camp of Henri Lagace and his whiskey traders, the Council of Forty had met to vote on Touch the Sky's fate: Half had voted to expel the youth for disobeying Black Elk and infiltrating the camp alone; half had voted to let him stay because, despite his disobedience, his courage had won the fight.

The tie-breaking vote had gone to Black Elk as war leader. After agonizing indecision, he had selected a white moonstone from the pouch—signifying his decision to let Touch the Sky stay. But now, how he regretted that decision! He could never have foreseen it: The inept, ignorant youth who couldn't even make a proper fire or sharpen a knife Indian fashion had developed into a dangerous, hard-edged warrior keen to raise his enemy's hair.

So what if Honey Eater loved the tall young buck? She is *my* property, he reminded himself fiercely. He had paid the bride-price for her, and a handsome bride-price it was—not only a string of fine ponies with hand-stitched bridles, but two travois piled high with valuable goods. This Touch the Sky did not even own meat racks!

But the young warrior's blood was hot with plans to put the old moccasin on—for everyone knew that inexperienced bucks wanted squaws who had been married once before.

But Black Elk vowed again to kill both of them before he let Touch the Sky rut on his squaw.

Now he scanned the vast canyon walls, trying to spot some sign of Touch the Sky's band. But if they were out there, they were hidden well.

He watched the sun, a fiery-orange orb, descend further toward the western horizon. And as it dipped toward its resting place, Black Elk made up his mind.

It was a dangerous plan, but it would have to be done. He realized now that rescuing all of the prisoners was out of the question. Yet if he stayed hidden here much longer in the brush, cowering like a white-livered Ponca, Honey Eater and the others would be taken away. Clearly there was only one solution.

It would be foolish, he told himself, to return from this mission without at least getting his wife—and thus, his manly respect—back. He had seen which jacal was Honey Eater's prison—the lone one which stood between the camp clearing and the river. The one which was always heavily guarded—often, by the same fierce, swift-riding Comanche warrior who had sent Black Elk's band scurrying from a hailstorm of deadly arrows.

But his mind was made up. He would slip into camp after dark by himself and rescue just Honey Eater.

"Look!" Wolf Who Hunts Smiling said to Swift Canoe. "Over there, toward that redrock pinnacle to the east. I saw Little Horse!"

Swift Canoe narrowed his eyes to slits, but could see nothing. His vision was not as keen as that of Wolf Who Hunts Smiling, whose swift-as-minnow eyes missed nothing.

"Brother, I see nothing but rock and brush, and plenty of that."

"He showed himself only for a moment," Wolf Who Hunts Smiling insisted. "But it was Little Horse."

"That means Touch the Sky cannot be far away. They are like a rock and its shadow."

Wolf Who Hunts Smiling nodded. "Now we know where they are. That may become useful to know."

For his own reasons, Wolf Who Hunts Smiling's eagerness to see Touch the Sky dead matched that of the insanely jealous Black Elk. The young Cheyenne was even more ambitious than his cousin. He dreamed of soon leading his own soldier society within the tribe, of someday leading the entire Shaiyena nation. But this Touch the Sky, he was trouble. Clearly Arrow Keeper and some others—foolishly swayed by this supposed "vision" of Touch the Sky's greatness—were grooming the white man's dog for leadership in the tribe.

Wolf Who Hunts Smiling knew he and Touch the Sky would eventually have to fight—and fight to the death. The two of them represented entirely different courses for the tribe's future. This Touch the Sky, he carried the white man's stink on him. Thus he preached that some whites might be trusted, that the Indians must try to cooperate to survive. Wolf Who Hunts Smiling would have none of this womanly talk—he had watched, numb with horror, when bluecoat canister shot had turned his father into stew meat. The red nation must wage a war of extermination against the white nation! And he himself dreamed of raising the lance of leadership for that great battle of all battles.

A twig snapped, just to their left in the gathering twilight, and instantly both Cheyennes had their knives clutched in their hands.

But it was only Black Elk.

"Stand easy, brothers. Any word?"

"Good news, cousin," Wolf Who Hunts Smiling said. He pointed toward the redrock pinnacle, now a silhouette. "I saw Little Horse, just moments ago. Touch the Sky's band must be hiding near that pinnacle."

Black Elk said nothing, but a mirthless smile touched his lips. His crudely sewn-on flap of dead ear made him look fierce in the dying light.

"Perhaps they plan to move closer after dark," he said, thinking out loud. "I must make my move first."

Quickly he explained his reckless plan to the other two. Wolf Who Hunts Smiling remained quiet after his cousin had spoken, thinking. Then he smiled the furtive grin that had earned him his name. He said:

"Cousin! Now have ears for *my* plan. Swift Canoe and I will not only provide a distraction to cover your movement. We will also finally send Touch the Sky under for good!"

Night descended over the canyon, dark as black agate. While Black Elk prepared to move into the heart of the enemy stronghold, Wolf Who Hunts

Smiling and Swift Canoe were making their way toward the redrock pinnacle at the rim of the canyon.

They moved on foot. Their skin had been darkened with river mud, their eyes conditioned to darkness by keeping their heads wrapped in their buffalo robes. They wore double moccasins against the sharp-edged rocks.

They knew they faced two enemies, the Kiowa-Comanche marauders and their own fellow Cheyennes. So they moved carefully by predetermined bounds, pausing often to listen and look and smell. Each time the wind shrieked, covering them, they moved in quick spurts.

They had no intention of confronting Touch the Sky or his companions. Their goal was to reach the dry, wind-whipped bunchgrass and creosote above them.

Wolf Who Hunts Smiling was in the lead. He disappeared inside a thicket. Moments later, Swift Canoe heard a soft owl hoot signal from him and hurried forward to see what he wanted.

"Maiyun has smiled on us, brother," Wolf Who Hunts Smiling whispered in the darkness, pointing to the small group of Cheyenne ponies tethered behind the thicket. "Cut the tethers!"

They removed their knives and sliced through the rawhide strips, freeing the ponies. Then they resumed their arduous climb up the canyon slope toward the plain above.

They encountered no further sign of the others. As smooth as cloud shadows, they slipped over the rim of the canyon and ran further back into the dry grass and creosote.

They stooped and began making little piles

from the punk, tiny wood shavings, they carried in their possibles bags. They heaped bigger sticks and handfuls of grass over these. Then each youth removed the flint and steel from his bag and struck sparks into the piles of kindling, the wind quickly flaming them into life.

"Quickly!" Wolf Who Hunts Smiling said, his voice gloating with triumph. "Back into the canyon, and steer well clear of Woman Face and the others. They are too close under the rim of the canyon and will not see the flames as soon as the Kiowas and Comanches will.

"Quickly!" he urged again when Swift Canoe paused to watch a small spear tip of flame swell in the wind until it was like a flaming tumbleweed, igniting more grass as it bounced along. "In moments our enemy will send riders to investigate!"

Chapter Twelve

Touch the Sky, still ignorant of the fire above them, signaled for a council soon after dark. Little Horse, Tangle Hair, and Two Twists gaped in unbelieving astonishment when they showed up at their leader's position and saw him squatting side by side with an Apache.

"This is Victorio Grayeyes," he told the others. "The same man you just watched pinching our women has killed his parents and stolen his brother and sister. He knows this area and can be useful to us."

"You are letting him join us?" Little Horse said doubtfully. "I am sorry for what happened to his people, truly. But his tribe, how many times have they come north to steal our ponies?"

"We would not have to come so far north," Grayeyes replied when Touch the Sky had trans-

118

lated this, "if combined Sioux and Cheyenne might had not driven us so far south."

"No sense licking old wounds," Touch the Sky said impatiently. Now he was almost convinced that Honey Eater had been killed by their enemy. A flat, dead anger had been growing inside him, a powerful thirst to save the rest and get revenge on these murdering, drunken pigs.

"We have a common enemy now. If we move quickly, we might save our people *and* the Apache children. No matter what grudges exist between our two tribes, surely we all agree that the children are not to blame? Let us join for this battle and get them back."

All agreed to these sensible words. But before they could begin discussion of a plan of action, bad news arrived. Touch the Sky had sent Two Twists below to check on their mounts. Now he returned, out of breath from running. He held up the cut strips of rawhide.

"Brothers! They have found our horses! I found these in the thicket, but no sign of our ponies. They are either stolen or scattered."

The seriousness of this shocked the others into silence. Without horses, this far out on the Llano Estacado, they were food for the carrion birds.

But their troubles were just beginning. Even before Touch the Sky could speak, excited cries broke out from the camp below them. They could see, in the flickering penumbra of the camp fires below, braves pointing up toward their position near the redrock pinnacle.

"What is happening?" Little Horse said. "They cannot possibly see us!"

Touch the Sky, who had just detected the first

acrid whiff of smoke, now turned to look up the steep slope behind them. The flames were still not visible from this angle. But the night sky held an unnatural glow.

"No, brother," he said grimly, "they do not see us. But I suspect Wolf Who Hunts Smiling and Swift Canoe have been playing the fox again. Look up there behind us! The prairie is on fire!"

Now they could hear the faint crackling and snapping sounds, the deep, hollow roars when gusts of wind caught pockets of fire and whipped them into huge walls of flame.

Already braves from the camp below were mounting and racing up to check on the fire. They would ride right through the Cheyennes' hiding place.

"Without ponies, how will we flee?" Tangle Hair said.

"There will be no fleeing," Touch the Sky replied grimly. "We could never outrun them, even if we can get around that grass fire up there. Nor is there any shelter outside the canyon. Yet we cannot give up this spot."

The others nodded, knowing he was right. One of the first laws of warfare, ground into them from their earliest training, was *take to the high ground and never surrender it.*

Now the flames had reached the edge of the canyon and were licking over the rim, casting an eerie orange glow down onto their position. Touch the Sky made up his mind.

"Here they come! They know we are here now. If we merely hide in the rocks and bushes, they will flush us out like rabbits and kill us for sport. Better that we take a bolder step. We have a good position with light to aim by. Spread out and take up a secure position. Then, as soon as our enemy ride into effective range, bring them down! One bullet, one enemy. Do not waste a shot, or we had all best sing our death songs!"

Quickly they fanned out, forming a skirmish line. Touch the Sky had his percussion-action Sharps, Little Horse his four-barrel shotgun. Tangle Hair and Two Twists were both armed with small-caliber but sturdy British trade rifles, Victorio Grayeyes with a captured cavalry carbine.

Touch the Sky had seen the nervous but determined frown on Two Twists' face when the young buck left to take up his position. He was still inexperienced in combat, and now Touch the Sky called out to him:

"Hold steady, Two Twists! Just as you did at the hunt camp when our enemy bore down on us. You are a fighting Cheyenne from the north country—show these dogs that you are *for* them!"

Now they could hear the hollow pounding of hooves as the first riders neared their position. The fire behind them was a roaring inferno now, lashed to a howling fury by an unrelenting wind.

"When you can see their faces," Touch the Sky called out to his men, "let them taste lead!"

In their excitement, the Kiowas and Comanches were loosing their yipping war cries. A brave rounded a rock formation below, bearing straight for the redrock pinnacle. Touch the Sky, ensconced in a slight depression behind a low wall of stones he had hastily erected, drew a bead on the man's chest and fired. The warrior flung both hands to the sky and flew off the back of his horse.

To Touch the Sky's left, the Apache's carbine spat fire into the night and a Comanche's face exploded. There were sharper, thinner cracks as the British trade guns fired, bringing down more horses and men.

This sudden and unexpected resistance slowed down the charge. But as the rest of the braves below saw their companions riding into trouble, more of them mounted and joined the fray.

Their enemy was not well supplied with long arms. But their cavalry pistols were plentiful and deadly at short range. Now the Kiowas and Comanches began to take up positions as they learned where the Cheyennes were hidden. Soon there were at least ten enemy braves for every hidden defender.

Desperately, Touch the Sky slipped another percussion cap behind the loading gate of his rifle. But while he was reloading, two Comanches suddenly rushed his position.

He saw them in the flickering firelight from above, their faces twisted with savage war cries. In a moment his throwing ax was in his hand and whirling through the air. It caught one of the Comanches in the chest and split it open, blood spuming in a wide arc. But the second drew a bead on Touch the Sky while he was exposed to throw the ax.

Two Twists stepped out into the open, exposing himself to withering fire, and his trade rifle cracked. The second Comanche dropped dead from his horse. For a moment Touch the Sky met the youth's eyes in the wavering firelight.

"One bullet, one enemy!" the boy said triumphantly, slipping back behind his rock to reload.

Touch the Sky leaped forward, grabbed the fallen brave's loaded pistol, dove for cover again. He had just barely made it when a literal wall of arrows cracked into the rock and whumped into the ground all around him. He risked a quick glance and saw him: the ferocious warrior who wore two arrow quivers and a roadrunner skin tied to his pony's tail.

Again, despite his hatred and fear, Touch the sky felt a grudging sense of admiration as he watched the fearless Comanche bounce atop his pony as if connected by invisible sinews, never once bothering to hang on. He was one with his horse. He strung and fired, strung and fired, so rapidly that Touch the Sky could not believe a man could move so quickly.

Even with Big Tree on hand, however, the attackers were not eager to rush high ground against deadly long arms. For the moment, at least, the attack had been stemmed. But the enemy was massing, clearly intent on a charge when its numbers were even greater. And now, Touch the Sky realized, he and his companions were caught between the sap and the bark: a raging fire closing in from the plains behind them, a hail of lead closing in from the canyon.

Black Elk felt his face tugging into a grin as the Kiowa and Comanche warriors first caught sight of the flames up above.

He had already swum across the river and hidden himself in a small cutbank from which he could watch the camp. At first, when they spotted the fire, the enemy leaders sent only a handful of braves up to investigate. But as the shots broke

out above, more of the camp had cleared out—
including the formidable warrior called Big Tree,
who had been guarding the entrance to Honey
Eater's jacal. A youth with perhaps 16 winters
behind him was left to watch the hut.

Black Elk moved from cottonwood to hawthorn
bush, from boulder to hummock, entering the
nearly deserted camp. He skirted the light of the
huge fires, coming up on Honey Eater's mesquite-
branch hut from behind.

His bone-handle knife was in his hand. He
picked up a small stone and tossed it out in
front of the hut. When the sentry's attention was
momentarily diverted by the sound, he grabbed
him by the hair, jerked his head back, and opened
a second mouth deep into his neck, slicing down
deep through the jugular.

The dead Comanche fell like a sack of grain.
Black Elk stepped over him, grabbed the buffalo
hide, lifted it aside, and stepped inside.

A small fire blazed in the firepit. Honey Eater
gasped when he suddenly appeared before her.
She had been standing in the middle of the hut,
wringing her hands in desperate agitation, since
the sounds of battle had broke out. She knew it
must be her people trying to save them.

"Black Elk!"

Despite the trouble between them, she was
relived right now to see her husband. Certainly
other braves must be freeing the others! But even
in the confusion, she could not help wondering:
Had the Comanche named Big Tree spoken the
straight word? Was Touch the Sky truly dead?

Black Elk said, "The light in your eyes tells me
that, for once, you are glad to see me."

"I will be glad enough to be out of here! But quickly, we must help get the children! How many are with you?"

Even as she spoke, Honey Eater was heading for the entrance of the hut. Now Black Elk caught her arm, halting her.

"There are no others. Not here in camp with me. They are hidden out in the canyon."

Honey Eater looked confused. "You came alone?"

He nodded.

"But—but some of the others are too weak to walk. They will need ponies."

"They will need nothing. They are not going. Only you are."

For a long moment Honey Eater stared as if he had spoken an incomprehensible joke. Then, slowly, she shook her head.

"This thing cannot be. I will not leave unless the others go with me."

"Woman, have you eaten strong mushrooms? Your husband just risked death to enter this camp. Now you tell him you are going to stay?"

"Yes, if the others are not going."

Anger smoldered in Black Elk's eyes. "The cow does not bellow to the bull. You will go with me."

But defiantly she shook her head. "Black Elk, hear me! I am your wife, but I am also a Cheyenne. From birth on I have been taught that we live on through our tribe. My father was Yellow Bear"—here she made the cutoff sign, as one did when speaking of the dead—"of the Roaring Bear Clan, one of the greatest peace chiefs who ever led the Shaiyena people. There are children in this camp with me, scared girls who still wear their knotted ropes. I am one with them. I cannot escape to safety and leave them behind."

Now the rage in Black Elk's blood twisted his face into an ugly mask. The hot, black jealousy was back, twisting his thoughts into ugly words.

"No, you will not leave with me. But if your tall, randy buck Touch the Sky stood here in my place, you would be happy enough to run off with him."

For a moment, hearing these words, Honey Eater's heart raced with hope. Black Elk had spoken as if Touch the Sky were still alive. But his next words struck her like ice-cold water.

"You can stop dreaming of rutting with the white man's dog. He is dead!" Black Elk lied.

The shock of hearing it stunned her. Then, before she could stop them, tears welled up in her eyes.

"Make water with your eyes, your tears will not bring him back. He died hard, his guts in his hands, without singing the death song. Now he wanders forever in the Forest of Tears, a soul in pain."

"I have no ears for this," she said weakly, the ground suddenly swaying under her as if she were trying to stand up in a canoe.

"I care not what you have ears for. I am your husband, and I have spoken. Now you are coming with me."

She backed up as he approached her. "Do not force me," she warned him. "I will scream and alert the enemy."

He stopped. "You would kill me?"

"I would if you force me to leave the others."

"You would stay here with those who would bull you to death? Or perhaps they have already bulled you, and you enjoyed it?"

His words were incredible, and she refused to rise to such bait. But as he continued to back her toward the wall, she did indeed prepare to scream.

However, a woman outside the hut beat her to it. She had just discovered the dead Comanche sentry and now called for help.

Black Elk leaped to the entrance, glanced out, and saw what was afoot. The alarm was spreading—a moment's delay, and he was a dead man.

"Then stay here!" he snarled at Honey Eater. "I will be back for you, and you *will* come with me! If not, I will kill you with my own hand."

A moment later, he had disappeared into the tumultuous night.

Chapter Thirteen

The discovery of the dead sentry not only forced Black Elk to flee for his life. It raised the alarm throughout camp, and drew the warriors back from the attack against Touch the Sky's band.

But the Cheyennes knew this was only a temporary respite. Now that their enemies knew their location, it was impossible to stay in this area. And with Kiowa and Comanche riders now honeycombing this section of the canyon, the only way out was up over the canyon wall—straight into the teeth of the fire.

"It is a dangerous move," Touch the Sky told the others in a hasty counsel beneath the redrock pinnacle.

They could still hear the grass fire crackling, the noise rising to an airy roar each time the wind gusted.

"We will be out in the open and without horses. But we must use the cover of night to move further down the rim, then enter the canyon again where the riders are not so thick."

Victorio Grayeyes spoke in English to Touch the Sky. "I know a place further to the north, a well-protected spot under the rimrock where there are some small caves. Perhaps we can operate from there and steal some horses to replace yours."

Touch the Sky translated this for the others.

"Brother," Little Horse said, "what if we cannot move around the fire?"

"We will have to move through it. We must get out of this place. They will be back to collect their dead, and they will have blood in their eyes. Also, clearly Black Elk has made some kind of move, or why else was the attack called off? We need to find out if he was successful in rescuing any of our people."

"It is a strange kind of rescue," Tangle Hair said bitterly, "that uses us as a lure to save them. That fire did not set itself."

"No," Touch the Sky agreed. "Many odd 'accidents' seem to happen when Black Elk and his cousin are nearby."

Even as the little band prepared to move up over the rim and brave the fire, Touch the Sky could not help again thinking: Honey Eater must be dead. He had seen no sign of her since that awful night when their enemy had tortured a Cheyenne woman. But if she had been sent over, he would move heaven and earth in his efforts to avenge her death. And if Black Elk or Wolf Who Hunts Smiling's rashness had contributed to her

death, they would be included in that revenge—
even if it meant sullying the sacred Cheyenne
Medicine Arrows by drawing tribal blood.

More important: For her sake, the others must
be saved. And had Two Twists not saved his life
just now? The youth had only 16 winters behind
him, but he was risking his life to save his sister Singing Bird. Even if Honey Eater was dead,
Touch the Sky knew the fight must continue.

Moving in single file, carefully watching their
back trail, the four Cheyennes and the lone Apache
brave moved closer to the rim of Blanco Canyon.
The wind rose in a howling shriek, making speech
impossible. As they finally neared the brim, light
from the flames above traced their grim features
in its eerie, blood-red glow.

Touch the Sky felt the heat in his face, animal
warm at first, now uncomfortably hot as they
drew closer. But there could be no hesitating
now—already the riders below were massing for
another strike.

He met the eyes of the others one by one:
Little Horse, Tangle Hair, Two Twists, Victorio
Grayeyes.

"Hi-ya!" he rallied them. "Hi-ya hiii-ya!"

The shrill war cry still on his lips, Touch the
Sky led the charge into the raging inferno.

Tom Riley had stalled his horse for the night
and finished filing his daily report at the company headquarters. After a meal of beef, beans,
and sourdough biscuits in the officers' mess, he
returned to his quarters. He was seated at a crude
deal table, sipping coffee and cleaning his pistol
in the light of a coal-oil lamp, when three deaf-

ening knocks sounded on the door.

"C'mon in, Rain Dancer," he said, recognizing the knock.

The Papago Indian scout stepped inside the cramped quarters but went no farther than the doorway.

"What's on the spit?" Riley said.

"I have been watching the Blanco as you told me."

"Good man. Seen anything?"

Rain Dancer nodded. "Come outside, Lieutenant. There is a thing I would show you."

Curious, Riley slipped his long, smoothly polished boots back on. He followed his scout outside. They walked to the main gate, which still stood open and would until taps sounded at ten p.m.

"Look out there," Rain Dancer said, pointing to the south and the direction of the Blanco.

At first Riley noticed nothing in the vast dark tableau of the night. Then, gradually, he became aware that a slight orange haze discolored the night sky.

"Fire?"

Rain Dancer nodded. "Big fire."

"Was it set?"

Again Rain Dancer nodded. "No lightning for many days now."

"Are the Comanches and Kiowas trying to flush the Cheyennes out? But why set a fire on the plains if they're hiding in the canyon?"

"The *Cheyennes* set it," Rain Dancer replied.

"The Cheyennes? Why?"

Rain Dancer shook his head.

"It could be," Riley speculated out loud, "that

they set it as a distraction. Meaning they made some kind of move."

He fell silent, thinking again of his friend Matthew Hanchon. The Cheyenne had shown great courage riding into that Blanco hellhole. But it would take more than courage to get their people back and successfully transport them across the Llano—it would take a major miracle. And miracles happened in the Bible, not on the Staked Plain.

Riley made up his mind. It was time to see what he could see.

"Ride over to the enlisted barracks and find Sergeant McKenna. Tell him to form a squad up for a night mission. Tell him to ask for volunteers and that I will authorize the men who go for a day off tomorrow. We're going to ride out to the Blanco."

"More of our men are down," Hairy Wolf said angrily. "You said a few Cheyennes in this canyon would be less than gnats. But so far those gnats have proven to be great pests."

Iron Eyes only nodded, too angry to speak. Both men stood over the dead sentry in front of Honey Eater's jacal.

Both braves stared through the entrance at Honey Eater. She sat on a buffalo robe in the corner, indifferent to their presence. Now she was accompanied by Singing Bird and several other young Cheyenne women. Worried about security, their captors had hurriedly decided to herd the prisoners into larger groups and increase the guard.

Honey Eater was alarmed by Singing Bird's

appearance. The frail young beauty wore a permanent shocked glaze over her eyes, and had been unable to eat the meager rations of crushed-ant soup and hardtack. She trembled constantly and started at the least noise. Honey Eater knew she was not long for this world unless she soon got away from here.

Ever since Black Elk too had claimed Touch the Sky was dead, Honey Eater had forced herself to accept the report as true. She glanced up when Big Tree joined his leaders outside the jacal, and for a moment her eyes went livid with hate as she stared at the man who had killed Touch the Sky. For herself, with Touch the Sky gone, she desired only suicide to end this intolerable misery. But she was still responsible for the others in her tribe and must watch for an opportunity to help them escape.

She would also, she vowed to herself, look for an opportunity to kill Big Tree. He had taken the breath of life from the man she loved; now he would pay with his own before she left this world for the Land of Ghosts. But that meant she would have to do more than sit wringing her hands.

So when Iron Eyes stepped aside for a moment to give an order to one of his braves, Honey Eyes met Hairy Wolf's eyes and smiled briefly. Surprised, the big Kiowa smiled back.

A moment later, when Hairy Wolf wasn't looking at her, she gave the same smile to Iron Eyes. It was a smile that said to each man: *You* are the one I choose. And thinking of her vow to kill Big Tree, she also managed to meet his eyes with the same promise.

"Tomorrow we move out to meet Aragon," Iron

Eyes said. "Then we will be rid of all this trouble-some baggage."

"Most of it," Hairy Wolf corrected him, looking at Honey Eater.

"Most of it," Iron Eyes agreed. "After that is done, we will have to come to an arrangement."

The two men exchanged a long glance, then each looked away. It was becoming clearer and clearer to each of them that no satisfactory "arrangement" would be reached. Sharing this beauty was out of the question. If she were indifferent to both of them, then perhaps they could simply share her or gamble to see who would own her. But each man was secretly convinced by now that she wanted only him.

"You know," Hairy Wolf said, "that we cannot leave her here while we transport the rest?"

"Of course not, Kaitsenko. My wives would kill her."

"My thought too. She will ride with us while we deliver the women to Over the River, then take the children to the Comanchero camp."

The Comanche war leader turned to Big Tree. "For now, the camp is safe. Ride back up and flush those Cheyennes out."

Heat seared his face even before Touch the Sky stepped over the lip of the canyon.

But now it was impossible to turn back. Below, the enemy were again rushing their old position, preparing to flush them. Now the fire which had exposed them promised their only escape. One way or another they must put those flames between themselves and their pursuers.

At first, as he hurled himself toward the searing

wall of flame, he could hear the others echoing his war cry. But in only moments the roar of the wind and flames isolated each of them in a swirling, smoking confusion.

There was no point in trying to skirt the flames on either flank—it had spread too wide. The only choice was straight into the heart of the fire. Touch the Sky could only hope the belt of flames was not as wide as it looked, or they would never make it through without roasting their own flesh.

He took one last, hungry mouthful of air as he plunged into the firestorm. Sudden, searing heat singed his hair and eyebrows. His eyes had been tearing from the smoke, but now the heat was so intense it dried not only the tears but the film of moisture on his eyeballs.

The sudden heat made it feel as if every nerve ending in his body had been stripped raw. Hot coals singed through his moccasins, flaming grass whipped against his legs, thick smoke crawled down his throat and tried to suffocate him.

For a moment he glimpsed Little Horse and saw that the feathers fletching the arrows in his foxskin quiver were aflame. Then he saw nothing again except the vast, orange brightness. The heat increased, blistering Touch the Sky's skin. His feet hardly touched the ground now as he flew across the burning strip.

He needed air now, bad, and it felt like knife points were ripping his lungs open from inside. Another step, another, the heat now forcing a roar of pain from his lips. But that roar cost him more precious air, and now he understood that he was about to die.

Dizziness washed over him, he staggered, the pain was so great he almost buckled. Then, even as he uttered the first words of the death song, he felt a blessed tickle of cool air against his face.

The orange wall gave way to the dark pall of night as he suddenly broke out of the flames. At the same moment, on either side of him, the others also broke through.

Touch the Sky was about to raise a cry of triumph. But then his eyes cleared enough to see what was waiting for them.

A line of blue-bloused pony soldiers sat their mounts just before them, carbines at the ready.

Chapter Fourteen

Riley had already ordered his men to hold their fire if they encountered Cheyenne Indians. Still, at the moment when Touch the Sky's little band burst out of the flames, several soldiers instinctively inserted their rifles into the hollow of their shoulders, preparing to fire.

At first Touch the Sky was caught flush with surprise and had no time to distinguish individual faces. He knew only that yet another enemy was upon them, ready to strike.

Like the others with him, he raised his rifle and prepared to kill the first bluecoat who fell under his sights.

"Touch the Sky!" one of the soldiers shouted in English. "You soft-brained fool, hold your fire!"

The young warrior had already inserted his finger inside the trigger guard and taken up the slack. Now, as he glimpsed the speaker's boyish face in the firelight, the tow hair visible beneath the raised brim of his cavalry hat, Touch the Sky shouted to his band:

"Hold!"

Victorio Grayeyes spoke English and had already lowered his weapon when he heard the officer shout. Now the rest, staring at Touch the Sky in amazement, nonetheless followed their leader's example and lowered their weapons.

Tom Riley dismounted and approached his friend. He knew Indians too well by now to offend them by offering his hand to shake. But a wide smile of greeting told the Cheyenne he was glad to see him again.

"Seems like every time I meet up with you, you're bucking trouble," Riley said.

The soldiers still held their carbines at the ready. They watched, suspicious and curious, as the white and red leader parlayed. The Indians stared back, never taking their eyes off the dreaded pony soldiers. More than one soldier had shot an Indian while handing him a cup of coffee.

"I don't think I can buck it this time," Touch the Sky replied, his voice dejected.

While they spoke, the sergeant named McKenna had ridden forward to look down into the Blanco. The flames had consumed all the grass and creosote and were now finally blowing themselves out, having reached the lip of the canyon.

"There's Innuns riding this way!" he shouted back. "And damn my Irish eyes if they ain't loosin' war whoops!"

"Form the men in a skirmish line right at the edge of the canyon," Riley ordered. "Fix bayonets and hold your weapons high so they can see them. Let them know they'll never make the high ground if they insist on charging. Numbers won't help them, we can pick them off like prairie chickens when they come up the narrow trail."

"You heard the captain!" McKenna shouted in his rough bray. "Let's go, laddiebucks, form up! There's no glory in peace! Put at 'em, and show those red Arabs that Soldier Blue is the boy they'd better give the slip to!"

While Riley's squad formed a defensive line, Touch the Sky turned to his band and explained in Cheyenne who Tom Riley was—the officer who had befriended his boyhood friend Corey Robinson, known to the tribe as Firetop, the red-headed white boy who had saved the Cheyenne people from Pawnees. While stationed at Fort Bates near Bighorn Falls, Riley and Corey had helped Touch the Sky and Little Horse defeat the hard cases hired by Hiram Steele to drive Touch the Sky's white parents from the territory.

"I know why you're here," Riley said. "My scouts have given me reports on the Cheyenne prisoners."

Touch the Sky nodded, misery clear in his fire-smudged face. "I thought we were up against a hopeless fight in Bighorn Falls," he said. "But this trouble here, I see no hope. It is not just the enemy, but my own tribe I must survive."

He explained about Black Elk's band, how the jealous, hotheaded young warrior's band was working at cross purposes with Touch the Sky's.

Riley nodded. "So that explains why we spotted two groups. I thought you had it planned that way."

"I tried to combine the groups. Together we might have done something." Frustration and anger were clear in Touch the Sky's voice. "But we have done nothing beyond kill and wound a few of our enemy. All we can do is sneak around the edge of the canyon like hungry coyotes circling the fringe of a buffalo herd. And now they have scattered our ponies. We are not strong enough to attack the main herd."

While they spoke, Riley had been curiously watching the Apache, Victorio Grayeyes, who clearly understood their English. Touch the Sky saw the curiosity in his face.

"This is Victorio Grayeyes," he explained. "Juan Aragon is his cousin. Aragon has played the turncoat, leading soldiers to their cave. Not only did Aragon kill his parents, but he has stolen his brother and sister and plans to sell them."

"The word from my scout is that they're preparing to move the prisoners, the women anyway, to Over the River. Soon. Probably tomorrow or the next day," Riley said.

Touch the Sky nodded. "We saw signs of this too. That is why we wanted to strike now. Once the prisoners are formed up between defensive columns of Kiowas and Comanches, we can never hope to free them."

"They've spotted us, Cap'n!" McKenna said from the rim of the canyon. "They're turnin' back. Don't look like we'll be busting caps tonight."

Riley was silent a long time, thinking about this situation.

"I've been wanting for a long time," he finally said, "to do something about all this damn slave trading. It makes trouble for red men and white men alike. But the thing of it is, the War Department figures it's an Indian matter. The commanders who try to stop it are labeled as Indian lovers, and there goes their careers in the Army.

"I can get away with bringing a squad out here. But it would take a platoon-size formation to attack the combined bands. And not only would some of your women and children be killed in the battle, but some of my men. That means everything would have to be on record, filed in a report. I'd never get authorization, not in time to stop them tomorrow. You're right, attacking them on the trail would be a bad piece of business."

Touch the Sky nodded, agreeing with this. But time was nearly up. If an attack was out of the question, what else could possibly work?

"There's only a few of you. I can get you some horses, I think," Riley said. He was gazing thoughtfully at his men. A plan was forming in his mind. A plan which would tell him once and for all how loyal his men were to him.

Now Riley walked closer to the squad where they were deployed at the edge of the Blanco.

"Men," he called out, "you don't know this Cheyenne, but I do. His people call him Touch the Sky, but he grew up as Matthew Hanchon in Bighorn Falls in the Wyoming Territory. And I'll tell you this much right now: I've fought rustlers and murderers beside him. He's all grit and a yard wide. He's solid bedrock, and I'd trust him with my life.

"You men know me. You know I'm no Indian lover. I've killed my share of Kiowas and Comanches and Pawnees and it hasn't cost me any sleep. But I believe in live and let live, and I don't hold with this policy of exterminating all Indians just because some of them are killers. You also know that there's not a one of you I wouldn't die for if I had to. Though don't try to get that in writing."

A few of the men laughed.

"Now I'm telling you this: I need five volunteers to join me for a dangerous mission. It's a mission that will have to remain off the record. You'll wear civilian clothes, and you will not be acting in your official capacity as soldiers. Some of you might not come back. Any takers?"

There was a long silence while the last of the dying flames snapped and sparked, an occasional ember blowing off over the vast opening of the Blanco.

"Ahh, *this* mother's son didn't join the Army for three hots 'n' a cot," Sergeant McKenna said, stepping his horse forward a few paces. "There's no glory in peace. Whatever's cooking, Cap'n, serve me up a helping."

One by one, four more soldiers nudged their horses forward a few paces.

Riley grinned. "Well, nobody ever credited you boys with any brains, but you don't lack for sand."

He turned to Touch the Sky. "All right. Let's move you and your men to a new position while I · tell you what I've got in mind. It's crazy, I reckon, and we'll have to move quick. But I've been aching for a chance to lock horns with Juan Aragon and his Comancheros."

On the morning after the grass fire on the Llano Estacado, the bustling town of Silverton shook itself to life like a sleeping horse rising from the ground.

Businessmen rolled out their green canvas awnings; a stagecoach rolled into town, tug chains rattling in the traces; miners, their hobnailed boots thick with dried red clay, showed up early at the land office to register new claims.

A dry tributary stream, once officially a river, marked the southern edge of Silverton. In marked contrast to the activity north of this boundary, the little shanty-and-sod hovel to its south known as Over the River was settling into sleep. By day it was nearly deserted. But after dark the usual denizens would take over: Indians employed by nearby Fort Union, half-breeds and criminals on the dodge from the law in the U.S. and Mexico, a few adventuresome soldiers with a taste for Indian women.

But as usual, the respectable citizens of Silverton ignored this blighted area nearby. Each side kept to itself, the way a snake and a badger might coexist in the same area: wary, suspicious of the other, but keeping their distance.

The heart of Silverton was a park in the center of town, a Spanish style promenade known as El Paseo. Surrounded by a spiked-iron fence and lancet-arched gates, this exclusive area was the meeting place for the white citizens of Silverton.

By mid-morning the park was busy as usual, alive with gossiping women, screeching children, and idling men discussing business and politics and the growing trouble between the North and the South.

The area around Silverton was rich in silver and minerals. Thus the boomtown drew many businessmen and speculators from back East. So no one paid much attention to the little knot of six men who sat conversing on iron benches around a spewing fountain, dressed in the familiar linsey-woolen and broadcloth suits of men of commerce.

Had an experienced eye studied the men more closely, some odd details might have been noticed. For example, the dark tan lines around their skulls which did not match up with their hats, or the rough-and-ready look about their eyes—watchful eyes trained to scour vast distances for enemies, not to add up columns of figures in a ledger. Also, as a group they were far younger than most of the speculators who visited the town.

But few paid any attention to them. This was the frontier, where few questions were asked and prying men seldom died of old age.

The men had chosen benches close to the spiked-iron fence. Gradually, the hollow thunder of hooves grew louder, approaching the park. More and more people began to glance up curiously as a furious yellow dust cloud boiled closer down the main street.

The pounding hooves drew closer, a horse whickered, and suddenly a group of five riders leading remounts broke into view outside the fence. A woman screamed when, one by one, the riders suddenly leaped the fence into El Paseo.

"Indians!" somebody shrieked.

Touch the Sky, leading the others on horses supplied by Riley, vaulted the fence and bore down on the "businessmen," his rifle at the ready.

"Throw down your weapons, or die right now!" he shouted in English.

The men rose from the bench in confusion, but were suddenly surrounded by the savages. A few of them drew hideout guns from inside their suits and dropped them into the lush grass.

"Search them," Touch the Sky said to Victorio. "Kill any who kept a weapon." When this was done, he indicated the spare mounts on lead lines and said, "Mount up! Quickly, or we kill one of you now to teach the others some respect for the Cheyenne people!"

He spoke loudly enough to make sure plenty of the gaping witnesses could hear him. The account of this "kidnapping" would be reported later in circulars and the local newspaper, and he wanted to make sure it was colorful—and that the Cheyenne people were mentioned.

One of the businessmen made as if to run. Touch the Sky appeared to reach out and kick him. Now the rest, their faces draining white with fear, hastily complied with the order.

The Indians discharged their weapons in the air as they left, again vaulting the fence. The entire raid had taken little more than a minute. But already frightened citizens were racing in

Judd Cole

every direction, some running for safety, others to the sheriff—and one to the offices of the *Silverton Register*, the town's daily newspaper.

Chapter Fifteen

"Of course I heard the story," the old Mexican named Valdez said. "How could I not? It has brought down the wrath of the entire white community of Silverton. So? It means nothing. We made a deal."

"In a pig's ass, you fat sack of suet. We talked terms, that's all."

Aragon paused to sip milky white *pulque* from a cracked pottery mug. The two men occupied the pair of nail-keg chairs in the slope-roof partition built off the side of Valdez's saloon. A special edition of the *Silverton Register* lay on the table between them. CHEYENNE RENEGADES INVADE NEW MEXICO blared the triple-deck headline on page one.

"This is no coincidence," Aragon said. "Tonight

147

the delivery is set, so this morning Cheyennes nab white hostages? No. It is no coincidence. They hope to trade those white prisoners for their own people."

"So what if they do?" Valdez fumed. "By the twin balls of Christ, we made a deal."

Aragon laughed, a harsh, protracted bark of derision. "You fat brown whore! You know damn good and well what the Territorial Commission will pay me, no questions asked, for the safe return of six white men. They're scared spitless that investors will be scared away from this area. You top their offer, and I'll tell the Cheyennes to kill their businessmen and go to hell."

Old Valdez was livid with rage. The dark brown adobe huts out behind his clapboard saloon now stood mostly empty. Women didn't last long in Over the River. But he was losing money every night. He desperately needed an infusion of fresh woman flesh.

"Have you heard from these Cheyennes?" he demanded.

Aragon sipped his *pulque* and shook his head. "Not yet."

"So you're still coming tonight as planned?"

"Did I ever say otherwise, old man? I'm just telling you now: I'll sell the female prisoners to you if the Cheyennes don't make contact with me first. Otherwise, they go to the highest bidder. Money talks and horseshit walks."

"All the women?"

"They won't leave any behind, you fool. However, as I said, I have a fine young Apache girl for you."

"Very fine indeed, eh? I hear it's your own cousin, you flint-hearted bastard. Still a child."

Aragon's dead-as-driftwood eyes held the old Mexican's. "That won't stop you from pointing her heels to the sky before you lock her up out back, will it, you filthy old goat?"

Before Valdez could reply, a knock sounded on the leather-hinged plank door.

In a heartbeat, Aragon's hand snaked to the machete in his shoulder scabbard and slid it out.

A half-breed named Guadalupe stepped inside.

"I have a message," he said in Spanish, looking at Aragon. "Bring the prisoners to Over the River tonight, as planned. But be prepared to exchange them for the white businessmen."

Only through an effort did Aragon repress a smile of satisfaction. Old Valdez cursed.

"I will be there," Aragon said.

"There is more," Guadalupe said. "Bring the Apache children too."

Aragon lost the urge to smile. A cold sense of dread seeped through him.

"Who gave you these messages?" he demanded.

"A tall Cheyenne with chest and shoulders like an Apache and your cousin, Victorio Grayeyes."

Aragon's cold sense of dread gave way to a moment of outright fear. So his suspicion had been right, after all. Grayeyes had survived the attack in the cave. And now he had somehow thrown in with these scalp-taking fools from the north.

He slowly slid the curved machete back into its scabbard. So—at least he was warned.

"Tell the Cheyenne *and* the Apache that I will be there," he said.

* * *

From their new position further north along the canyon rim, Touch the Sky and his little band watched below in the Blanco as preparations were made to transport the Cheyenne prisoners. Huge camp fires were augmented by a full moon and a star-spangled sky.

Anxiously, although in his mind he had given her up for dead, Touch the Sky watched for a sign of Honey Eater among the prisoners.

"There is Singing Bird!" Two Twists said excitedly. "There is my sister! But brothers, look at her! They have used her badly, she is not long for this world."

"If she can hold on a bit longer, little brother," Touch the Sky replied, "she will soon be safe in her clan circle."

He refused to let Two Twists see the pain in his own face as he strained, unsuccessfully, for a glimpse of Honey Eater.

"All right, you prisoners," Riley called out to his men, "check your weapons. Then come over here so I can tie you up."

Touch the Sky saw Victorio gazing down into the valley with a grim, determined set to his lips. The Cheyenne did not like what he saw.

"I know how you feel," he said. "I know how much you lust for revenge. I too want it, and worse than you could ever know. They have killed the woman who was the soul of my medicine bag. But know this, Apache. I have other people to save first before my thoughts can turn to revenge. Do *nothing* to interfere with the return of my people."

Touch the Sky's bitter, saddened tone made

the Apache look at him closely. "Do not shed so much brain sweat worrying, buck. I too want my brother and sister back. But neither will I forget that my parents now lie under heaps of stone, dead by Aragon's hand."

"Brother!" Little Horse interrupted them. "Look!"

Below, the Kiowa and Comanche leaders had just stepped outside of a mesquite-branch hut—and Honey Eater was between them!

For a moment Touch the Sky only stared, unable to believe what he was in fact seeing. A massive stone was suddenly rolled off of his chest. Honey Eater was still alive!

Again he looked at Victorio. This time the sadness in his tone was replaced by a note of urgent command.

"Do *nothing* to interfere with the return of my people."

Hairy Wolf of the Medicine Lodge Creek Kiowas surveyed the two long columns of warriors with approval. Between them, each lashed at the wrists and mounted with another brave, were the Cheyenne prisoners.

"Have ears for my words," he said to the Comanche leader Iron Eyes. "There could be trouble. We cannot let this one"—he nodded toward Honey Eater, whose eyes were cast downward in defiant silence—"ride on her own pony. I will take her up with me."

"Nonsense, Kaitsenko," Iron Eyes said. "You are a big man, the size of a bear. I am little. Let her ride with me."

"Quohada, how could this thing matter? She is

little, but a mere reed. I will take her up with me."

Big Tree stood nearby, grinning as he understood the real meaning of this strained politeness between the two leaders. In case something did happen, and flight proved necessary, each wanted to be assured of having her.

"A pity you cannot understand them," he said now to Honey Eater in Cheyenne. "They are deciding which one will bounce you in his lap. Perhaps *I* shall hold you close on *my* pony? I can do many things while riding at breakneck speed."

Honey Eater made no sign that she understood. But even without Big Tree's remark, she knew the two leaders were again arguing over her. Now, as she glanced at the knife in Hairy Wolf's beaded sheath, she reminded herself that big men generally moved slower than little ones. So far no one had remembered to bind her wrists. She also reminded herself that this journey might be her last chance to act before the rest were sold. Time was a bird, and the bird was on the wing.

Iron Eyes, anger deepening the furrow between his eyes, turned to Big Tree.

"Tell her," he said, "to pick the one she wishes to ride with."

Big Tree spoke, and Iron Eyes and Hairy Wolf released their grips on her.

Again Honey Eater cast an imperceptible glance at the knife in the Kiowa leader's sheath.

Then she stepped close to Hairy Wolf's big sorrel with the handsome hand-tooled saddle.

"Do not worry, Quohada," he assured Iron Eyes, trying to keep the gloating from his voice. "It is only my horse she likes better than yours."

"Do you think *I* am worried?" said Iron Eyes, his voice tight with irritation. "I have more wives than I can service now. I am a Quohada Comanche, a Red Raider of the Plains. I have killed Texans and Mexicans and stolen horses from every tribe north of the Platte River. Just remember this. She goes with us tonight only because she is not safe here alone. She is *not* for sale."

Once Grayeyes was sure the Kiowa-Comanche band was headed toward Over the River, he showed Touch the Sky a shortcut through a series of cutbanks leading up from the Rio de Lagrimas. It was too narrow to allow easy passage for a larger formation. But Touch the Sky's small band managed the cutbanks easily in the moonlit darkness.

Despite his elation at finally spotting Honey Eater alive, Touch the Sky was plagued by another thought: Where were Black Elk and his band? There had been no sign of them since the deliberately set fire. But he feared they had more reckless plans in store—and the last thing they all needed now was anything that would place the Cheyenne prisoners in danger on the trail, or interfere with their arrival in Over the River.

They picked their way carefully through the rock-strewn canyon, their faces grim in the milky moonlight. Riley and the rest of the prisoners rode in a tight group, hands loosely tied behind them in fake knots that would allow them to free themselves from the rawhide whangs in a second.

Despite his tangled thoughts, Touch the Sky had not forgotten Arrow Keeper's admonition:

Stay attuned to signs, portents, and the language of the senses. They were about to emerge from a long cutbank when, abruptly, it felt like a cool feather was tickling the bumps of his spine.

Touch the Sky pulled back on the reins, halting the well-trained cavalry black Riley had loaned him. He glanced all around them, slowly, his head lifted as if sniffing the wind.

Moon wash glimmered on the sterile peaks and pinnacles surrounding them. The wind was quiet here, the only noise the steady singsong of cicadas and the occasional snorting of the horses.

"What it is, brother?" Little Horse said, watching his face.

Victorio Grayeyes too watched him with curiosity. The Apache believed in no gods and was skeptical of those who claimed to have visions and read signs. Yet something about this tall young Cheyenne was different—he seemed marked for some great destiny.

Touch the Sky finally settled his stare on a huge sandstone shoulder just to their left. It overlooked the main part of the canyon and the wider trail their enemy would follow to reach Over the River.

"I am not sure," he finally told Little Horse. "Humor me, brothers, and ride with me while I look at something."

Leaving Riley and the soldiers behind, the four Cheyennes and the Apache let their horses set their own pace toward the sandstone shoulder. They rounded it carefully in the moonlight and emerged onto a wide limestone shelf on the other side.

"Look!" Tangle Hair said, pointing.

A clump of ponies had been hobbled just in front of them. Touch the Sky recognized Black Elk's paint and Wolf Who Hunts Smiling's pure black. He also spotted his chestnut and the rest of the ponies that had once belonged to his band.

Further down the shelf, perhaps a double stone's throw away, lay Black Elk, Wolf Who Hunts Smiling, Swift Canoe, and the Bull Whip named Battle Sash. Below them, the trail emerged from a thick copse into an open, exposed flat.

"I see how the wind sets," Touch the Sky whispered. "They must have seen word-bringers coming this way and learned the path to Over the River. This is Black Elk's last desperate plan: to ambush them as they emerge from the copse."

"He is a fool," Little Horse said. "They could kill a few, certainly. But chances are good their bullets, at this range, will also kill our people."

Touch the Sky nodded. This thing could not stand. "We need their weapons," he decided, "and their horses. A snake without venom loses its courage."

Moving quietly in the moonlit darkness, relying on double moccasins to quiet their feet, they slipped up to the horses and undid the hobbles. Then, while Two Twists and Victorio led the horses back to their own string, Touch the Sky and Little Horse and Victorio crawled closer along the hard shelf. Intent on watching for the enemy below, no one in Black Elk's band heard them until Touch the Sky called out:

"Black Elk! You and your men, lay your weapons down beside you or you cross over tonight!"

Lying flat on their stomachs, the Cheyennes

were in no position to quickly whirl and fire. They glanced up, saw the rifle and shotgun bores staring at them, and wisely downed their weapons.

Tangle Hair moved forward and collected them.

"You squaw-stealing dog," Black Elk fumed. "I am your war leader! I taught you the arts of combat. You will stand before the Council of Forty for this."

"Perhaps. But when I do, I will explain to them how my first concern was to save my people, not to play the big Indian no matter how much I recklessly endanger my tribe."

"Save your people!" Black Elk spat back bitterly. "You speak in a wolf bark! Your blood is hot to rut on Honey Eater, this is all."

Touch the Sky bit back his reply. He had just heard the faint noise of hooves ringing on rock below. Their enemy approached. Now it was time to ride ahead to Over the River.

"Bluster all you want to," he said, "roar and howl like the north wind. There was a time when I respected you. That time is passed. If we survive this place, we will surely meet again. I warn you now, your life is nothing to me. There was a time when I spared you because you were Honey Eater's husband. But now I see that I only spared you to make her life more miserable. I will not make that mistake again. Place my words in your sash."

He signaled, and his men started dropping back, clutching all the weapons.

"Woman Face!" Black Elk roared. "I will tear out your guts for this!"

But as he retreated into the night, Touch the

Comancheros

Sky couldn't help reminding himself: Their plan for tonight was far from foolproof. Chances were good the Kiowas and Comanches would not leave Black Elk an opportunity for revenge.

Chapter Sixteen

Seven riders leading a string of packhorses entered Over the River as they usually did, through the series of cutbanks which led down from the Comanchero camp in the nearby hills.

Pale moonlight the color of bleached bones reflected off the boulders and alkali sand and made them glow like foxfire. The shod hooves of their horses echoed in muffled drumbeats as they rode through the crude graveyard of those who had died in Over the River: row after row of shallow, unmarked graves with stones piled on them to ward off predators.

Juan Aragon rode at the head of his Comanchero band. The last man led the packhorses by a lariat snubbed around his saddlehorn. Aragon's young cousins, Delshay and Josefa, shared the first packhorse.

A SPECIAL OFFER FOR LEISURE WESTERN READERS ONLY!

Get FOUR FREE Western Novels

Travel to the Old West in all its glory and drama—without leaving your home!

Plus, you'll save between $3.00 and $6.00 every time you buy!

GET YOUR 4 FREE BOOKS NOW— A VALUE BETWEEN $16 AND $20

Mail the Free Book Certificate Today!

FREE BOOKS CERTIFICATE!

YES! I want to subscribe to the Leisure Western Book Club. Please send my 4 FREE BOOKS. Then, each month, I'll receive the four newest Leisure Western Selections to preview FREE for 10 days. If I decide to keep them, I will pay the Special Members Only discounted price of just $3.36 each, a total of $13.44. This saves me between $3 and $6 off the bookstore price. There are no shipping, handling or other charges. There is no minimum number of books I must buy and I may cancel the program at any time. In any case, the 4 FREE BOOKS are mine to keep—at a value of between $17 and $20! Offer valid only in the USA.

Name_____

Address_____

City_____ State_____

Zip_____ Phone_____

Biggest Savings Offer!

For those of you who would like to pay us in advance by check or credit card—we've got an even bigger savings in mind. Interested? Check here. ☐

If under 18, parent or guardian must sign.
Terms, prices and conditions subject to change. Subscription subject to acceptance. Leisure Books reserves the right to reject any order or cancel any subscription.

GET FOUR BOOKS TOTALLY *FREE*—A VALUE BETWEEN $16 AND $20

PLEASE RUSH
MY FOUR FREE
BOOKS TO ME
RIGHT AWAY!

Leisure Western Book Club
P.O. Box 6613
Edison, NJ 08818-6613

AFFIX
STAMP
HERE

Comancheros

"Are you sure, *jefe*," said the Comanchero half-breed named Benito, "that this is a wise idea, this plan with one big meeting? That is too many enemies eyeball to eyeball. Enemies from tribes that have blackened their faces against each other."

Aragon's vigilant eyes never stopped scanning the landscape while he replied.

"It is best to take the bull by the horns, Benito, else he will gore you every time. I am not worried about the Kiowas and Comanches turning on us. True, neither tribe can be trusted any more than you might trust Valdez with a young virgin. But they are a crafty lot with a keen head for business matters. They will not raise arms against us. Soon they will have more prisoners to sell, and they will need us again. We are more useful to them alive.

"No, Benito. It is Victorio Grayeyes we must watch, and these Northern Cheyennes. That is why I arranged for one big meeting. There are only seven of us. I am told there are five Cheyennes. With Grayeyes, that makes six. But an Apache bent on revenge is good for five warriors. And what if more Cheyennes are in hiding, waiting to mount a revenge strike? The runners claim there is a second small band near the Blanco."

Benito nodded, understanding. "The presence of the Kiowas and Comanches will prevent a Cheyenne strike."

This time Aragon nodded. "Once those white men are in our hands, why should we cry if Hairy Wolf and Iron Eyes decide to massacre the Cheyennes? Then Valdez will be a happy old whoremonger because he will get his woman after all and we will profit twice."

"But what about your cousin?" Benito said. "Surely you cannot let him live? Getting his sister and brother back will not quench Victorio's thirst for revenge."

Aragon felt the reassuring weight of the machete in its shoulder scabbard. "No, it won't, will it. I think you are right, 'mano. Certainly no Cheyennes are going to grieve at his death. And as surely as there are flames in hell, I cannot let Victorio live."

Iron Eyes now hated the beautiful young Cheyenne girl. And he hated Hairy Wolf for playing the fox against him all this time.

The Comanche leader had seethed with jealous rage ever since the girl chose to ride with Hairy Wolf instead of him. For that choice was also symbolic. She was also announcing her preference between the two war leaders.

Was it not as plain as fresh tracks in mud? he asked himself. Without doubt Hairy Wolf had been sneaking into her jacal, whispering the honeyed words which bent her in his direction.

The short, homely, bandy-legged Iron Eyes was fully aware of the sorry figure he must cut next to the handsome Kiowa. Now, as the double column of combined warriors picked its way through the Blanco, his eyes cut furtively to Hairy Wolf. The smug warrior held the slim girl before him with one brawny arm encircling her waist.

Now that the girl was lost to him, Iron Eyes was bitter with resentment at the loss of profit. Aragon had said she would be worth as much as the rest combined! Now he realized how foolish it would be not to sell her with the others.

Certainly Hairy Wolf would object. Clearly he looked forward to many comforting nights with this copper-skinned Cheyenne beauty warming his sleeping robes. Iron Eyes hoped to avoid killing his longtime battle ally. Though he hated him for this treachery, he did not wish to gain the enmity of their best allies, the Kiowas.

But if it came to that . . . Iron Eyes glanced back at Big Tree, riding just behind him in the column. The warrior's two quivers were stuffed full of new, fire-hardened arrows. The roadrunner-skin good-luck charm swung rhythmically from his pony's tail.

If it came to that, Big Tree was a Comanche, after all. He would side with his own.

Big Tree saw his leader glance back toward him, and the swift-riding menace of the plains barely suppressed a knowing grin.

He had eyes to see and ears to hear. Hairy Wolf and Iron Eyes had been circling each other like jealous stags over this little Cheyenne tidbit. And she had cleverly played the two-face with them, getting each man's blood hot. But Big Tree had also seen the secret looks she cast at *him*, and he knew whom she really preferred.

She had seen his riding prowess. She had seen him unleash arrows so quickly that barely an eyeblink separated each shot. Too, he spoke her language. Why should she *not* choose him over the others?

Now he nudged his pony up a little closer to where the girl rode with Hairy Wolf.

"Little bob-tailed one," he said in Cheyenne, "I see the game you are playing. Even now Hairy Wolf holds you close and feels his blood singing for you. Iron Eyes looks on, murderous blood filming his eyes. You are pitting one against the other, hoping they will send each other over. You are a clever little vixen!"

Hairy Wolf frowned, not understanding the words nor liking the taunting look on Big Tree's face. But he said nothing. Even a member of the elite Kaitsenko warriors did not provoke Big Tree. It was said he was born during a thunderstorm, and now he was crazy deep in his eyes.

Honey Eater understood the words, however, and boldly met Big Tree's eyes. Her look did nothing to discourage his arrogant belief. After all, she told herself, this was the murderer who killed Touch the Sky. If she could get close enough, with a weapon in her hand, his blood would surely stain this earth before she left it.

Aragon had sent word to meet him in a small canyon just south of Over the River. Now, as Touch the Sky's band and their disguised prisoners approached the canyon opening in the moonlight, Tom Riley ran through the instructions again with his men.

"Remember, nobody draws steel until I give the command. Keep your heads down, your hands behind your back. We don't know how many we're going up against, so let's wade in slow."

"No firing," Touch the Sky said, "until the women and children have been handed over and bunched behind us, out of the line of fire."

He spoke the same words in Cheyenne. Then he looked at Grayeyes.

"I know there is a fever in your heart to kill Aragon. He sent your parents under. I understand this thing you must do. But remember what I told you. Until our people have been handed over, make no play against him. After the shooting starts, he is yours."

Victorio nodded. But as they rode closer to the canyon, he squinted his eyes to carefully study the shape-changing shadows surrounding them.

"It will not be as simple as the words you use to describe it," he said with grim conviction. "Juan Aragon does not ride carelessly into deathtraps. If you Cheyennes believe in a god, pray to him now."

Because Aragon did not warn either group of the other's presence, the exchange of goods and prisoners was even more dangerous than he expected.

He had not anticipated that the Kiowas and Comanches would bring the little beauty—the one they refused to sell. Now the Cheyennes had spotted her. What would happen when they found out she was not part of the deal?

For their part, the Kiowa and Comanche warriors watched intently, their eyes greedy in the moonlight, as Aragon's men unpacked the goods for inspection.

They opened cases of brand-new Colt revolving-cylinder rifles, still packed in oil. They opened kegs of black powder and ball, crates of primer caps. From the panniers and packsaddles they pulled twists of rich brown Virginia tobacco, packets of coffee and sugar. There were also several cases of good whiskey.

Finally, Hairy Wolf and Iron Eyes nodded.

"It is all here, as you promised," Iron Eyes said.

Aragon nodded. "I always do as I say. You know that. It's good for business."

Despite his calm tone, Aragon was worried. The Cheyennes and Victorio Grayeyes sat their horses in a line to his right, just inside the entrance to the narrow canyon. The much-larger formation of Kiowas and Comanches was grouped on his left. The Cheyenne prisoners, and Delshay and Josefa, were bunched into a tight ring between the two groups—all except for the beauty, whom Hairy Wolf kept close to him. Aragon and his Comancheros circled them, rifles at the ready.

But the white prisoners—something about them felt wrong to Aragon. But he couldn't find word shapes for his feeling. He had tried to get a close look at their faces. However, the tall, broad-shouldered Cheyenne wouldn't let him ride very close.

What was it? Aragon wondered. What was wrong about the white hostages?

"If you are satisfied," Aragon said to the war leaders, "take your goods and load them onto your horses."

Braves scurried to pack the supplies. Aragon interrupted his worrying about the white hostages long enough to again stare at the Cheyenne beauty clutched in Hairy Wolf's arm.

Aragon spoke in Spanish. "Include the girl, and I will match all these goods."

"Accepted," Iron Eyes said almost immediately.

Hairy Wolf gaped at him in astonishment. "Accepted? But we agreed. She is not for sale."

"Speak with your brain, Kaitsenko, not your man gland! Have you not guessed by now that she is the woman of that tall buck, their leader? Have you looked at these Cheyennes? One is still a child, true, but even he is clearly ready to sell his life dearly. Now that they have seen her, do you think they will not die to get her? Aragon is willing to take her. Let *his* men pay the price in blood!"

"You milk liver!" said Hairy Wolf. "You were keen to hold her back, then she chose to ride with me! You are a jealous child. These few Cheyennes are not gods! Big Tree will let moonlight into all of them before they have drawn a drop of our blood!"

While this argument ensued in Spanish, a Comanchero was escorting the first prisoners— the Apache children—to a predesignated spot beside the Cheyennes. Aragon, under cover of this movement, managed to get a longer look at the white hostages.

Even in the moonlight, it was clear that all had well-tanned faces.

But now Aragon knew what bothered him even more. They were all young, all but one of them in their twenties. Aragon knew the type of man who came out here from the East to speculate—rarely were they this young. And rarely did they carry what these men seemed to carry: a sense of powerful and sudden danger about to be unleashed like a tightly coiled spring.

And that Cheyenne leader, the one the Pawnees called Bear Caller and claimed was blessed with strong medicine—he radiated the same sense of danger.

Aragon met his eyes, and suddenly he *knew*.

"*Es una trampa!*" he shouted in Spanish to his men and the Kiowa-Comanche force. "It's a trap! Shoot to kill!"

Aragon's long-muzzled cavalry pistol seemed to leap into his fist. He had no time for aiming, and only meant to bring down Touch the Sky's pony, killing the Cheyenne with his machete before he could even stand up. But at the moment he fired, Delshay stepped into the line of fire. The big-caliber bullet shattered the boy's skull.

Victorio, still mounted, uttered a harsh cry compounded of rage and grief as his little brother fell dead to the ground. He slid the Spanish bayonet from his sash, leaped to the ground, ran hard toward Aragon. At the last second his corded thighs strained with his leap, the bayonet held out before him in both hands.

Aragon's machete flashed in the moonlight, sliced into Victorio's neck less than a heartbeat before the long bayonet punched straight into Aragon's heart.

Victorio's head flew from his shoulders, the cry still on his lips as Aragon's body twitched and staggered before collapsing as if the bones had suddenly turned to water. Even in the heat of battle, Touch the Sky could not help marveling as the Apache died the glorious death—not falling on the ground, but on his enemy's bones.

"Fire!" Riley screamed to his men.

Honey Eater had almost fainted with joy and relief when she spotted Touch the Sky with the others. Big Tree and Black Elk had lied after all about his death! But the first flush of joy passed quickly when she realized the hopelessness of their situation.

Now she knew the time had come—the moment she had been planning for. Even now she was less than an arm's length away from Hairy Wolf's knife.

At the first shots, he pushed her aside to raise his rifle. Now she lunged at him, pulled out the knife, and drove it deep into his belly, feeling steamy warmth emerge from the wound.

Iron Eyes gaped in astonishment as Hairy Wolf dropped to his knees, blood blossoming from his stomach.

"Kill the she-bitch, Quohada!" Hairy Wolf gasped. "She has gutted me!"

Iron Eyes raised his carbine to shoot her even as Big Tree closed on her with his stone skullcracker. Touch the Sky aimed his Sharps and dropped Iron Eyes with one shot. But now Big Tree was about to pulverize her skull. Touch the Sky kicked his horse into motion even as he drew his spiked tomahawk back for the throw.

"Hi-ya, hiii-ya!"

He had his chestnut back now, but she had been badly used by Black Elk's band and Touch the Sky had opted to ride the Army horse Riley gave him. But he was not used to this mare, trained by white men, and the throw was off. The solid hickory handle of the tomahawk caught Big Tree at the base of the skull, toppling him to the ground and stunning him but not killing him.

The scene in the canyon was total pandemonium as Touch the Sky continued riding forward and scooped Honey Eater up with him. Despite their huge advantage in numbers, the Kiowa and Comanche braves had been eagerly inspecting their new bounty. Suddenly, the white hostages had pulled weapons from under their suit coats— weapons they were employing with the deadly accuracy of seasoned troopers used to staying calm and shooting plumb under fire.

The leaders of the Kiowa and Comanche were dead, and many others went down in the first volley of fire. Little Horse's shotgun roared, roared again, again, each blast dropping a man or a horse. Loosing the war cry, Two Twists leaped into the confused knot of prisoners and grabbed his sister Singing Bird.

Riley's men, as ordered, had first brought down the Comanchero slavers. Now they joined their Cheyenne allies, laying down withering fire on the confused Kiowas and Comanches.

Leaderless, concerned only with their new wealth, the enemy seized whatever they could carry and fled, leaving their dead.

Touch the Sky spirited Honey Eater to the safety of a packhorse. Now he saw Big Tree moving sluggishly, managing to get up from the ground. But the little Apache girl, Josefa, stood crying over her dead brother, exposed to danger. Touch the Sky was forced to watch Big Tree mount and flee while the Cheyenne grabbed up the crying girl and took her to Honey Eater's side.

Once, before he raced ahead into the night, Big Tree turned to meet Touch the Sky's stare. The look he sent the Cheyenne seemed to promise that they *would* meet again.

"Never mind that!" Touch the Sky exclaimed when Two Twists loosed another war cry and started chasing the fleeing enemy. "You've earned enough glory for one battle, buck! Now let us get our people back to their tribe before our enemy drinks that strong water and starts hungering for revenge!"

The Cheyennes and Riley's soldiers delayed only long enough to dig shallow graves for Victorio Grayeyes and his young brother Delshay. Riley agreed to take the girl to live with the Apaches at the reservation at nearby Mater Dolorosa. No Apache was happy on a reservation, but at least she would be with her own blood.

Knowing they might be pursued, Touch the Sky carefully watched their back trail. He pushed his band as quickly as he dared across the Llano Estacado, forced to pause often to rest the weakened women and children. Finally, Touch the Sky heaved a huge sigh of relief when the hunt camp came into view below them in the valley of the Red River.

The rest of the tribe was elated at the return of the prisoners. Touch the Sky and his band were greeted as heroes and a Sun Dance was given that same night. But hard upon the heels of this heady joy came cold reality for Touch the Sky. The very next day, Black Elk and his band returned on horses they had managed to steal from the Comanche herds.

Black Elk, Wolf Who Hunts Smiling, and Swift Canoe felt humiliated in the eyes of the others—especially Black Elk, whose face flamed with hot blood as he thought about the sight of Touch the Sky riding triumphantly into camp, *his* squaw on the tall dog's lead line.

"Home is the mighty warrior, one day later than his squaw!" some whispered. And though Black Elk could not hear their words, he heard the derision in their laughter, saw the scorn in the slanted glances they shot at him. After all, had he not strutted about camp before he left, playing the he-bear? Indians did not mind a boaster unless he failed to match his brag.

On the night before the tribe was set to begin the northward trek to their summer camp, Black Elk caught Touch the Sky in front of his tipi.

"Gloat, Woman Face. Once again you have played the big Indian at my expense. But know this. Our lances will cross yet, and only one of us will ride away. And I have just told Honey Eater what I am now about to tell you. She is *my* squaw, not yours. If she shames me one more time in the eyes of my people, I am going to kill her."

"She has never shamed you and never will. But I have already spoken on this matter, and my words have not eroded. I tell you again. Since you have violated Cheyenne law in the treatment of your wife, *I* do not recognize Cheyenne law in the matter of your rights as a husband.

"Lay a hand on her," Touch the Sky continued, "and you had better sing the death song yourself because I will feed your liver to the dogs."

Black Elk grinned, his flap of dead ear gruesome in the flickering camp fire. "Fine, White Man's Shoes. Feed as many dogs as you wish. At any rate, that will not bring your Honey Eater back, will it? I will gladly die, if it keeps you from bulling my squaw."

Before Touch the Sky could reply, his war chief had disappeared into the darkness. But the truth of his words mocked the tall young Cheyenne long into the night. Touch the Sky no longer feared what Black Elk might do to him. However, clearly Black Elk was truly insane with jealous rage. And Honey Eater was virtually his property, to do with as he pleased.

There was a time when Black Elk, a better man, had truly loved Honey Eater. But from this day onward, she was sleeping with a rattlesnake in her tipi. And that rattlesnake might strike at any moment—to kill him *or* Honey Eater.

WAR PARTY

Prologue

In 1840, when the new spring grass was well up, a Northern Cheyenne named Running Antelope led his wife, infant son, and 30 braves on a journey to counsel with their Southern Cheyenne kin living below the Platte River.

Running Antelope was a peace leader, not a war chief, and his band rode under a white flag. Nor had they painted or dressed for battle, nor made the all-important sacrifices to the sacred Medicine Arrows. Nonetheless, they were forced to fight when blue-bloused pony soldiers attacked them in a pincers movement near the North Platte.

It was the Cheyenne way to flee during battle until a pursuing enemy's horses faltered. Then the Cheyenne would suddenly turn and attack. But a hard winter had left their ponies weak. Nor were their stone-tipped lances, fire-hardened

5

arrows, and one-shot muzzle-loaders any match for the Bluecoats' percussion-cap carbines and big-thundering wagon guns that shot screaming steel.

Still, the braves fought the glorious fight, shouting their shrill war cry even as they sang their death song. When flying canister shot cut down their ponies, they used them for breastworks and fought on. But eventually Running Antelope, his squaw, and all 30 braves lay dead or dying. The only survivor was Running Antelope's infant son, still clutched in the fallen chief's arms.

Pawnee scouts were about to kill the child when the lieutenant in charge interfered. He had the baby brought back to Fort Bates near the river-bend settlement of Bighorn Falls in the Wyoming Territory. John Hanchon and his barren young wife Sarah, owners of the town's mercantile store, adopted the child. His Shaiyena name lost forever, he was raised as Matthew Hanchon.

His parents were good to him, and at first the youth felt accepted in his limited world. He worked for the Hanchons, earning hostile stares and remarks from some customers, but also making friends in Bighorn Falls. Then came his sixteenth year, when tragedy struck his safe little world.

Matthew fell in love with Kristen, daughter of the wealthy rancher Hiram Steele—the Hanchons' most important customer after Fort Bates itself. Caught in their secret meeting place, Matthew was severely thrashed by one of Steele's hired hands. And Steele warned Matthew: Stay away from Kristen or he was a dead man.

Afraid for Matthew's life, Kristen lied and told him she never wanted to see him again. But even then the youth's misery was not complete. Seth Carlson, a jealous cavalry officer with hopes of marrying Kristen, issued an ultimatum: Either Matthew left Bighorn Falls for good, or Carlson would use his influence to ruin the Hanchons' mercantile contract with Fort Bates.

Saddened, but determined to know if the tribe of his birth would accept him, Matthew fled north to the up-country of the Powder River—Cheyenne hunting grounds. Captured by braves from Chief Yellow Bear's tribe, he was declared a spy for the hair-faced soldiers and sentenced to death. But at the last moment Arrow Keeper, the tribal shaman, interfered and ordered the prisoner freed.

Arrow Keeper had just returned from a fateful vision quest at sacred Medicine Lake. His epic vision promised the arrival of a mysterious Cheyenne youth—one who carried the mark of the warrior on his body. And one who would eventually lead the entire Shaiyena nation in one last, great victory against their enemies. For despite the prisoner's white man's clothing and language, Arrow Keeper had spotted a mulberry-colored birthmark buried well past his hairline: a birthmark in the perfect shape of an arrowhead, the mark of the warrior.

Arrow Keeper insisted that the youth must be allowed to live with Yellow Bear's tribe, to train as a warrior. His white name was buried forever, and the tall youth was given the Indian name Touch the Sky.

This infuriated those who wanted him executed as a spy. These included Black Elk, the fierce young war leader who hoped to marry Chief Yellow Bear's daughter, Honey Eater. Black Elk noticed the glances Honey Eater gave this handsome stranger. And early on, Black Elk's younger cousin, Wolf Who Hunts Smiling, stepped between Touch the Sky and the camp fire, thus announcing his intention of killing the white man's dog.

From the beginning of his training, Touch the Sky faced many trials and much suffering in his quest for acceptance in the Cheyenne world: He helped to save his tribe from destruction by Pawnees and white whiskey traders and land-grabbers; he fought against Crow Crazy Dogs, Comanches, and bloodthirsty Kiowas. But throughout all of this, the hatred and jealousy and mistrust of his tribal enemies only strengthened.

Now Black Elk, hard but fair at first, has finally succumbed to jealous rage over Honey Eater. Touch the Sky's recent rescue of Honey Eater, when she was a prisoner of Kiowa and Comanche slave traders, has further humiliated Black Elk in the eyes of his fellow warriors. And Wolf Who Hunts Smiling, realizing that Touch the Sky is the main obstacle to his ambitions for tribal leadership, has vowed to eliminate this obstacle once and for all.

Chapter One

"Brother," the young warrior called Little Horse said, "a thing troubles me greatly. I would speak with you about it."

Touch the Sky glanced up from the new bow he was fashioning out of green oak. He sat in front of the elkskin entrance flap of his tipi. Their sister the sun had already gone to her resting place, and now Uncle Moon owned the sky. A fire burned in a circle of stones. Orange spear tips of flame illuminated Touch the Sky's strong, hawk nose, pronounced cheekbones, and long, loose black locks. Though he was seated, it was clear that he was tall and broad-shouldered, even for a Cheyenne.

"You know I always have ears for your words," Touch the Sky told his best friend in the tribe. "Sit and speak of this thing."

Little Horse had brought his favorite clay pipe,

filled with kinnikinnick—a mixture of coarse tobacco and fragrant red-willow bark. He sat beside his friend and lit the pipe with a piece of glowing punk pulled from the fire. Little Horse was much smaller than his friend, but built strong and sturdy like a good war pony. Unlike Touch the Sky, he wore his hair wrapped tight in a single braid, the style preferred by men of his clan.

As was the custom, the two young braves did not immediately broach the subject on Little Horse's mind. Instead, they smoked for several minutes, speaking of insignificant things and watching the camp come to life as darkness descended.

There was no established "bedtime" in the Cheyenne village, now located in the lush grass at the fork where the Powder River joined the Little Powder. Often the camp stayed lively and loud all night long. Braves placed bets on pony races and wrestling matches; children played at taking scalps and counting coups; sad old grandmothers keened in grief for sons and husbands whose bones had been strewn on battlefields from the Missouri River to the Marias.

Finally Little Horse set the pipe between them, the sign that he was ready to begin talking.

"Brother, you are no white-livered Indian. I have fought beside you when you waded into battle fighting as fierce as a she-grizzly protecting her cubs. You have defeated many enemies, as the scalps dangling from your coup stick prove. But sometimes the most dangerous enemies live closest to home. Even the fierce badger has been killed in his own burrow."

Touch the Sky met his friend's eyes but said nothing, only listening. Beyond the well-lit circles of the clan fires, a coyote raised its ululating howl to the heavens, a howl that ended in a series of yipping barks. The tall young brave knew full well what his friend was hinting at.

"Black Elk has always been covered with hard bark," Little Horse said. "But there was a time when he tried to be fair to you. That time has long passed, thanks to his jealous rage over Honey Eater. Now, since you saved her from the Kiowas and Comanches down south in Blanco Canyon, the other braves in his Bull Whip Society goad him on. They tell him, 'This Touch the Sky, he wants to put on the old moccasin with your squaw!'"

Touch the Sky nodded, watching sparks float up from the flames like fireflies. "Putting on the old moccasin" was a reference to a young, unmarried brave who was eager to rut with a married woman.

"I fear greatly for Honey Eater's safety," Touch the Sky admitted. "Black Elk has already cut off her braid to shame her, and he has beaten her. Now, since he failed to rescue her, he threatens to kill her if she so much as looks at me."

"You speak straight-arrow. But buck, it is not only Black Elk you must watch. His young cousin is enraged since the Council of Forty punished him. Wolf Who Hunts Smiling hates you as never before—I have heard warnings from

11

Tangle Hair and other Bowstring soldiers friendly to you.

"Wolf Who Hunts Smiling now speaks in a bark against you every chance he finds. He tells the younger warriors you are a white man's dog. That because palefaces raised you, you have the stink of the whites on you for life. He has made it the mission of his life to destroy your name within the tribe."

Again Touch the Sky could only let silence acknowledge the truth of these words. During a recent buffalo hunt far to the southwest, Wolf Who Hunts Smiling had served as a hunt soldier: one of the braves who enforced the strict Hunt Law which governed buffalo hunts. Using his authority to arrest, he had falsely accused Touch the Sky of illegally employing a buffalo jump— driving part of the herd over a blind cliff to their death, a serious violation of Hunt Law permitted only if horses were not available.

But Wolf Who Hunts Smiling was not content with the severe whipping this false accusation earned Touch the Sky. He went on to bribe an old squaw of the Root Eaters Clan. He convinced the addled old grandmother—known for her prophetic medicine dreams—that she had experienced a "vision" concerning Touch the Sky. She then announced, before the entire tribe, that the youth must set up a pole or else his white man's stink would ruin the hunt.

Tribal belief in such medicine dreams was strong. Touch the Sky had no choice but to undergo the grueling penance. Bone hooks were driven into his breasts, and he was suspended for hours from a pole atop a hill. But later, Arrow Keeper discovered Wolf Who Hunts Smiling's treachery and reported it to Chief Gray Thunder.

Recently, by a formal vote of the clan headmen comprising the Council of Forty, Wolf Who Hunts Smiling had been stripped of all his coup feathers—a serious blow to a haughty, proud warrior who constantly boasted of his battle prowess. Now there were no white eagle-tail feathers in his war bonnet. Now admirers could not count how many times he had defeated his enemies.

Even as Touch the Sky was about to answer his friend, three shadowy forms passed near the edge of his fire.

"Steady, Cheyenne," Little Horse said in a hushed tone. "Here come your enemies now, traveling like curs in a pack."

Touch the Sky recognized Black Elk, Black Elk's younger cousin Wolf Who Hunts Smiling, and a brave from the Wolverine Clan named Swift Canoe. Swift Canoe had played the dog for Wolf Who Hunts Smiling and wrongly accused Touch the Sky of killing his twin brother, True Son.

The trio stopped, their stern faces outlined in the flickering flames. Black Elk was the oldest. He looked especially fierce because of the dead, leathery flap of skin where one ear had been severed in battle, then crudely sewn back on with buckskin thread. Like the others, he wore a soft kid breechclout, buckskin leggings, and beaded elkskin moccasins. A small rawhide medicine bag dangled from his clout. It held a set of lethally sharp panther claws—the special totem of his Panther clan.

"Look here, stout bucks!" Black Elk called out to his companions. "Here sit two of the white men's favorite spies, plotting new ways to play the big Indian while they sell tribe secrets to hair-mouths!"

"Indeed, cousin, I smell the stink of whites all over Woman Face," Wolf Who Hunts Smiling said. He was smaller than Black Elk, and younger, but his strength and agility were fearsome. His dark, furtive eyes constantly moved like minnows, missing nothing.

Touch the Sky said nothing at the allusion to "Woman Face," refusing to rise to such familiar bait. This was a mocking reference to his former habit of permitting his feelings to show in his face—a white man's trait despised by Indians as unmanly.

"Even the buffalo run from this stink," Black Elk said.

"But the red men have run from it long enough," Wolf Who Hunts Smiling added. The young brave had looked on, horrified, when a burst of Bluecoat canister shot turned his father into stew meat. Now tight anger sizzled behind every word. "It is time to feed all the white men and their dogs to the carrion birds."

It was Little Horse who next spoke up.

"You three speak of white men's dogs until I am weary of hearing it. The first scalps to dangle from *our* clouts were those of hair-faced whites."

"So you say," Black Elk replied. "But you yourself saw *this* one"—he pointed at Touch the Sky—"drinking strong water with hair-faces at the trading post. Both of you were seen holding secret council with blue-bloused soldier chiefs, and leaving talking papers for them in the forks of trees."

"During a bad flood, a snake will share a dry rock with a rat. This does not make them lodge brothers. What is seen and what is true are not always the same."

"Hold, brother," Touch the Sky said, gripping his friend's shoulder. "Do not waste time arguing with words. Words are the coins spent freely by old squaws. These talking magpies are nothing. Men let their war lances speak for them."

"*Men*," Black Elk said, "find their own wives instead of holding another man's in their blanket."

"No man can steal that which is his by right," Touch the Sky replied.

Absolute silence greeted this remark. All four braves clearly understood Touch the Sky's point. Despite having undergone the squaw-taking ceremony with Black Elk, Honey Eater's heart belonged to Touch the Sky alone. Only her mistaken belief that he had deserted her and his tribe had led her to accept Black Elk's bride price. And then only because tribal law forbade her living alone after Chief Yellow Bear, her father, had crossed over.

Black Elk's fierce dark eyes glowed with the hatred of blood-lust. His hand moved to the bone-handled knife in the beaded sheath on his sash. Wolf Who Hunts Smiling and Swift Canoe followed suit.

As one, Touch the Sky and Little Horse rose to meet the attack.

"I will not stain the sacred Arrows by being the first to let Cheyenne blood," Touch the Sky said. "But close against me or Little Horse, and I will leave your warm guts steaming on the ground."

"Cousin, I for one am weary of this bloodless sparring," Wolf Who Hunts Smiling said, moving a step closer. "This make-believe Cheyenne would rut with your squaw! I say we make maggot fodder of him now!"

Cheyenne village life centered around a huge clearing, in the center of which was a hide-covered council lodge. On a lone hummock at the river edge of the clearing stood the tipi of old Arrow Keeper, the tribe shaman and keeper of the sacred Medicine Arrows. A pony with markings unfamiliar to Gray Thunder's camp was hobbled before the tipi.

Inside, a fire blazed in the stone-lined pit in the middle of the tipi. The buffalo-hide tipi cover was almost stretched transparent with age, and was now transformed into a dull-orange cone by the fire within. Old Arrow Keeper sat across the fire from a young Cheyenne brave named Goes Ahead.

Goes Ahead was a word-bringer who had ridden south from the camp of the Cheyenne Chief Shoots Left Handed. It was located far to the north in the mountains near the Land of the Grandmother—the land called Canada by the whites.

"Now, little brother," the old medicine man said after they had smoked to the four directions of the wind, "unburden your heart to me and speak straight-arrow. I can see, from the trouble clouds in your eyes, that the news from my old friend Shoots Left Handed is not good."

"Not good, Father, not good at all. Trouble has infected our band like the red-speckled cough. I do not even know if the rest will be alive when I return."

These somber words deepened the sharp creases of the old shaman's face. He already knew the situation must be bleak indeed—Shoots Left Handed had instructed this word-bringer to go directly to Arrow Keeper, not Chief Gray Thunder or the headmen. This suggested there was no time for the usual, lengthy proceedings of a council.

"What is this trouble, little brother, that places such a weight of age and sadness over your young face?"

"Our band has been blamed for several attacks on white stagecoaches and freight wagons. Paleface passengers have been wounded, goods and money stolen. White settlers in the region have blood in their eyes against the Shaiyena people. Now we live on the run, driven higher and higher into unfamiliar mountains."

Arrow Keeper's brow creased in a puzzled frown. "Southern Cheyenne Dog Soldiers sometimes raid this way. But no Indian loves peace more than Shoots Left Handed. Surely no Cheyenne from his band would do this thing?"

"None, Father. We are certain of this, yet we are blamed."

"But little brother, the area where you live is crawling with Blackfeet, not Cheyennes. Everyone knows Blackfeet attack whites at every opportunity. Why, then, are Cheyennes being blamed?"

Goes Ahead shook his head. "No one understands this thing. Soldiers and vigilantes come for us in the night. We move our camp often now. But our meat racks are empty and game is scarce in the high country where we are forced to hide. There is no grass for our ponies, the children and elders are sick, pregnant squaws are losing their babies. Worse yet, we have little strong medicine to fight back since Scalp Cane was killed."

Both Cheyennes automatically made the cut-off sign, as one did when speaking of the dead. Now Arrow Keeper was deeply troubled. Scalp Cane gone, crossed over! For more winters than Arrow Keeper could recall, Scalp Cane had served as medicine man for Shoots Left Handed's band. How could a tribe face trouble such as this without strong medicine? Indeed, perhaps the loss of Scalp Cane's big magic was behind the current trouble.

And perhaps, Arrow Keeper told himself, the hand of Maiyun, the Good Supernatural, was in this thing.

Old Arrow Keeper thought again, as he did often lately, about his young apprentice, Touch the Sky. The tall youth's existence with the tribe had proven difficult since that first day, many winters gone now, when he had been captured, taken before the Council of Forty, and pronounced a spy for the hair-faces.

However, recent events had endangered Touch the Sky more than ever before. It was as clear as blood in new snow that Black Elk's jealousy over Honey Eater had finally driven him insane with suspicion and rage. And being stripped of his coup feathers had left the mean-spirited Wolf Who Hunts Smiling keen to punish his enemy. Either brave would gladly sully the sacred Medicine Arrows—and thus the entire tribe—by killing Touch the Sky.

The old brave had been thinking, even before Goes Ahead rode into camp, that perhaps it was time, once again, to send Touch the Sky away for his own safety. For one thing, despite Touch the Sky's youth, Arrow Keeper knew his medicine was strong. He also knew the youth possessed the gift of visions. What better Cheyenne than he to send north to help Shoots Left Handed, whose people had no spiritual guide through this difficult time?

Besides, Arrow Keeper had intended to eventually send the youth north anyway. The elder had experienced a powerful vision at Medicine Lake. One which told him that Touch the Sky must be prepared for eventual leadership of the entire Shaiyena nation. He must meet their northern allies and familiarize himself with the land of the short white days.

"Wait here, little brother," Arrow Keeper said,

rising with a popping of stiff kneecaps. "I must speak with someone."

His mind a riot of troubled thoughts, Arrow Keeper headed across the central camp clearing toward Touch the Sky's tipi. He pulled up short when he viewed the tense scene which awaited him. Touch the Sky and Little Horse stood shoulder to shoulder in front of Touch the Sky's tipi. Facing them, hands on their knives, were Black Elk, Wolf Who Hunts Smiling, and Swift Canoe.

"Cousin, I for one am weary of this bloodless sparring," Wolf Who Hunts Smiling was saying, moving a step closer. "This make-believe Cheyenne would rut with your squaw! I say we make maggot fodder of him now!"

There was a quicksilver glint in the firelight when Wolf Who Hunts Smiling slid the polished obsidian blade of his knife from its sheath. His companions too drew their weapons.

"Then close the gap!" Touch the Sky said, his knife leaping into his fist. Little Horse too drew his blade. "I am *for* you!"

"Hold! I command it in the name of the Arrows!"

Arrow Keeper's voice was cracked and old, but carried the stern authority of age and wisdom. All five braves stared at him. One glance at the scene had convinced Arrow Keeper that his decision to send Touch the Sky north was the right one.

"You three," he said, his hatchet-sharp profile directed at Black Elk and his companions. "Return to your clan circles!"

But Wolf Who Hunts Smiling's blood was up to kill this white man's Indian who had cost him his coup feathers. More and more he had been openly challenging Arrow Keeper's authority.

"This old one has grown doting in his frosted years!" he said scornfully. "His brain is soft with age."

Black Elk, however, recalled the many times that Arrow Keeper's medicine had blessed his war bonnet and shield.

"Cease this unmanly disrespect, cousin, and do as your Cheyenne elder commanded! In good time we will settle with Woman Face."

After they had left, Arrow Keeper turned to Touch the Sky and Little Horse.

"You two. Ready your battle rigs and equip yourselves for a long ride. But keep your preparations secret. I want *no one* in the tribe to know that I have sent you north on a dangerous mission."

Chapter Two

The Milk River Stage and Freighting Line operated the only stagecoach service between the Bear Paw Mountains of northern Montana and Fort Buford in the remote Dakota Territory.

The desolate stretch between Fort Randall and Birch Coulee was especially treacherous. In the higher elevations, rock slides occasionally wiped out the wagon road; below on the plains, sudden downpours could mire the wheels up to the axles in minutes. There was also the constant threat of Indian attack.

Jeanette Lofley knew all of this very well because her husband, Colonel Orrin Lofley, was the commanding officer at lonely Fort Randall. He had finally agreed, reluctantly, to send for her despite the considerable dangers of the long journey in this far-north country. The War Department had recently notified him he was being kept at Fort Randall for another two years. Upon learning this, Jeanette told him bluntly she would rather be a widow than an Army wife. It was she who'd insisted on her leaving Michigan to join him.

But now, watching the seamed bottom of a steep canyon slide by just a few feet to the right of their narrow, twisting trail, she missed the placid shores of Lake Erie.

She was a pretty, dark-haired woman of perhaps 30, her pale and serious face still unlined. She shared the six-passenger coach with a portly, bald-headed major named Carmichael—an administrative officer returning to Fort Randall after temporary duty in the Dakota region—and two civilian cattlemen headed for the railroad spur at Milk River.

"We're nosing into the rough stretch now," said one of the cattlemen, a lanky, rawboned man named Legget. "This next twenty miles is where the last two attacks took place."

"What gripes me," said Starret, his companion, "is how the Army buckles under to the Indian lovers in Congress. They just sit back and let the redskins rule the roost hereabouts. Blackfeet, Mandans, now Cheyennes. My wranglers know this north country. They ain't too eager to push beef through it. I have to double their wages once we cross the Yellowstone."

The officer named Carmichael frowned. "It's no use to blame the Army. You can blame that goddamned—excuse me, ma'am—you can blame the Fort Laramie Treaty. *That's* what ties the Army's hands hereabouts. According to that treaty, whites are to punish white criminals, Indians are to punish Indian criminals. The Army has no legal jurisdiction against aboriginals on the road through Indian country. That's why Colonel Lofley can't even send out a detachment to protect his own wife."

"Blamed fool treaty," Legget said.

"I'll grant that, sir. The Army doesn't like it either. You can thank the Quakers back East for it, what with all their Noble Red Man and brotherly love claptrap."

"What's that?" Starret said, craning his neck out the window on his side.

Legget paled a bit, then stuck his head out too. "Where?"

Starret caught Jeanette's eye and winked. "Oh, I reckon it's just a stand of trees. I thought maybe it was a group of Indians."

Starret chuckled as his friend frowned and shot him a disgusted look. "Don't be playing the larks with me like that, Jim. It ain't funny."

"Well anyway," Carmichael said, again letting his gaze fall to the creamy white skin at the neck of Jeanette's shirtwaist. "Even if the colonel couldn't provide a detachment of guards, he did the next best thing. The man riding shotgun is named Jay Maddox, and he's a sharpshooter from Fort Randall. He can shatter a shaving mirror at five hundred yards, shooting over his shoulder."

Jeanette gripped the pleated leather armrest as the stage shifted to climb a steep incline. She heard the steady jangle of the traces, the driver cursing the team and lashing them with his light sisal whip. The coach was equipped with iron springs and leather braces, but still jolted and bounced roughly on the rock-strewn trail. Behind, the boot was stuffed with luggage. Overhead, the iron-reinforced security box was lashed tight to the roof. It contained a gold shipment bound for the huge trading post at Pike's Fork.

By standing agreement, the only people who knew when such shipments were coming were the traders at Pike's Fork, Colonel Lofley and his immediate staff, and the men at the stage line. Despite recent Indian attacks, it was generally believed that red men this far north had no concept yet of the value of gold. The colonel had explained all this carefully to Jeanette. But still she glanced nervously to right and left, suspicious of every cloud shadow or hidden gulch.

"No need to fret, ma'am," Major Carmichael said deferentially, taking her slim white hand between his own pudgy fists to pat it reassuringly. "Young Corporal Maddox is the pride of the Army. And as you can see, I'm armed too. You're well protected."

Legget opened his linsey suitcoat to reveal a six-shot pin-fire revolver in a leather holster over his right hip.

"Made for me special-order in Philadelphia," he boasted. "There's a fold-away knife blade under the barrel. You can—"

"What the hell?" Starret said, his face stiffening with fear as he stared toward the rimrock overhead.

"Jim," Legget said, "Don't wear it out. I like your barroom josh as well as the next fellow. But there's a lady with us now, and you—"

Jeanette watched Starret flinch violently. A moment later she heard an insignificant little popping sound. Not until Starret flopped back in his seat, a neat hole in the middle of his forehead, did she realize the popping sound was gunfire arriving a heartbeat after the slug's impact.

"Good God a-gorry!" Legget said, even as a geyser of blood spurted from his friend's forehead and splashed Legget's coat.

"Hi-ya! Hiii-ya!"

Hearing the fierce, shrill cries from without, Major Carmichael shouted, "That's the Cheyenne war cry! Christ on a crutch, we're being attacked by Cheyennes!"

Now it was clear to all that the Indians had picked a perfect place to attack from above. The stagecoach was halfway up a steep rise, the team laboring in the traces. Perpendicular walls of smooth mica on both sides of the trail kept the passengers from getting a clear aim from inside.

"Gee up!" the frightened driver called out, lashing his team to a frenzy. "Haw, gee up!"

More gunfire sounded from above, and Jeanette heard the slugs thwacking into the japanned wood of the coach. She heard the sharp, precision crack of Maddox's carbine, once, twice; then abruptly his weapon fell silent and a body slumped past the window. Jeanette watched, horrified, as the seriously wounded young sharpshooter lost his hold on the box and fell directly in the path of the right front wheel. It snapped his spine like a dry twig, the coach momentarily jolting as it rolled over him.

Another flurry of slugs, and she heard the driver cry out. Major Carmichael, his soft face as pale as alkali dust, made no move to draw his Army .44. Legget had his pin-fire revolver in his hand but could spot no target.

"We're being attacked!" Carmichael repeated uselessly, almost blubbering. "Cheyennes! We're being attacked! Maddox is dead, we're being attacked—"

"Shut up, you fat, white-livered coward and draw steel!" Legget growled. "Ma'am, you get the hell down!"

His warning came too late. The next flurry of slugs ripped into the leather seats, and Jeanette felt a white-hot crease of pain in her left side.

"She's been hit!" Legget shouted to Carmichael even as Jeanette almost fainted. "Tend to her!"

But the blubbering major ignored her. "Maddox is dead!" he said. "Oh, sweet Jesus, Maddox is dead, Cheyennes killed him!"

"You talk too damn much," Woodrow Denton said.

The man he spoke to was called Lumpy because of a huge goiter distending the side of his neck.

"The hell you mean, Woody? I swear by the twin balls o' Napoleon I ain't opened my mouth onc't since we vamoosed with the swag!"

"I mean during the holdup, you fool. You're

spozed to be an Indian. Indians don't talk so damn much."

Denton, Lumpy, and four other men nearly filled the single room of a run-down ,shack. It was hidden high on a remote ridge well behind Fort Randall. One of the men was a cavalry captain in full field uniform. The rest were all dressed as Northern Cheyenne braves. Their authentic masquerade included horse-hair "braids" and skin darkened by berry juice.

"What the hell," Lumpy told his leader. "Don't I toss in plenty of Cheyenne words? Anyway, it was your big idea, seein' as how I can palaver a little Cheyenne, that I should do the talking."

"You're spozed to sound like a Cheyenne that speaks a little English. That means plenty of grunts and baby talk. Hell, soon as you opened your mouth that woman stared at you like she twigged the whole game."

"She didn't twig a damn thing. She had other problems," Lumpy said. "Hell, she was bleedin' like a stuck pig."

When he heard this, the cavalry officer's jaw slacked open in astonished disbelief. He had been perched on the edge of a deal table, portioning out piles of gold dust while the others spoke. Now he slowly laid down a chamois pouch he was filling and rose from the table. He was big and powerfully built, with blunt features and a permanent sneer of cold command.

"You *shot* Jeanette Lofley?" Captain Seth Carlson demanded. "It wasn't enough you killed the guard and a passenger? One of you idiotic, horseshit-for-brains morons also *shot* the Old Man's wife?"

"Don't get all your pennies in a bunch," Denton said. "It was a accident, is all. We had to spray 'em good with lead before the driver and all the passengers would throw down their irons. She just got in front of a stray round, is all."

"Is *all*? You fools! *I'm* the one in charge of the new mountain company. These Indians are my direct responsibility. Why do you think I know about all the shipments? You know damn well the treaty outlaws military patrols along the wagon road, but not elsewhere. Until now the Old Man's been more or less content with my progress in hunting down Shoots Left Handed's band. Now that you've shot his wife, he's going to want Cheyenne guts for garters. Did you kill her?"

Denton shrugged, looking ridiculous now that he had removed his bonnet and fake braids. The berry dye stopped where his bald white head took over.

"Hard to tell. I couldn't see if she was gut-shot or caught one in the cage."

Everyone there knew what he meant. A gut shot would bleed internally. This far from civilization, such wounds were often fatal. A shot to the rib cage bled less and was usually easier to survive.

"If she dies," Carlson said, "you can put this down in your book—our little gold mine has just run dry. Lofley knows he doesn't stand a chance of making the general's list, so he's not exactly champing at the bit to fight savages. But he dotes on his wife. Even if she doesn't die, he won't rest until every Cheyenne in this region has been hunted down. That means more pressure on me."

"What I don't get," Denton said, "is why it's so all-fired important to you to pin this on Cheyennes? Most of them are concentrated down around the Powder and the Rosebud. It'd be more sensible-like to hang it on Blackfeet or Mandans. Then you could just kill off a few 'n' show their scalps to your boss, tell him you got the renegades."

Carlson frowned impatiently. "Think about it. There's thousands of Blackfeet in this area, fewer than two hundred Cheyennes. What happens if you're a Blackfoot warrior and you hear somebody is dressing up like your tribe to rob whites? You go on the warpath. This Cheyenne band is too weak."

All this was true. But neither Denton nor any of the hardcases riding for him knew the secret history of Carlson's one-man war against the Cheyenne nation. Indeed, they knew nothing of the humiliating debacle which had sent him to this godforsaken outpost.

It had begun years earlier, at Fort Bates in the Wyoming Territory. While still a shavetail lieutenant, he had fallen in love with Kristen, daughter of the wealthy mustang rancher Hiram Steele. Then he had discovered, about the same time Hiram did, that Kristen was meeting secretly with Matthew Hanchon—a full-blooded Cheyenne in spite of his white name.

Enraged, Hiram Steele ordered one of his wranglers to savagely beat Hanchon. And Hanchon was warned he would be killed if he ever met with the girl again. But Carlson took no chances. He looked the youth up on his own and warned him: Either Matthew left the territory for good, or his white parents' lucrative contract with Fort Bates went to another mercantile.

The plan worked. Then everything went to hell in a hay wagon. Hiram Steele went on to drive the Hanchons out of their mercantile business. When they sold out and started a mustang spread, Steele decided to run them off with Carlson's help. What they hadn't counted on was Matthew Hanchon's return as a Cheyenne warrior.

Even now, just thinking about what had happened made Carlson's face flush warm with shame and anger. Hanchon had humiliated him at every turn! While attacking the buck on the open plains, the officer's horse had stepped into a prairie-dog hole and thrown Carlson ass-over-applecart in front of all his men. Then the buck and his renegade companion had whipped Carlson and three men from the dragoons, thwarting the effort to drive the Hanchons from their spread. Worse yet, a subsequent investigation had turned up Carlson's falsified reconnaissance reports designed to create an "Indian menace." As punishment, he'd been sent to this northern hellhole where, in winter, piss froze before it hit the ground.

Denton had watched Carlson's face closely. Now he shook his head and said, "Whatever you say, trooper. 'Pears to me, though, you're nursin' a grudge agin the Cheyenne."

"Well, iffen he is," Lumpy said, fingering his goiter and eagerly watching Carlson fill another pouch with gold dust, "he's got a perfect job for grinding axes."

Carlson commanded a new mountain company which represented the U.S. Army's latest Indian-fighting strategy. Hitherto the Army had tried to engage the savages in combat on the plains. But this had proved suicidal. By warm weather the new grass left Indian ponies strong and agile, and they could cover up to seventy miles a day relying on water holes known only to them. Once they fled into the mountains, there was no finding them. The Army's response was to equip smaller, lighter, faster units for high-altitude fighting and hunt the Indians down, concentrating massive firepower on them and exterminating them without allowing surrender or taking prisoners.

"Maybe he has," Denton said, "but so far ol' Shoots Left Handed has slipped through his fingers slicker 'n grease through a goose, ain't that the straight?"

Denton's mocking tone irritated Carlson. The man looked like a sinister clown, his face painted dark beneath the fish-belly white of his pate. He was scum, and Carlson would gladly air him in a minute if he weren't so useful. And one glance around at his filthy companions, all hardcases on the prod, reminded him that only Denton could control these animals.

"So far he has," Carlson admitted. "But time is a bird, my friend, and the bird is on the wing."

Chapter Three

For three full sleeps Touch the Sky and Little Horse rode hard, bearing north toward the Always Star and the Land of the Grandmother.

The sacred Black Hills constantly behind their left shoulder, they forded the Little Bighorn, the Bighorn, and the Yellowstone. Following Arrow Keeper's urgent instructions, they pushed their mounts to the limits of endurance. Cottonwood groves and open, rolling plains slowly gave way to towering evergreen forests and deep coulees still moist with snow runoff. Fortunately, water and lush grass were plentiful. On the third day, the Bear Paw Mountains loomed up on the distant horizon.

Little Horse had been absorbed in deep thought for some time.

"Brother," he said when they paused to water their ponies at the Milk River, "I know Shoots

Left Handed and most in his band. You saw them at the annual Sun Dance, again at the Chief Renewal. They are a generous and peaceful group and always bring many blankets and horses for the poor during the dances."

"I remember them well. They were the only Cheyenne band still wearing fur leggings in spring."

"At one time they lived closer to our Powder River hunting grounds. But Shoots Left Handed married an Assiniboin and fell in love with the north country. His wife died, but he stayed in the north. Soon other members of his Cheyenne clan migrated to join him. Now he is a peace leader of his own band.

"He fought beside Arrow Keeper at Wolf Creek and saved his life from a Kiowa throwing ax. So I am not surprised that Arrow Keeper is quick to send us during this trouble. But that is not the only reason he wanted us—*you*—out of camp immediately. And why was our leaving a secret, unless he does not want your enemies within the tribe to follow you?"

Touch the Sky listened carefully to all this, saying nothing. While he listened he gazed off at the distant mountains. From here they did indeed resemble bear paws, huge and blunt with snowcapped toes. Looking at them made him recall the time a grizzly had trapped him in a cave at Medicine Lake.

"Yes," he finally replied, "Arrow Keeper knows the danger well. When he sent me by myself to Medicine Lake, Wolf Who Hunts Smiling and

Swift Canoe followed and tried to send me under. This time Arrow Keeper wants to make sure the dogs do not return to their vomit."

By now their ponies had nearly drunk their fill. To avoid suspicion as long as possible, Arrow Keeper had instructed them to leave their own ponies with the herd. Instead, he had them cut out two from his own string. Little Horse rode a ginger buckskin, Touch the Sky a blood bay with a pure white blaze on its forehead. Like all ponies owned by Arrow Keeper, these had been taught special tricks and blessed with strong medicine.

"You are worried about Honey Eater," Little Horse said, not making it a question.

Touch the Sky nodded. His lips were set in a grim, determined slit. "I am worried, buck. Your words fly straight-arrow. Black Elk is sick with jealous hatred. At least in camp my presence served as a constant reminder that he must pay dearly for hurting her. Now I am gone, and who knows for how long?"

"Is this why you took Two Twists aside before we rode out?"

Again Touch the Sky nodded. Two Twists was a junior warrior in training. He had fought gallantly alongside Touch the Sky and Little Horse in freeing Cheyenne prisoners from the Comanche stronghold in Blanco Canyon. Touch the Sky had instructed him to keep a close eye on Honey Eater, especially when Black Elk was around. Touch the Sky had already served notice to Black Elk. Unlike the barbaric Comanche, Cheyenne law did not permit wife-slaughter and wife-beating. If he laid a hand on Honey Eater one more time, he was carrion fodder.

Touch the Sky's bay snorted and backed away from the water, having drunk its fill. Now, as they prepared to ride on, both youths again gazed toward the Bear Paws.

Again they were riding into the maw of unknown danger. Not only was this area crawling with Blackfeet and other hostile tribes, but with blue-bloused soldiers too. And with Cheyenne being blamed for the recent attacks Arrow Keeper spoke of, they were open targets for vigilante fire.

Therefore they had come well-armed. Touch the Sky's percussion-action Sharps protruded from his scabbard, Little Horse's four-shot, revolving-barrel shotgun from his. Both braves were also armed with knives, stone-headed throwing axes, and new green bows. Their foxskin quivers were crammed with fire-hardened arrows.

"It is time to ride, brother," Touch the Sky said, gripping his pony's hackamore.

The tall, broad-shouldered youth cast one last, long glance south toward their Powder River camp. His eyes were clouded with trouble as he thought about Honey Eater. Then, pointing their hair bridles toward the Bear Paws, they rode on into the gathering twilight and unknown trouble.

Almost three sleeps had passed before Wolf Who Hunts Smiling was sure of it. He turned to Swift Canoe and suddenly said, "Brother, we have less brains between us than a rabbit. Woman Face and Little Horse are gone!"

Swift Canoe glanced up, startled. The two youths sat before Wolf Who Hunts Smiling's tipi. Their sister the sun had gone to her rest earlier. Now the two braves were filing arrow points in the light of a bright cottonwood fire.

"Gone? What do you mean?"

"Buck, do I suddenly speak Arapaho? What else does 'gone' mean? I mean gone, they are not in camp! Have you seen them?"

Swift Canoe thought about it hard, the furrow between his eyes deepening. Then he shook his head. "You are right, Panther Clan."

They had been sent out secretly by Arrow Keeper. Wolf Who Hunts Smiling knew that. Once before, the wily old shaman had sent Woman Face away to avoid danger in camp. Only this time, he had not announced his decision at council. And the two friends had taken different ponies.

"It would be foolish," Wolf Who Hunts Smiling said, "to trail them now. The sign will be cold. And Arrow Keeper would miss us and know."

"This time," Swift Canoe said, disappointed, "they have played the fox and outwitted us."

"Perhaps not, Cheyenne. Only think on this thing. Did Arrow Keeper announce the departure from camp of Little Horse and Woman Face, as is custom and law?"

Swift Canoe shook his head, confused. "You know he did not. You just said—"

"And the others in camp? Soon now these two

must be missed. When they are, the people will be furious to know. After all, these two have never cleared their names from serious charges that they have spied for Long Knives. But what if, before Arrow Keeper can concoct a story, *another* story flies through camp on the wind?"

"What story, brother?"

"Put those points down and follow me, buck. I know my cousin will want to counsel with us on this matter."

The two youths stayed in the apron of shadows at the edge of the main clearing. Slipping behind tipis and lodges, they avoided the groups where soldier societies had gathered to smoke and talk. Soon they stood before Black Elk's tipi. A bright fire burned within, and they could see two long, distorted shadows: Black Elk and Honey Eater.

Black Elk's voice raged from within.

"You will *not* take this tone with me and make me a squaw, haughty Cheyenne she-bitch! I am your husband and this tribe's war leader. I have cut off your braid before, and what man has done, man can do."

"Brother," Swift Canoe said nervously, "Black Elk has blood in his eyes. This is not a wise time to interrupt."

"You are wrong, brother," Wolf Who Hunts Smiling said, his furtive grin dividing his face. Anger seethed inside him. His coup feathers had been the soul of his medicine bag, and thanks to Woman Face they were now a memory smell, a thing of smoke.

"No better time," he added. "This hatred in my

cousin's voice, who do you think has caused it? None other than Woman Face!"

Wolf Who Hunts Smiling stepped boldly forward and stood before the entrance flap.

"Black Elk! I would speak with you."

The flap was thrust wide and Black Elk stared out at the visitors, scowling. The fire inside backlighted his face and braided hair. The wrinkled, leathery flap of sewn-on ear made him look fierce in the eerie orange light.

"Well?" he demanded. "Are you a totem pole, or is there a bone caught in your throat? Speak!"

But the younger brave had hesitated because Honey Eater stood close to the entrance. Even Wolf Who Hunts Smiling, whose great ambition for leadership left him indifferent to women, was suddenly impressed yet again with her frail beauty. High, delicately sculpted cheekbones framed an oval face and full lips. Her hair had finally grown back long enough to braid with her usual white columbine petals. Her huge, wing-shaped eyes watched the three braves suspiciously, knowing some new treachery was afoot.

Wolf Who Hunts Smiling signaled to his cousin with his eyes, then looked at Honey Eater again.

"Back off, mooncalf!" Black Elk snapped at her.

When she was gone, Wolf Who Hunts Smiling said, "Black Elk, have you seen Woman Face or Little Horse these past several sleeps?"

Slowly, Black Elk's frown turned into a look of wary curiosity. His cousin was not one to make small talk.

"Woman Face I rarely see anymore," he said. "He wisely avoids me and my clan circle. But now I recall that Little Horse should be riding herd guard, yet I have not seen him. Do not be coy. We are not girls in their sewing lodge. Why do you ask this thing?"

"Cousin, two of Arrow Keeper's best ponies are missing. So are Woman Face and Little Horse. Yet nothing was said at council. Do you see? The old shaman has sent them on a secret mission in violation of tribal law. Even Chief Gray Thunder cannot authorize missions without a vote of the Headmen. Only the Star Chamber can do this, and they have not convened."

For many heartbeats Black Elk was silent, thinking about this.

"Cousin," Wolf Who Hunts Smiling continued, speaking faster in his gathering excitement, "you know there is bad feeling within the tribe for these two. This, ever since they deserted their people to fight for Woman Face's white family. Now, any time they ride out, the people talk. They say, 'This Touch the Sky, why does he ride off so much without the camp crier announcing it? Why so much secret business for this one?' "

Black Elk was catching on. A faint smile touched his stern lips. There was grudging admiration in his tone when he said, "I have ears for this, cousin. As you say, nothing was told at council."

"Nothing. And cousin, do you recall? River of Winds recently scouted the Valley of the Greasy

Grass for buffalo sign. He spotted blue-bloused soldiers camped there."

Black Elk nodded, suddenly very impressed by his younger cousin's scheming mind. He said, "No one would believe either of us. It is commonly known we would gladly feed his liver to the dogs. But cousin, you and I have brothers in our Bull Whip soldier troop. They will gladly claim to have seen Woman Face and Little Horse playing the white man's Indian for soldiers."

Touch the Sky and Little Horse rode as far into the mountains as they could before night settled over everything like a dark cloak. They made a cold camp beside a runoff stream. A meager meal consisted of cold water, and pemmican and dried plums from their legging sashes.

The next morning, as the word-bringer Goes Ahead had promised, they found signs where Shoots Left Handed's band had blazed a trail to their latest camp. For the better part of a day the two youths climbed steadily higher and higher. The trees held as they rose, but grew thinner and more wind-twisted. Deadfalls, piles of rock scree, mud slides caused by spring runoff blocked the way. But all this also, the two young braves realized, made it tougher for enemies to find this camp.

Finally, climbing up out of a long cutbank, they were greeted by the owl hoot of a friendly Cheyenne sentry. He led the new arrivals to the high-altitude camp which had been made in the lee of a well-protected ridge.

The squalor of the place shocked and saddened both youths. Dogs were always numerous in Cheyenne camps because of their usefulness as sentries, but they had all long since been eaten. The few ponies which remained were starvation-thin, their ribs protruding like barrel staves. It was foaling time for the mares, but they were too weak to birth. The pony-loving Cheyennes would cry openly as they were forced to kill the mares and cut the new foals out.

Nonetheless, life went on. Water haulers made the long trip from the nearest stream, full bladder-bags sloshing. Old women sat in a circle preparing precious chokecherries, gathered earlier after hours of hard scouring. There was no other food.

"Tonight," Shoots Left Handed said, soon after meeting the new arrivals, "we will eat another pony."

His words shocked them into silence. Tribal history told of times, of course, when Cheyennes had been forced to kill and eat ponies. And they knew that such tribes as the Apache ate horse meat as casually as they might eat buffalo or elk. But never had they seen Cheyennes forced to such barbarism.

They sat in a small circle in Shoots Left Handed's tipi, a fire blazing in the pit to counter the cold mountain air. The group included Pawnee Killer, the band's battle leader.

"Our band has lost many warriors because of these attacks against whites," Pawnee Killer said.

He was a brave with perhaps 40 winters behind

him, still vigorous and strong though his braids were traced with silver. He wore a leather shirt adorned with the intricate Cheyenne beadwork admired throughout the West.

"Warriors are not the end of it," Shoots Left Handed said. The old peace chief had left his snow-white hair unbraided, and a milky cataract clouded one eye. Hunger had emaciated the entire tribe, and their leader had not been spared. Touch the Sky winced when he noticed that the fingers clutching the old man's blanket about him were as thin as twigs.

"These constant attacks by pony soldiers," he continued, "have forced us further and further into these barren mountains. This is intolerable. We are Cheyenne, plains-loving horsemen! My people are sick, miserable, hungry, and tired of eating fish."

"Too," Pawnee Killer said, "all this constant moving to new camps puts us at risk from attack by the Piegan."

Touch the Sky and Little Horse nodded, recognizing the name by which the Blackfoot tribe called itself.

Touch the Sky said, "Would the Piegan disguise themselves as Cheyenne and attack whites?"

"As a people," Pawnee Killer said, "they are as low as the lice-eating Pawnee. Yes, they are capable of such a thing. But for many winters now they have stayed well south of the Milk River Road. Nor are they a tribe to bother with such games as dressing up."

"Truly," Touch the Sky said, nodding, "I know

of no red tribe that plays at such games, though our Lakota cousins will dress in a blue blouse after they kill a soldier."

Pawnee Killer watched the tall newcomer closely, his eyes slitted in an approving scrutiny. "As you say, young Cheyenne. I see that your mind flies on the same wind with mine. This painting and dressing for crime is more of a white man's game."

Outside the tipi, the cold mountain wind whipped up to a blustering frenzy, driving everyone for shelter. Touch the Sky heard a starving horse nicker piteously, heard a sick baby crying with a steady, faint tone of utter hopelessness. Hot tears threatened his eyes as he realized: All around him, the people who shared his blood were dying.

"We must find out at once who is making these attacks," he declared with conviction. "And the tribe must be blessed with strong medicine. When were the Arrows last renewed?"

Pawnee Killer shook his head, making the cut-off sign as he mentioned the dead. "Scalp Cane was our Arrow Keeper. But he lay sick for several moons before he crossed over, unable to renew the Arrows."

Alarm tightened the young shaman apprentice's face. "Are they safe?"

"Of course. They are with White Plume of the Sky Walker Clan. But he is not a shaman. We have no priest to conduct the ceremony."

"I will conduct the renewal soon," Touch the Sky said. "Not just for the warriors, but to cleanse the entire tribe."

Chief Shoots Left Handed nodded. His milky eye glistened in the flickering firelight.

"This is a good thing, little brother. I knew Arrow Keeper would send the right brave. But I fear strong medicine alone cannot spare us from the new Bluecoat mountain troop. Even now their turncoat Ute scouts are sniffing out this camp, and soon the attack will again be on us."

Chapter Four

Colonel Orrin Lofley said, "You know my motto, Carlson: The shit rolls downhill."

"Yes, sir," Captain Seth Carlson replied, thinking to himself as usual: *Why don't you set it to music, you tiresome blowhard?* But the silver eagles perched on Lofley's epaulets stared at the captain with stern, unblinking authority.

"That was my *wife* who got shot in this last attack, Carlson!"

"Yes, sir. The colonel has my deepest regrets. Is Mrs. Lofley doing better?"

"She's going to survive, Carlson, no thanks to you. Your deepest regrets aren't worth a plug nickel. You're in charge of what's supposed to be the best Indian-hunting company in the Far West. I don't want regrets from you, I want action."

"Yes, sir."

War Party

The commanding officer of remote Fort Randall was a short, barrel-chested redhead with coarse-grained skin and a weak chin disguised by a goatee. His left arm had been partially paralyzed during the Sioux campaigns. He could not lift it above his shoulder and required assistance in taking his jacket off. But if a man could walk and still had one functioning trigger finger, Army regulations permitted him to serve.

"Carlson, this fort is already the butt of jokes back East. Every shitbird recruit who can't open his mess kit gets posted here. I'm sick of cringing every time the newspapers arrive, crammed full of stories about how the goddamn aboriginal hostiles are making a mockery of the U.S. Army! Now that my own wife has eaten an Indian bullet, you think the papers aren't rawhiding me mercilessly?"

"Yes, sir. I mean, no, sir."

Carlson knew damn well that Lofley only had himself to blame for his troubles. He had ended up at Fort Randall because his inept battlefield tactics were infamous in military circles. In one campaign against the Hunkpapa Sioux, a regiment directly under his command had expended 25,000 rounds of ammunition in killing five Sioux, all women and children. Carlson's unit of mountain-trained sharpshooters, in contrast, had once wiped out an entire Assiniboin camp and expended only 500 rounds. The trick, Carlson knew, was to hit them in their sleep and shoot plumb for their vitals.

"The Army is caught between the sap and the

bark on this Indian question," Lofley said, standing up from his desk. Behind him on the wall was a Mercator map of the United States. The all-important 100th meridian was marked with a heavy black line. This was the crucial boundary where rainfall dramatically slacked off and the tall grasses gave way to the shortgrass prairie—marking the official beginning of Plains Indian country.

"If the damned Indian lovers back East hadn't tied my hands in Congress, I would by God put paid to it *now*, Carlson, and make this region safe for white women like Jeanette to travel."

"Yes, sir."

"But even if that damned Laramie Accord forbids a major command offensive, it permits punitive actions away from the wagon road right of way. That's where your new company comes in, Carlson. Damn it, Soldier Blue, find those heathen Cheyennes and kill every man, woman, and child! That's an order!"

"Yes, sir. We've been trying."

"My grandmother *tries*, Carlson. You don't seem to understand me here. It's not just the fact that those mother-rutting savages almost killed my wife. The War Department is giving me six sorts of hell, not to mention the local vigilantes who cry about how soft the Army is on Indians. So help me Hannah, I want those red devils exterminated. Your unit's been crackerjack when it comes to routing out Mandans and such. Why so much trouble with one raggedy-assed band of Cheyennes?"

Carlson felt the irony of his situation. The plan to blame stagecoach and freight-wagon attacks on Cheyennes had served two very useful purposes: It made him rich, and it built a strong case to justify his eventual slaughter of Shoots Left Handed and his band, thus appeasing Carlson's vendetta against Matthew Hanchon and the Cheyenne nation.

So in the beginning, he had deliberately not tried to wipe out the band quickly. Their continued existence guaranteed scapegoats for the attacks by Woodrow Denton and his gun-throwers. But when the pressure to punish the Cheyennes had finally mounted, the band had slipped off to more remote regions. Now they had to be tracked down. But scouts were on the trail and due to report any day now.

Lofley turned to the map and jabbed at it with an angry index finger.

"*Look* at this region, Carlson. We're responsible for thousands of square miles of mountains and forests and canyons so deep you can't see the bottoms on a clear day. I have one special mountain company—yours—outfitted for the field. The rest are regular cavalry.

"Does anyone care that the goddamn manual says twenty-five miles a day is the maximum for the regular cavalry? I said twenty-five miles a day. And we're locking horns with Indians who ride with as many as five remounts on their string, remounts as clever and well-trained as circus ponies. They carry nothing but their weapons, they live on bark and insects if they have to, and they ride up to eighty miles a day."

Carlson mechanically said his "yes, sir" again, his eyes glazing over. Lofley was a bitter man with an ax to grind. He had repeated all of this so often he sounded like a salivating bible-thumper.

Finally he dismissed his subordinate. But as Carlson was about to escape through the office door, Lofley called his name.

"Sir?"

"You know the Officer Promotion Board meets next month at Fort Union?"

"Yes, sir."

"You have enough time in grade. If I sign the recommendation, the promotion to major is almost guaranteed."

Carlson nodded, liking what he was hearing.

"I also know how bad you want to get transferred back East. Just remember, appointment to major makes you a field-grade officer. That means you post out to a new command. I can't guarantee the East. But if you were to exterminate these Cheyennes, that would give you a Letter of Merit in your file, maybe even a Letter of Commendation. That would strengthen your request considerably."

Carlson nodded again, liking it even better. The scheme with the attacks was about played out anyway. If he could not only kill his enemies, the Cheyenne, but also earn a promotion and a transfer, so much the better.

"They shot my wife," Lofley repeated before he dismissed him. "Carlson, kill those damn hostiles. And bring me their scalps to show the paper-collar newspaper boys!"

"Goes Ahead should have returned by now," the battle chief named Pawnee Killer said.

He, Touch the Sky, and Little Horse were crossing toward the tipi of White Plume. The tribe elders had agreed with Touch the Sky that a Renewal of the Arrows should be held immediately; any strategy to combat Bluecoats or the highway raiders was doomed to fail without good magic.

Goes Ahead had been sent south to Powder River with news of this disaster. He was to have returned immediately, circling by way of Fort Randall to scout the soldier's activity.

"If enemies have slain him," Pawnee Killer added, "our tribe has lost a warrior who fights like ten men."

It was mid-morning of Touch the Sky's first full day in the high-altitude camp. Nights in the Bear Paws were cold, and he had shivered even in the depths of his shaggy buffalo robe. The cries of the hungry children were piteous. In the morning he and Little Horse had refused their portion of cooked meat, knowing it was horse flesh. They'd subsisted on the last of the pemmican and dried fruit in their sashes.

Now, as they picked their way across the sloping, rock-strewn ground, Touch the Sky glanced warily all around them. The camp seemed safely located, at first glance. They were deep in the lee of a sheltered ridge, cut off from sunshine but also from sight below. Three approaches were blocked by cliffs, landslides, and steep escarpments of rock. Night and day vigilant sentries watched the only path leading into camp.

All seemed secure enough. Yet during the night Touch the Sky had followed Arrow Keeper's advice: He had closed his mind to all thought and simply listened to the language of his senses. And then abruptly, like being plunged naked into a snowbank, his entire body had felt a bone-numbing chill of premonition.

Some danger lurked near this camp. He was sure of it. Lurked very near. And Little Horse, who had long ago recognized his friend's big medicine and the mulberry birthmark buried in his hair as the mark of the warrior—he too saw this knowledge in Touch the Sky's troubled dark eyes.

Something else had plagued him during the cold, windy night—a gnawing in his belly as sharp as a rat's incisors. For how could he forget that Honey Eater was living with a man who was on the feather edge of killing her? Leaving her with Black Elk was like deserting her in a grizzly's den.

But he forced his thoughts back to the here and now when the group of braves reached White Plume's tipi. White Plume, a brave with perhaps 50 winters behind him, looked at the two visitors with genuine respect when he learned Arrow Keeper had sent them. He ushered them into his tipi. His wife filled a clay pipe for them. Then she discreetly ducked outside to visit her clan while the men counseled over their important business.

"You are a shaman?" White Plume asked Touch the Sky after all had smoked to the directions.

He shook his head. "I assist Arrow Keeper at the ceremonies, and he is teaching me the shaman arts."

White Plume was satisfied with this response. "I know Arrow Keeper, buck. When I was a limber sapling even younger than you, he was once my battle chief in a fight against Crows. With so many arrows in him he looked like a porcupine, he rallied thirty Cheyennes to victory against twice as many stub-hands. If he chose you to assist him, this means you surely have the gift of visions and are blessed with strong medicine. He would not have chosen you otherwise."

He did not press the issue. It was understood among Indians that spiritual matters were powerful and mostly private. A person who possessed the gift of visions was not expected to speak of this thing, nor were others welcome to mention it.

White Plume crossed to the rear of his tipi and lifted aside a flat buffalo-hide saddle he'd won in a pony race with a Dakota. He pulled aside a blanket, then returned with a soft coyote-fur pouch.

All four men fell silent as he unwrapped the Medicine Arrows in the flickering firelight. There were four of them, painted in bright blue and yellow stripes and fletched with scarlet feathers. Ten sets in all existed, one for each of the ten bands of the Shaiyena nation.

Arrow Keeper had explained carefully how the secret of the Arrows had first been revealed to the people by the High Holy Ones who lived in the northern lights, The Land Where the Food Comes From. The fate of the Arrows was the fate of the entire tribe. Therefore, it was the Arrow Keeper's solemn responsibility to not only protect them with his life, but to keep them forever sweet and clean. Certain serious crimes—such as murder and adultery—stained the Arrows and thus the tribe. The Renewal of the Arrows was held to cleanse them after a crime or to strengthen them before a battle.

In the presence of the Arrows, Touch the Sky unconsciously lowered his voice. "Tell your warriors," he said to Pawnee Killer, "to paint and dress and bring their gifts to the Arrows. But tell the rest too to bring gifts. The entire tribe must renew its medicine and dance."

Pawnee Killer nodded, but his voice was heavy with doubt. "I will certainly tell my warriors, Touch the Sky. What few remain to us. Arrow Keeper is right, our strong medicine must be renewed. But medicine or no, this new Bluecoat mountain troop, they are wild and crazy like dogs in the hot moons. If our camp is located one more time, there will be one less band of Cheyenne."

The Cheyenne brave died hard.

Rough Feather, a huge Ute scout employed by Fort Randall, had nearly been taken by surprise. For many sleeps now, Rough Feather had painstakingly hunted down this camp. The Utes were a mountain tribe, nimble as goats and highly useful to the U.S. Army. After numerous false starts and miles of useless back-tracking, he had finally gained sight of Shoots Left Handed's camp.

Eluding the sentries in the gathering twilight had been tricky and required long patience. Finally, after crawling on his belly for hours over rocks, he knew right where the heart of camp was. He made a mental picture of everything so Carlson could plan a precise strike: the layout of the tipis, the number and location of sentries, any possible escape routes.

That Captain Carlson, thought Rough Feather—*here* was no white devil to fool with. The motto of his Indian-fighting company was known to every tribe in the region: *Take no prisoners!* The Utes had seen this coming early on, and wisely decided to nail their streamers to the Bluecoat mast.

Thinking all of these things, intent on looking ahead at the camp, he had almost missed the approach of a rider behind him.

The young Cheyenne did not spot him until he was almost on him. His pony suddenly snorted and pulled up short, tossing its head violently. In a heartbeat the Cheyenne's streamered lance was raised for the throw.

Rough Feather was faster. There was already a jagged rock in his hand. The big Ute rose to his feet and sent it flying hard. It chunked into the Cheyenne's forehead with an ominous sound of bone splitting. He slid from his pony like a heavy sack of grain. Moments later the young buck's moccasined heels futilely scratched the dirt as Rough Feather's French dagger opened his throat from ear to ear.

Rough Feather cursed this bad luck. He wiped his blade in the grass, then quickly hobbled the pony to keep it from wandering on into camp. But hiding the body, this close to camp and with such barren ground cover, was not worth the risk. Now he would have to leave immediately.

But soon Rough Feather calmed down. After all, even though the raggedy band would be alerted, what could they do? They were at the end of their tether. Moving an entire camp was a major enterprise. So many sick elders and infants made it far harder. Now they were trapped between the last mountain strongholds and the approaching Bluecoats.

Even as Rough Feather began to ease back down the trail, the night wind rose to a shriek like the howl of wolves mating.

Chapter Five

That night, while young women kept time with stone-filled gourds, everyone in Shoots Left Handed's band danced at the Renewal of the Arrows ceremony.

Touch the Sky directed that even the outlying sentries should be relieved long enough to join the dance. He had feared, at first, that the people would be too weak from hunger to dance. But hunger did not matter once the rhythmic cadence of stones and the steady *"Hi-ya, hii-ya"* chant started sounding. Everyone old enough to dance was soon circling a well-hidden ceremonial fire.

Touch the Sky watched them, his clay-painted face gruesome, yet magnificent, in the wavering glow of the fire. Their knees kicked high, higher, the starvation-lean bodies wrapped in furs against the mountain chill. And as they danced their misery out of them, hunger made the trance-state happen faster.

For a moment, watching them, Touch the Sky felt the power of his epic vision at Medicine Lake. Again the images were laid over his eyes: He saw red men, thousands of them from every tribe west of the river called Great Waters, all dancing as one people, dancing out their misery and fear and utter hopelessness. And on the horizon behind them, guidons snapping in the wind, sabers gleaming in the blood-red sun, the approaching hordes of blue-bloused soldiers.

When all seems lost, the voice of the dead Chief Yellow Bear had warned him, *become your enemy.* Touch the Sky felt the bitter sting of the present irony. Clearly, an enemy of the Cheyenne had become *them.*

After the dance, Touch the Sky unwrapped the Medicine Arrows and laid them on a stump in the center of camp. He had donned his mountain-lion skin, a gift from Arrow Keeper. It had been blessed with strong medicine, the shaman insisted. Touch the Sky could not swear to this. But he had worn it during a vicious Comanche raid, drawing all their fire onto himself, and not one bullet or arrow had found his flesh.

For this ceremony, he had painted his face as Cheyenne braves paint for war: forehead yellow, nose red, chin black. He also wore his single-horned war bonnet, its tail long with coup feathers. As the tribe lined up to leave their gifts to the Arrows, the crying of hungry babes rose to join the keening wail of the night wind. The misery of this people was evident in their lean bodies and empty stares.

For this reason, Touch the Sky recited the sacred Renewal Prayer in his clearest, most powerful voice, a voice meant to inspire the people with hope:

> *Oh, Great Spirit of Maiyun,*
> *whose voice we hear in the winds,*
> *and whose breath gives life to all the world,*
> *hear us! We are small and weak, we need*
> *your strength and wisdom.*

"Let this be so," the people said as one.

> *Let us walk in beauty, and make our eyes*
> *ever behold the red and purple sunset.*
> *Make our hearts respect the things you have*
> *made and our ears sharp to hear your voice.*
> *Make us wise that we may understand the*
> *things you have taught the people.*

"Let this be so," the others repeated.

> *Let us learn the lessons you have hidden*
> *in every leaf and rock.*
> *We seek strength, not to be greater than our*
> *brothers, but to fight our greatest enemy*
> *—ourselves.*
> *Make us always ready to come to you with*
> *clean hands and straight eyes.*

"Let this be so," the tribe sang as one.

Now Touch the Sky's voice rose above the shrieking of the wind, concluding the Renewal Prayer in a powerful tone that echoed downridge.

So when life fades, as the fading sunset,
our spirits may come to you
without shame.

A long, profound silence followed the prayer. Then Touch the Sky's voice again rang out: "Cheyenne people! The Arrows have been renewed! Now leave your gifts!"

One by one, every member of the tribe with more than 12 winters behind him knelt beside the Arrows to leave a sacrifice. The tribe's desperate situation was mirrored in the value of the gifts. Though everyone left something, there were no valuable pelts, no rich tobacco, few weapons. Instead, there were brightly dyed feathers, decorated coup sticks, moccasins with beaded soles.

The last gift had just been placed near the stump when there was a frightened shout from the direction of the only entrance to camp.

Everyone stared toward the narrow path. One of the sentries, who had been relieved and was riding into camp to leave his gift, frantically beckoned to them. As one, the tribe hurried across to him.

Darkness had descended, but a full moon owned the unclouded sky. The dead brave, Goes Ahead, was clear in the luminous white moonlight. He lay sprawled on his back, arms far-flung, his neck opened up like a second mouth. His pony was hobbled nearby. The huge gash in Goes Ahead's forehead told how he had been dropped from his pony.

Raven's Wing, the dead brave's young bride, cried out. She dropped beside her man and blindly groped for a sharp piece of flint in the rough dirt. No one stopped her when she began savagely gouging her arms with it, drawing ribbons of blood. But several of her clan sisters automatically formed a ring around her, blocking access to more serious weapons.

A few other Cheyennes made the cut-off sign while an old grandmother began keening in grief for the fallen youth.

Touch the Sky and Little Horse locked glances in the moonlight. The awful significance of this death, so near camp and the time of the sacred Renewal, could not be denied.

Shoots Left Handed and Pawnee Killer were clearly thinking the same thing. They crossed to join the young Cheyennes.

"The Arrows have been renewed," Shoots Left Handed said. "Good. It was a good ceremony, a good prayer. But clearly, Goes Ahead did not fall on his knife. He was murdered. That means our camp has been discovered yet again. Our enemy knows where we are—soon comes the attack!"

Touch the Sky and Little Horse shared a tipi provided by Pawnee Killer's clan. They slept little that night, counseling over this new trouble.

"We have been bearded in our den," Touch the Sky said. "Whoever sent Goes Ahead under, he was able to slip past a tight ring of experienced Cheyenne sentries. What does this tell you, buck?"

"That he was an Indian, brother. A mountain Indian. A turncoat Ute, perhaps, or a Blackfoot."

"And if it was a Ute," Touch the Sky said, "he surely plays the dog for Bluecoat whiskey and tobacco."

"And thus, Shoots Left Handed is right. Soon comes the attack."

Touch the Sky nodded glumly. At this point, there was little they could do to prepare for an attack except pray and wait. The only hope lay in thwarting the whites disguised as Indian raiders. But could they move in time to prevent the annihilation of Shoots Left Handed's camp?

The first opportunity to try presented itself soon after sunrise the next morning.

The two visitors to the north country were counseling with Pawnee Killer and White Plume when a sentry raised a shout. He was hidden in the rimrock of the ridge which sheltered the camp from view below. From his position he could see all the way to Fort Randall and beyond, to the Milk River.

"Other sentries, far across the river valley, are in touch with him with mirror signals," Pawnee Killer explained. The battle leader squinted as he spoke these words, watching carefully as the sentry above now used his fragment of mirror to transmit the message to the main camp.

Pawnee Killer finally nodded. "As I thought. Our 'Cheyenne' raiders have been sighted again!"

"Where?" Touch the Sky demanded.

"There is a white way station on the Milk River Road, near Roaring Horse Creek. The wagons and coaches always stop here to water their horses. It would seem our pretend Cheyennes—five of them, as always—are lurking in a coulee nearby, waiting to strike when that happens."

"Five of them," Little Horse said. "Could we not form a war party and ride hard, and perhaps stop them?"

"I understand you are keen for them," Pawnee Killer said. "So are we, buck. But only think on this thing. How would a war party get from here to there without being spotted by whoever killed Goes Ahead? Even now, Bluecoats are closing in on our camp. We are no longer free to move in this area."

Touch the Sky nodded, his lips set in a straight, determined slit. "I have ears for this. A war party is no good. But two riders might stand a chance. Arrow Keeper did not send me here only to pray. Little Horse and I will ride out."

"Now goddamnit, Lumpy, remember. Don't talk so much. Just point your iron and grunt a lot. You're an Indian, not a damn jaw-jacking Frenchman."

Woodrow Denton looked at the rest of his men, checking their disguises.

"You, Noonan! Get rid of that damn quid, Indians don't chew. And you, Bell. Put some more of that berry juice on your face, you look like a spotted owl."

Denton, his four men, and Captain Seth Carlson sat their horses just inside the entrance of a deep coulee located a stone's throw from the Milk River Road. They had been waiting for hours. From here, they could see the approaching road and the way station built beside Roaring Horse Creek. It was a split-pine building surrounded by dilapidated outbuildings and a stone watering trough.

"Now remember," Carlson said, "they'll be looking for trouble. The freight company has hired two extra guards. They're riding in the coach with the passengers. Get the drop on them *after* they get out to stretch their legs. I'll be waiting back here in case there's any trouble."

A thin line of nervous perspiration dotted Carlson's upper lip. This holdup today would be even more lucrative than usual: The coach was carrying a cash shipment intended for the trading post at Pike's Fork. Now that Colonel Lofley was breathing fire to kill those "Cheyenne" attackers, Carlson knew this sweet little gold mine was almost played out. These last few strikes, with luck, might make his fortune, or at least guarantee an easy retirement.

"Shh," Lumpy said suddenly, cocking his head to listen. His tobacco-stained fingers probed at the goiter on the side of his neck. "Hear that?"

Soon the others did—the distant and steady jangle of approaching traces.

"Here she comes," Denton said, pulling a feathered bonnet on over his bald white pate. "Gotta die sometime, boys. Let's put at the sonsabitches!"

Pawnee Killer had quickly made a picture in the dirt for the two Powder River Cheyennes, showing them the country all around. Now, as their sister the sun tracked ever higher in a seamless blue sky, they discovered the merits of Arrow Keeper's ponies.

The country between the hidden camp and the Milk River Road was mostly a series of folded ridges. Heavily timbered, with few trails, they were a constant challenge to riders in a hurry. But Touch the Sky's blood bay and Little Horse's ginger buckskin seemed to sense, in the urgent pressure of their riders' calves and knees, the need to fly on the wind.

They strode the ridges almost as effortlessly as if they were open plains, racing at breakneck speed into seemingly unbroken walls of timber, yet always somehow sensing an opening. Their endurance, even for Cheyenne ponies, made the two riders exchange dumbfounded glances and foolish grins despite the danger they rode toward. How could any pony climb ridge after ridge, leap streamlet after streamlet, and not even spray foam on its rider?

"There!" Little Horse said, pointing as they crested the final swayback ridge before Milk River and the wagon road which followed it.

"See them, brother? They are just now moving into position in the last line of trees near the white man's lodge."

"If those are Cheyennes, I am a Ponca. I have eyes for them, brother," Touch the Sky assured him. "Our ponies are keen for sport, let us give them warriors for riders! If we ride hard, we can arrive before the stagecoach and scald some dogs."

Their mounts laid back their ears and put on a final burst of speed. Quickly the two Cheyennes cleared the ridge and emerged onto the badly rutted wagon road. Riding the smoother ground just to either side, they raced toward the way station. Each brave had pulled his long arm from its scabbard, and now held it at the ready in one hand.

Touch the Sky spotted it first.

A brief glint of military brass, emerging from the opening of that coulee on their left. And even as he spotted it, his newly emerging shaman's sense told him it was too late.

He pulled hard on the blood's hackamore, turning her toward the coulee. A moment later he was staring straight into the shocked eyes of Seth Carlson.

Carlson, shaken to the core of his being by this completely unexpected appearance of his worst enemy, held fire for just a second. Then, before Hanchon could lower his Sharps and snap off a round, Carlson pointed his carbine dead-center on the tall Indian's torso and squeezed the trigger.

Only a heartbeat after Touch the Sky made the discovery, Little Horse too spotted the officer.

"Brother, leap!"

But it was too late to jump out of the way. Even as Carlson pressured the last fraction of trigger resistance, Little Horse lunged off his pony and into the path of his friend.

Touch the Sky felt his face drain cold when, with a sound like taut rawhide bursting, the bullet struck Little Horse in the chest.

Chapter Six

"Little brothers! I have a thing I would speak to you."

Wolf Who Hunts Smiling allowed a rare note of cordiality to seep into his tone. It was his responsibility to train a group of the junior warriors in the arts of combat, tracking, and survival. Now his young charges were gathered about him while their tired ponies drank their fill from a nearby stream. A hard day of training was ending, and Sister Sun was a ruddy glow behind the Bighorn Mountains.

"You have done well today! You, Bright Hawk! Five times you aimed your throwing ax at a cottonwood while at full speed on your pony. And five times you sank the blade deep into hard wood!

"You, Two Twists! You launched fifteen arrows

in the time it might have cost a hair-mouth soldier to reload his carbine. And they flew straight, stout buck!"

Neither of the young braves thanked Wolf Who Hunts Smiling for this praise. Nor did they show gratitude or pride in their faces. They only held them stern, as the blooded warriors did around women and children.

Unlike Bright Hawk, however, Two Twists was suspicious. He respected Wolf Who Hunts Smiling as a warrior—only a fool would not. But any time the fierce brave became amiable, currying favor like this from the more popular junior warriors, it usually meant he had treachery firmly by the tail. Treachery involving Touch the Sky. Two Twists had only 14 winters behind him. But his brain was as quick as his bow. He saw clearly enough that Wolf Who Hunts Smiling was ravenous for power. And like two grizzlies circling before a savage territorial battle, Touch the Sky and Wolf Who Hunts Smiling were destined to clash.

"Little brothers," Wolf Who Hunts Smiling continued now, "you are doing your task as demanded by our Cheyenne Law Ways. But only think! Does everyone in the tribe respect the Law Ways? Do Touch the Sky and Little Horse? Does Arrow Keeper?

"I ask this, bucks, because it is common knowledge now that the old shaman sent these two riders out without benefit of Council. These two riders who have been seen counseling with white soldiers! I speak straight-arrow. Ask River of Winds. *He* saw them, and does he ever speak more than one way to any man?"

Two Twists felt heat rising into his face. He had to bite his tongue to keep from demanding: "And what of *you*, Wolf Who Hunts Smiling, who bribes old grandmothers into 'visions' against Touch the Sky?" But he tried to control his anger as warriors must. Touch the Sky had sworn him to secrecy about Two Twists' mission to watch Honey Eater. It was not wise to call attention to himself. But deep in his heart of hearts, Two Twists considered Touch the Sky the best and bravest Cheyenne warrior he had ever known. He would readily follow him into the very jaws of the Wendigo himself.

"Young brothers, only think. The wily old shaman can break our law, this Touch the Sky can break our law, even play the big Indian for the white dogs. But can you break any laws? Bucks, tell me. If you pull off an unmarried girl's rope, what happens?"

An uncomfortable silence greeted this remark. Wolf Who Hunts Smiling was referring to the knotted-rope chastity belt worn by all unmarried Cheyenne girls. Every young buck present knew full well the serious consequences of touching a girl's rope. The Bull Whip soldiers would beat them senseless; all their goods would be destroyed, their tipis would be shredded, their horses would be for those who took them; they could never again smoke from the common pipe or touch any common eating utensil.

"Your silence answers me well, bucks. You

know what happens when *you* break the law. But the doting old shaman and his white men's spies—they hold themselves above our Cheyenne Way. Remember this because *you* are the future of our tribe. Soon you may have to make a decision about which leaders to follow. Place my words in your sash and study them later."

Wolf Who Hunts Smiling fell silent. But his final words left Two Twists' heart stomping against his ribs. Clearly, something ominous was afoot! Often Wolf Who Hunts Smiling spoke with open admiration of Roman Nose and other young leaders of the Dog Men—the rebellious young Southern Cheyenne braves who had broken from the rest of the tribe which still followed the older chiefs and the Council of Forty.

It was as plain as blood in snow, Two Twists realized now. Wolf Who Hunts Smiling planned to eventually defy the established leaders and take over the tribe and its destiny. And now, somehow, some way, he was moving to eliminate the one man he sensed could stop him: Touch the Sky.

Two Twists knew he had to watch this thing closely. For a moment his eyes met those of Wolf Who Hunts Smiling.

I praised you publicly, but I know you play the dog for him, the older brave's mocking gaze seemed to say. *I may praise you to your face, double-braid, but watch your back-trail!*

While Wolf Who Hunts Smiling did his part to destroy Touch the Sky's standing with the tribe, Black Elk was back in camp doing his.

Like his younger cousin, Black Elk was a member of the Cheyenne military society known as the Bull Whips. It was their job to punish certain offenses and to police the tribe during ceremonies and the all-important buffalo hunts. They were quick to resort to their knotted-thong whips, and thus feared and despised by most of the tribe.

Now, as grainy darkness took over the camp and the clan fires sprang up, Black Elk stopped by the Bull Whip lodge. It was a smaller version of the main council lodge: elkskins and buffalo hides stretched over a bent-willow frame. From a pole in the front fluttered brightly dyed strands from enemy scalps.

Bull Whips filled the interior, smoking in little groups, gambling, discussing the news from the other soldier troops. Black Elk's keen black eyes searched out two of his favorite troop brothers.

"Stone Jaw! Angry Bull! One of my meat racks has collapsed. Come help me repair it."

The two braves, their highly feared whips tucked into their clouts, followed him across camp toward his tipi. They knew full well that Black Elk needed no help repairing a meat rack. But it was their usual excuse to counsel in private behind his tipi.

"Brothers," Black Elk said as soon as they were safely out of sight of the rest. "Do you think it might be time to replenish our troop's pony herd?"

Neither of his companions was noted for brains. They both stared at him in confusion.

"But Black Elk," Stone Jaw said, "the Bull Whip string has never looked finer."

"You yourself said so when Red Feather rode in with two more fine buckskins," Angry Bull added.

"You can never have too many fine ponies," Black Elk said impatiently. "The scouts report fine-looking mustang herds near the Valley of the Greasy Grass."

He paused, turning to look behind him toward his tipi. Like the others, it glowed dull orange from the fire within. He could make out the long, distorted dark line of Honey Eater's shadow. But he couldn't tell if she was listening or not. He lowered his voice.

"Have ears, brothers. Bluecoats are on maneuvers near the Valley of the Greasy Grass. If you were to ride in that direction, merely to scout the herds, you would of course have to be careful of the soldiers. And of course . . ."

Black Elk paused, adding emphasis to his next words. "If you happened to see the soldiers counseling with two Cheyennes, clearly you would be required to report this thing."

Stone Jaw was still lost, the puzzled furrow between his eyebrows deep. But Angry Bull had caught Black Elk's drift.

"Touch the Sky and Little Horse," he said. "No one knows where they are."

Black Elk nodded, letting this sink in. He had selected these two because they were among Touch the Sky's worst enemies in the camp. From the beginning, when he was first captured, they had argued for his death as a spy. Instead, the tall young stranger had won more and more respect within the tribe—but as he had, the hatred of his enemies had intensified.

Stone Jaw avoided Angry Bull's eyes, knowing the two of them might laugh and infuriate Black Elk. It was common knowledge throughout the Bull Whip troop that his wife loved Touch the Sky and he her. In fact, most of the Whips assumed the tall youth was holding her in his blanket for love talk, perhaps even bulling her. Of course, nothing was said in front of Black Elk. Perhaps his squaw had put the antlers on him; nonetheless, he was no brave to fool with.

Still, it would be satisfying to finally put an end to this arrogant stranger who grew up wearing white man's shoes and now played the big Indian with Gray Thunder's tribe.

"As you say, brother," Angry Bull finally said. "Our string could use a few more good ponies. Stone Jaw and I must prepare for a ride to the Valley of the Greasy Grass. Who knows what we might see there?"

Black Elk thought a moment. Then he added, "Do not swear to seeing this thing. Arrow Keeper might then force you to repeat your oath on the Arrows. Instead, paint broad strokes with your words. Say you could not get close, say only that you saw two Cheyennes. One was tall, the other smaller."

Black Elk thought of something else. He smiled, then added, "Say too that one rode a blood bay, the other a ginger buckskin."

"Arrow Keeper's ponies?"

Black Elk nodded. He knew his younger cousin

was moving to directly challenge the old shaman. At first Black Elk has resisted this out of respect for Arrow Keeper. But as his hatred for Touch the Sky reached a white-hot intensity, Black Elk could read the sign clearly. It was Arrow Keeper who protected Touch the Sky. Therefore, Arrow Keeper's power and influence must be hamstrung.

"We will ride out as soon as the Council agrees to it," Angry Bull decided.

"They will agree to it quickly," Black Elk assured him. "I am not just a Bull Whip trooper, I am this tribe's war leader. That pretend Cheyenne has somehow led a charmed existence so far. But even Arrow Keeper's big medicine cannot come between him and a bullet forever."

Hot tears welled up in Honey Eater's eyes, zigzagging down her pronounced cheekbones and dripping into the robes covering the ground inside the tipi.

She had seen Black Elk and his fellow Bull Whips duck behind the tipi. And though she could not make out their exact words, the treacherous tone alone told her that Touch the Sky's trials and sufferings were far from over.

How long could it possibly last? How long? He had suffered more than she would have believed ten men could endure. And that was only the suffering she knew of—what about the trials he faced when away from camp, as he was now?

A thousand times over she had regretted her marriage to Black Elk, yet what could she have done? Touch the Sky had apparently deserted the tribe forever, her father had crossed over, and tribal law forced her to marry. If only, through all of Touch the Sky's suffering, she could have been beside him!

Yet . . . and yet, she told herself with a burst of desperate hope, was there not the song sung by the girls in their sewing lodge? Though it did not mention their names, it sang of their love. And in this song, their marriage finally came to pass.

But how, she scolded herself now, could she be pining away about marrying Touch the Sky when his very life was in danger? Her own husband, assisted by two of the lowest and meanest braves in the tribe, was even now playing the fox against him. Even if it meant her life—and it well might, given Black Elk's insane jealousy—she must somehow thwart this plot.

More tears welled in her eyes as she thought of the stone in front of Touch the Sky's tipi—the piece of smooth white marble he had placed there as a symbol of his love. When that stone melts, he had assured her, so too will my love for you. There was a time when, by custom, she would check that stone each night when he was away from camp. And always, she found it intact.

But no longer. Black Elk had caught her kneeling before it and come within a cat's whisker of killing her. Now she could only think about it.

Outside, the big, mean warrior called Angry Bull raised his voice in sudden laughter.

I must watch and listen, Honey Eater told herself again.

She had already made up her mind when Touch the Sky rescued her from the Comanches and Kiowas in Blanco Canyon: Their two lives were one now. And though she would be banished forever, she would kill her own husband before she let him kill Touch the Sky.

Chapter Seven

Not sure if Little Horse was dead or alive, Touch the Sky grabbed him even as he slumped from his pony.

His face crumpling under the effort, Touch the Sky managed to haul his friend over onto his pony with him. But by now Carlson had recovered his battle wits. His next round flew past Touch the Sky's ear with a hum like an angry hornet. He felt a sharp tug on his foxskin quiver as a third shot passed through it.

More shots rang out, further away, and Touch the Sky realized that the fake Cheyennes were opening fire on their quarry at the way station.

Balancing his friend awkwardly with one arm, Touch the Sky finally pointed his Sharps in his free arm and snapped off a round toward Carlson. The situation was desperate: His first priority was Little Horse. Touch the Sky owed his very life to his loyal friend. So long as there was a chance that the vital force still beat inside him, the first obligation was to get Little Horse to safety.

Touch the Sky knew this without thinking, the way a she-grizzly fights for her cubs. So he also knew that Carlson had to be stopped from pursuit. And since Touch the Sky couldn't guarantee a killing hit with a one-handed shot, that meant he must do something repugnant to a Cheyenne and aim for Carlson's horse.

He dropped the big cavalry sorrel with a shot to the chest. Touch the Sky had the satisfaction of watching his old nemesis plunge to the ground hard, his hat flying off like a can lid—the second time he had dropped him unceremoniously from horseback.

Carlson! Even as he raced back down the road, leading Little Horse's pony, he found it hard to believe. And yet, it also made perfect sense. Now the young brave understood why Cheyennes were being blamed for the attacks. Carlson was again waging his one-man campaign against the tribe he hated most.

Touch the Sky was concerned with finding a place to shelter as soon as possible. Now and then a gout of blood spurted from the ugly, puckered flesh of Little Horse's wound. It had to be stopped, and soon. Otherwise, Little Horse was dead—if he wasn't already.

Touch the Sky couldn't tell how the raid was going. The shooting behind him had finally stopped. He raced through a sharp dogleg bend in the road, then spotted a thick pine copse well back from the road. Making sure they were out of sight from the others, he nudged his pony off the trail.

Every moment counted now, and Touch the Sky's mouth was set in its grim, determined slit. His movements were fast, sure, efficient. First, he gently laid his friend down on a thick carpet of pine needles. At least the bleeding had slowed. Still not sure yet if Little Horse was dead or alive, he quickly hobbled their ponies out of sight from the road.

Finally, he returned to Little Horse's side and knelt down near him.

It was time to find out if his best friend still belonged to the living or had crossed over to the Land of Ghosts.

He held his face impassive. But Touch the Sky's lips trembled imperceptibly as he lay his ear on Little Horse's chest, less than a handsbreadth from the wound.

Nothing.

Just a cold, hard wall of dead muscle. His Cheyenne brother had kept his vow to protect Touch the Sky's life with his own.

Touch the Sky's next breath snagged in his throat. His face went sweaty and numb.

A moment later, he felt it: a faint pulse in Little Horse's chest, weak as a baby bird's.

Weak, but Little Horse still clung to life!

"This is *not* a good day to die, brother!" Touch the Sky whispered. "You have not yet bounced your son on your knee."

Now there was no tribal crisis, no danger to Touch the Sky—every effort of his being was directed at saving his friend. First he raced down to the nearby Milk River and filled his watertight legging sash. He returned and washed the wound carefully.

Now came the hard part: removing the slug and cauterizing the wound, a process Touch the Sky had learned from Old Knobby, the former mountain man. He took the flint and steel from his possibles bag and gathered kindling for a small fire. When he had it blazing, using old, dry wood to cut the smoke, he unsheathed his knife and heated the obsidian blade.

Probing carefully but quickly, using just the sharp point, he managed to locate the slug quickly. Little Horse flinched, but never regained consciousness, as Touch the Sky removed the .52-caliber carbine slug. Next he heated the entire side of his blade until it glowed. When, all at once, he pressed it against the wound, the stink of singed flesh assaulted Touch the Sky's nostrils. Little Horse jerked violently, arching his back like a bow. But he neither cried out nor regained awareness.

Finally, Touch the Sky packed the wound with gunpowder and balsam. Soft strips of willow bark served as a dressing.

Touch the Sky tensed, making sure there was a ball behind the loading gate of his Sharps, when he heard hooves pounding past on the road. Then he realized it was probably Carlson and his thieving "Indian" cohorts, fleeing with whatever booty they had stolen.

The situation was bleak, bordering on hopeless. Another attack would now be blamed on Cheyennes; Shoots Left Handed's band was on the verge of being annihilated; and Little Horse lay balanced on the feather edge between life and death.

And behind all of it, Seth Carlson. The same corrupt, vicious, Indian-hating officer who helped to ruin his life as Matthew Hanchon, who tried to destroy his white parents' livelihood.

He glanced at his friend and told himself he would have to move him soon. It wasn't safe here this close to a road. Yet moving him in this condition might well kill him even though the bullet was out.

One way or the other, it had to be done.

Touch the Sky said a brief prayer to Maiyun, the Good Supernatural. Then he went to fetch the ponies.

"Things went badly," Pawnee Killer reported to Chief Shoots Left Handed. "Very badly."

The battle leader craned his neck to read the signals being flashed to him from the sentry in the rimrock above. He, in turn, was in communication with another sentry in clear view of the Milk River Road.

"The raid was not prevented. A white man was wounded. The youth Little Horse appears to be dead. Touch the Sky was forced to flee with his body. They are nowhere in sight now."

Pawnee Killer fell silent. Goes Ahead's widow was still sewing her husband's moccasins for the final journey, and now this new trouble.

He met his chief's glance. Shoots Left Handed's milky eye stared blindly back.

"This Touch the Sky," Pawnee Killer said. "I like him well enough. He carries himself like a man and seems to talk one way only. But Father, was Arrow Keeper right to send him?"

"His medicine is said to be strong. You have heard the stories: how his medicine can summon insane white men from the forest, enraged grizzly bears from the mountains."

Pawnee Killer nodded. "I have heard the stories, yes. But I also have eyes to see. I see that only moments after Touch the Sky renewed the Arrows, Goes Ahead was found murdered. Then he rode off to stop a raid. Now, once again, we are blamed for the raid. And now his friend Little Horse is apparently dead. If this is strong medicine, I would be spared such magic."

Shoots Left Handed said nothing for a long while. His good eye gazed out past the series of swayback ridges, toward the snowy peaks of the Bear Paws.

"I know Arrow Keeper, buck. If *he* sent these two braves, they were the right ones to send. Sometimes, we must wait for the flames to abate before we may read the embers."

Pawnee Killer cast a troubled glance back toward the spot where an intruder had killed Goes Ahead.

"As you say, Father. But even now we may be

in the sights of Bluecoat rifles. Sometimes, when the flames abate, the destruction is so complete there is nothing left to read."

The journey back to Shoots Left Handed's high-altitude camp was an agony for Touch the Sky.

Eyes and ears constantly alert to attack, he nonetheless kept a close watch on Little Horse. Touch the Sky had lashed him tight to his pony with buffalo-hair ropes. But each jounce in the trail, each stumble by the pony, caused Touch the Sky to wince.

Attack now, by Piegans or hair-mouth soldiers or vigilantes, would surely be fatal. But they managed to traverse the long series of ridges without incident.

Little was said when Touch the Sky rode into camp with his fallen comrade. Though no one aimed accusing eyes or words at him, he knew they had serious doubts by now about his medicine. But Touch the Sky cared little right now about their doubts. His best friend lay dying, the victim of a bullet intended for *him*.

Two braves helped him move Little Horse into the tipi he shared with Touch the Sky. Then began the long vigil.

Touch the Sky knew the immediate problem was sustenance for Little Horse. He had lost much blood, nor was there any nourishment in the destitute camp. Yet he would quickly die without something to replenish his system.

That night, when another pony was slaughtered to feed the people, Touch the Sky asked for a little blood and a few of the bones. He cracked the bones open on a rock and dug out the nutritious marrow with the point of his knife. He boiled this and the blood together in a potion. Then, painstakingly, using a bit of buffalo horn as a spoon, he fed it to Little Horn in tiny sips. Though the brave remained unconscious, his swallowing reflex worked.

That night, as was the custom with serious illness or injury, Touch the Sky stayed wide awake and recited the ancient cure songs he had learned from Arrow Keeper. All night long, the wind howled like the Wendigo while hungry babes cried. Finally, as the first rose-colored trace of dawn painted the eastern sky, Little Horse's eyes snapped open.

There was a long silence while they looked at each other.

"Brother," Little Horse said in a weak but clear voice, "I think you have saved my life."

"I hope so, Cheyenne, for you have certainly saved mine before."

"The pretend Cheyennes?"

Touch the Sky shook his head. "They got away."

"And now that Bluecoat is back. This Seth Carlson. I was sure we faced him for the last time in Bighorn Falls."

Already, Little Horse's eyelids were drooping with the effort of speaking.

"Sleep, buck," Touch the Sky told him. "Sleep long. You will need your strength. The battle has not even begun."

Chapter Eight

"Just remember, Carlson. The shit rolls downhill. That's not my cherished personal philosophy, Captain. That's the way the Chain of Command works. If I get thumped on from above, I thump on those below me. And I assure you, I *am* being thumped on."

"Yes, sir."

"I don't believe it! Two raids, practically back to back. Carlson, I was willing to overlook your miserable conduct and proficiency reports from Fort Bates. I happen to know the man who commanded your regiment there. Bruce Harding is a good enough clerk. As a soldier, he isn't worth the powder it would take to blow him to hell."

"My sentiments too, sir. He—"

Colonel Orrin Lofley frowned, nervously fingering his red goatee. "I'm not finished, Carlson, you're out of line! As I was saying, I was willing to overlook all that. But two raids mounted by a small group of renegades, back to back, and what's your battle plan? Has your company even pulled up its picket pins yet?"

"It's posted in the morning report, sir. My company deploys at 0500 tomorrow."

"Don't give me the smart side of your tongue, Soldier Blue. I know damn good and well when you deploy. That's why I called you in here. Those special weapons I requisitioned have arrived from Fort Union. Your men can pick them up at the armory after you sign the receiving orders."

Carlson felt a smile tugging at his lips. Since Matthew Hanchon and his stocky little companion had obviously thrown in with Shoots Left Handed's band, that was good news indeed. Anything was good news if it increased the chances of killing Hanchon.

"Very good, sir. I'm sure they'll be an efficient addition to the unit."

"They damn well better be."

Lofley shut up before he embarrassed himself. But Carlson knew he was thinking about that fiasco with the Hunkpapas—the infamous operation where 25,000 rounds of ammunition scored five kills, all women and children.

Lofley was even more agitated than usual, Carlson noted. Thanks to the newspapers making merry at his expense, humiliation had become Colonel Lofley's constant companion. Lofley confirmed all this with his next remark.

"I can't even look my own wife in the eye, Carlson. Her lying there in bed, so sore from a redskin bullet she can't move. And what does the horseshit-for-brains chaplain give her as reading material to pass the time? The Bible? Hell, no! He gives her the newspapers, full of scathing articles written by cowardly little scribblers who have to squat to piss. Articles about the supposed buffoon she married!"

Hell, Carlson thought, even a blind hog will occasionally root up an acorn. Why can't the newspapers be right now and then?

But he wisely held his tongue while Lofley wrapped up his tirade. "We're just goddamn lucky nobody got killed this time. But the paper-collar newspaper boys are reminding everybody over and over just how many gold double eagles were heisted. Carlson, you've got a history of fighting Cheyennes. I know that some tribes in the Southwest have learned about currency from the Mexicans. But since when does the Cheyenne tribe suddenly place such a value on white man's gold?"

This question was uncomfortable and made heat rise into Carlson's face. He realized, again, that his little scheme was played out. Ironically, Lofley hadn't asked that question until he'd read it in the very newspapers he hated so passionately.

"That's a puzzler, sir, it is. But the Cheyenne is a wily Indian with no lack of brains. They've found some use for that gold."

"Speaking of wily Cheyennes. Did you send Rough Feather back out as I ordered?"

"Yes, sir. As soon as I had his map and crystal-clear directions. He's been ordered to watch the camp constantly. If they move, he's to blaze a trail and follow."

"I see you ordered the band to remain in garrison for the deployment instead of marching out with you. No music?"

"That's right, sir. No music, no bugles, no flags. Just weapons and ammunition, all packed on the men themselves. The lack of fanfare is to remind the men of the mountain company's single mission—to kill Indians."

Lofley thought about that, fingering his goatee some more. Then he approved it with a nod.

"I mean it, Carlson. Don't let this explode in our faces while the eyes of the entire goddamn country are on us. When you do reach this camp, do *not* take all damn day in a complicated West Point maneuver. The longer it drags on, the more chance for something to go wrong."

"Don't worry, sir," Carlson assured him. "Nothing *can* go wrong. It'll be fast, it'll be efficient, and I guarantee, there won't be any Cheyennes left to report to the reservation."

"But why did Arrow Keeper send just us?" Little Horse said. "Without boasting, brother, I can agree he sent two of the tribe's best warriors. And perhaps, with luck and skill, two good braves might indeed stop these make-believe Cheyenne raiders. But buck, from all the sign *we* have read, the jaws of a death trap are already closing on this camp. Two braves are merely two more to die with the others."

Late afternoon sunlight slanted through the

tipi's smoke hole and the open flap of the entrance. Little Horse still lay resting in his buffalo-fur sleeping robe. His voice, like his body, was still weak. But the crisis had passed, and once again the sturdy little warrior had eluded Death's black lance.

"I too have given much thought to this thing," Touch the Sky said. "Arrow Keeper has entered the frosted years, truly. But brother, his mind is as keen as the blade of my ax. He has a plan."

"I have never known him to be without one, surely. But what kind of plan? Brother, you have eyes to see! These Cheyennes have reached the end of their tether. There is no place left to run, nor are they strong enough to flee if they could."

Touch the Sky nodded. "I know, brother, I know. You think that perhaps this time Arrow Keeper made us wade in before he measured the depths? Perhaps. Even the wisest owl can fall from its tree. But I do not believe Arrow Keeper sent us merely to furnish targets for the Bluecoat bullets. This time I do not think our battle skills were foremost in his mind."

Little Horse's forehead wrinkled in curiosity. He studied his tall young friend closely. Little Horse was among the few in Gray Thunder's tribe who had noticed the mark buried past Touch the Sky's hairline: a mulberry-colored birthmark in the perfect shape of an arrowhead. The traditional mark of the warrior. But such a sign also marked vision seekers and those whose medicine was strong.

"You mean, brother," he said slowly, "you

think the hand of the Supernatural is in this thing?"

But Touch the Sky refused to talk of such things openly. At any rate, he thought, his own supposed magic had done precious little to help their desperate kinsmen.

"Leave it alone, brother," he told Little Horse. "I can see that you are tired and need to rest again. Get strong, buck, find your fighting fettle! You are no good to me sleeping in this tipi," he added fondly.

Little Horse yawned hard. "I will soon be fighting like five braves," he assured Touch the Sky, his eyelids already closing.

"I never saw you fight any other way," Touch the Sky said, though he knew his friend was asleep.

Touch the Sky too felt the same sense of helpless frustration Little Horse had expressed. For now he was limited to constant scouts around the perimeter of camp, checking for more infiltrators. He had already helped erect breastworks of pointed logs, lining them across the one vulnerable entrance. Rifle pits had been dug behind these. But rifle pits were almost a meaningless gesture because the tribe owned only a few rifles and ammunition was critically short.

He stepped outside into the bright sunshine. The air, this high up, was rarified and clear, and he could see the mountains of the Land of the Grandmother to the north. As he passed through camp, some of the others cast odd looks at him.

Their looks were not exactly unfriendly. The Cheyenne people were too hospitable for such barbarity to visitors of their own blood. But the nods that White Plume and Pawnee Killer exchanged—clearly they said, "This stranger, so far he is a good nurse. Fine, but this is squaw's work. He seems useful for nothing else. As for his supposed medicine—add *his* magic to a rope, and all you have is a rope."

But Touch the Sky only held his face impassive in the warrior way, keeping his feelings private inside him. Slowly, as he made his way carefully down the narrow access trail, the camp began to recede behind him.

The sun was at its warmest and lay against his skin like a friendly hand. The cool mountain wind lifted his long black locks, feathering them out behind him like wings. It felt good after the close confines of the tipi.

Nonetheless, Touch the Sky sensed danger.

He glanced to his right, toward a wide swale—a low, moist tract of ground—overgrown with small bushes.

A tickle moved up the bumps of his spine, as light as a scurrying insect. Light, but it spoke of much danger.

Death lurked there at this moment, waiting. Just as it had waited somewhere around here for Goes Ahead. He was sure of it now.

Feigning interest in a point further down the trail, Touch the Sky moved on past the swale.

The Ute scout named Rough Feather flattened himself into the damp ground when the tall Cheyenne youth stared toward his position.

He cannot possibly see me, the big Indian told himself. This huge depression was covered with thick bushes. He had taken extra care in selecting it—after all, he was returning to an area where he had already killed one brave. They were alerted to his presence now.

Rough Feather had made his report to Carlson at Fort Randall. Then he had returned here at once, following orders to watch the camp closely until Carlson's special Indian-killing regiment arrived and turned this tribe's history into smoke.

This tall young brave—his buckskin leggings and low elkskin moccasins marked him as a stranger to this territory. But stranger or no, they all died the same.

Rough Feather eased his knife from its sheath. Because they were tall with especially long arms for Indians, Utes were noted knife fighters. Their style was to stand back and madly slash at an opponent's arms and hands in a flurry of wild passes. Then they closed for one perfect killing thrust when their opponent was disoriented.

But when he next peered out from behind the bushes, a line of nervous sweat broke out on his upper lip.

A heartbeat ago the Cheyenne had been there. Now he was nowhere in sight.

Touch the Sky made himself virtually invisible. Sticking to natural depressions and isolated bits of ground cover, he circled well behind the dish-shaped area formed by the swale.

Safe behind a tangled deadfall, he gathered up a pile of fist-size rocks.

One by one, he sailed the rocks high into the air over the swale. Each one thunked to the ground with a crashing of bushes. He covered the entire swale methodically, until one of the rocks chunked into something besides the ground—something human or animal that grunted in pain.

Touch the Sky didn't hesitate. The element of surprise was vital, but useless unless you followed through on it immediately.

His knife clutched in his fist, he leaped toward the spot where his rock had landed. The spy was fast for such a big man. He eluded Touch the Sky's grasp at the last moment and fled from his hiding place.

Touch the Sky recognized his tribe immediately from the brave's massive size and distinctive beaded headband. The Ute had at least three inches and 20 pounds on him. But it was his speed that truly amazed the Cheyenne. At one moment he was the pursuer; the next, the Ute had whirled and turned into the attacker.

The ferocity and speed of the knife assault caught Touch the Sky completely off guard. White-hot wires of pain sliced into his hands and arms before it dawned on him—he was being slashed! Again, again, hot steel sliced into him with the sting of a rattler's fangs.

The Ute's arms flailed like a white man's windmill gone Wendigo, his blade glinting cruelly each time the sun caught it. Touch the Sky took cuts to his hands, arms, face, chest, stomach, all the time backing rapidly away. Ribbons of his blood ran into the ground.

The Ute's exertions left his breath whistling in his nostrils. Touch the Sky's foot hit a rock and he went down. With a snarl of triumph, the Ute leaped for the death cut.

Desperately, Touch the Sky tensed his back like a bow and rolled aside just in time. The Ute crashed hard to the ground.

Touch the Sky, his lips a straight, determined slit, closed for the kill. His blade sought for the spot between the fourth and fifth rib, as Black Elk had taught him—from there it was a straight thrust to the heart.

But this finishing blow wasn't needed. The Ute lay on his face, immobile except for fast twitches of his legs. When Touch the Sky flipped him over, he saw why. The turncoat Indian's knife had landed against a rock and turned against him, driving deep into warm vitals.

Though he had been slashed many times— each cut like fiery bites—Touch the Sky's injuries looked worse than they were. Few of the cuts had gone deep into tender meat. But as he stared at the dead Indian's Army-issue shirt and trousers, he realized the awful truth.

No scout would have stayed in this dangerous area this long after discovering the camp and killing Goes Ahead. It would be a scout's mission to immediately return and report the camp's position. This Ute had already done that. Touch the Sky was sure of it. His job now had been to keep a close eye on the tribe until the soldiers arrived.

How long now before they arrived? Surely not long. Touch the Sky knew they wouldn't be riding in under a white flag—nor would they brook surrender.

It would not, however, be a battle. Not against Shoots Left Handed's dispirited, ill-equipped warriors.

It would be a massacre.

Blood streaming freely from his many slashes, Touch the Sky headed back to report this latest piece of bad news.

Chapter Nine

"Niece, no one ever told you marriage was a tender hump steak. Your problem is that you are a dreamer. I knew you were your mother's child, Honey Eater, as soon as you took to tying white columbine in your hair. You must remember that Black Elk is a warrior, tempered to lead when the war cry sounds. It is not easy for such men to show the soft side or be patient with girls who sigh and dream."

"Well, are not other men brave warriors too? Yet do they cut off their wives' braids or accuse them of treachery because they cannot bear their child?"

"Other men?" Sharp Nosed Woman said, watching her niece closely. "Just place these words in your parfleche, niece. *All* men gawp about and make the love-talk when their blood is hot for the rut. In time, they are all alike. The blood cools, and so does the love-talk."

"All men?" Despite her sadness, Honey Eater smiled gently as she recalled stories her aunt had told. "What about Grins Plenty?"

A rare softness seeped into the older woman's eyes. Both women automatically made the cut-off sign, as one did when discussing the dead. She had lost her husband Grins Plenty in the same Pawnee raid which killed her sister, Honey Eater's mother, Singing Woman.

"There was a man with hot blood and love-talk to spare," Sharp Nosed Woman confided, lowering her voice a bit and bending over her beadwork closer to her niece. "Did I tell you how he . . ."

She caught herself, looking at Honey Eater's innocent, distracted face. "Oh, but you'll blush and play the coy one. Never mind, never mind."

The next moment the entrance flap of Sharp Nosed Woman's tipi was lifted aside, and young Two Twists was staring at them.

"Sisters, may I come in?" he said, stepping hurriedly inside even before he had permission. He looked at Honey Eater. "I have a thing to speak to you."

Sharp Nosed Woman inhaled a deep breath, preparing to interfere. This was highly improper. Two Twists did not even belong to their clan; he should have announced his presence from outside. And to ignore an older woman, speaking directly to a younger—one who was married at that!

Honey Eater's confusion was mirrored in her

face. She knew Two Twists was a friend of Touch the Sky's, that this visit must have something to do with him.

Two Twists watched the older woman's face closely and saw her objections. Quickly he spoke up before she could.

"Sharp Nosed Woman, please find a soft place in your heart and forgive an ill-mannered Cheyenne! The women in my clan have long praised your beadwork. And the men, they say all the time, 'This Sharp Nosed Woman, how is it that a woman this comely is not marrying again?' I did not mean to be rude. It is just that I have important words for Honey Eater's ears. For her ears alone," he added meaningfully. "And I must speak them quickly."

He didn't need to add what all three of them understood: *Before Black Elk catches me.*

Although she knew the youth was openly flattering her, Sharp Nosed Woman had smiled gratefully at his praise. She knew he was here to talk about Touch the Sky, and she did not approve. At the same time, she too had heard the young girls in their sewing lodge—singing over and over of the great love between her niece and this tall young stranger marked out for a hard destiny. And despite her flint-edged practicality, tears always blurred her eyes when she heard it.

"Honey Eater," she said reluctantly, "I think I shall step outside and cut some turnips."

This was a thinly veiled sign that she was offering to keep watch. Grateful, Honey Eater nodded.

"Be quick," Sharp Nosed Woman added. "You know how dangerous this could be."

The moment she was gone, Two Twists said, "Sister, I have checked for you. The stone is still there."

Instantly, the tight bubble of a sob rose from her chest into her throat. But Honey Eater held it back. With that one remark, she realized, he'd meant the white marble in front of Touch the Sky's tipi. This was Touch the Sky's way of letting her know for sure that Two Twists was on their side.

Now she had someone to speak this terrible grief too! It was as if a dam suddenly gave way inside her.

"Oh, what do you know of him?" she pleaded.

"He is sworn to secrecy about his mission, sister. What passes at his end of things, I cannot say. From the look of the weapons he and Little Horse packed out of camp, I fear they are riding into great danger once again. But this much I do know. Thanks to his enemies here at home, especially Wolf Who Hunt Smiling, some terrible new trouble awaits Touch the Sky when he returns."

This was the first time he had managed to be alone with her. He told her about everything he had seen and heard, including Wolf Who Hunts Smiling's rebellious speech to the young warriors during training.

"This hotheaded young brave has the hunger of ambition blazing in his eyes," Honey Eater said when Two Twists had finished speaking. "These things he said, they are meant to do more than ruin Touch the Sky."

"You have eyes to see, sister, and your father's fine brain. He plans to lift his lance in leadership before the entire Shayiena nation. And their mission, under him, will be to kill as many whites as possible. He despises Touch the Sky and any others who believe some whites are decent."

"As you suggest," Honey Eater said, "Wolf Who Hunts Smiling is not alone in his treachery. My own husband and others in the Bull Whip troop are also playing the fox."

She, in turn, explained Black Elk's recent meetings with his troop brothers Stone Jaw and Angry Bull.

"No braves to fool with," Two Twists said glumly. "Something unspeakable is about to happen."

Time was short, the situation critical. Hastily they agreed on the only plan they could. At the very first moment when the plan of Touch the Sky's enemies was clear, both Two Twists and Honey Eater would appeal directly to the Star Chamber for justice and a chance to tell all they knew.

The Star Chamber was the Cheyenne's court of last resort. It met in secret at the request of Chief Gray Thunder, the only non-member who knew which braves belonged to the Chamber. Their decisions could override the Council of Forty. But although any member of the tribe could petition them, it was extraordinary for them to grant the request.

Two Twists was about to slip outside again when the urgent voice of Sharp Nosed Woman drifted through the entrance:

"Maiyun help us now, here comes Black Elk, and he has blood in his eyes! Do not try to come out now, either of you! Do not move or make a sound. If he catches you in there together, we are all heading for a funeral scaffold."

Honey Eater met Two Twists' eyes, fear widening her own.

"Good day, Black Elk!" they heard Sharp Nosed Woman call out cheerfully.

"It *would* be a good day, woman, if my squaw knew where she lived! Is she here?"

"No, Black Elk, I have not seen her this day."

"Then why is her beadwork missing? Whenever she takes it with her, she always comes to your tipi."

"As you say, Cheyenne. But she is not here."

There was a long pause while Honey Eater felt her heart pounding in her ears.

Abruptly, Sharp Nosed Woman laughed.

"Well, go ahead then, Black Elk! If you do not trust a woman who is your own clan sister by marriage! By all means, look into my tipi. This good widow has nothing to hide. Maiyun grant that someday she may."

Another long pause. Two Twists, sweat beading on his forehead, gripped the bone handle of his knife.

"I have no time to stand here and chatter with women," Black Elk finally said. "Nor interest in peering inside your tipi. If you see my squaw, tell her she knows where her tipi is and what time her husband likes his meals!"

Seth Carlson's new mountain company set out promptly at 0500 hours, deployed in two long columns of 30 troopers each. The grim purpose of this mission was suggested by the fact that no officer wore his saber—sabers rattled in the dead of night, warning Indian sentries.

Following their Indian scouts, the unit deployed south from Fort Randall toward a remote spine of the Bear Paws. It was here, according to the map furnished by Rough Feather, that Shoots Left Handed's band had found scant shelter beneath a ridge.

And it was *here*, Carlson was sure, that he would again meet Matthew Hanchon.

But this time, history would not repeat itself.

True, he may well have killed Hanchon's sidekick, that squat little Cheyenne whose war cry could scare the bluing off a gun barrel. But that slug had been meant for Hanchon himself. The only God Carlson believed in was gold dust. Sometimes, though, he suspected Hanchon had some kind of divine protection. Well, he'd need it for this next encounter, all he could rustle up.

Carlson let his sergeant assume the lead. He dropped back to ride up and down the columns, inspecting men and equipment. At first glance, they seemed a motley and unmilitary crew. Army dress regulations were strict only for garrison duty—in the field, men were mainly on their own. Experienced campaigners had learned to wear old clothes into combat. As a result, only a few of Carlson's troopers wore the highly feared and despised blue coats—most wore coarse gray cotton shirts and straw hats they had purchased from the sutler.

Despite their ragtag appearance, however, they were formidable indeed.

Each man was a qualified sharpshooter with the new seven-shot carbines tucked into their saddle scabbards. Each man had faced action against Cherokees back East, or Apaches, Sioux, or other tribes out West. Each man packed everything he needed on his own person or on a horse—there were no cumbersome supply and ammo wagons to hold this unit up.

"Ulrich!" Carlson called out, riding up beside a freckle-faced corporal on a huge claybank. "Are you clear on the operation of that new gun?"

"Yes, sir. I'll make 'er sing like a preacher on Sunday!"

The packhorse behind Ulrich carried one of the recently patented guns invented by Richard Gatling, as well as several long belts of ammunition.

"I fired it, sir, back East at Fort Defiance. This was when they was still testin' it. She's a reg'lar honey of a weapon."

Trotting beside the packhorse, Carlson curiously eyed the ten-barreled Gatling.

"She spits out three hundred fifty rounds a minute, sir! It's hard to credit even after you see it with your own eyes. But she does."

Carlson's jaw slacked open. "Stretching the blanket a mite, aren't you?"

"It's God's own truth, Cap'n. And there was plans on paper for one that'll double that rate. You just set the gun on its tripod and connect that magazine hopper thing right there. The barrels crank in a circle around that stationary spindle. You just feed the rounds into the hopper 'n' give the enemy jip! Hell, Mr. Innun ain't even dreamed of this gun yet. Gunna be some mighty consternated red Arabs, once this pup starts barkin' at 'em."

Carlson thought again about Hanchon's companion leaping in front of that slug. Let him leap in front of 350 of them!

"Well, you'll get your chance soon enough to impress me with it," Carlson assured the trooper.

He fell back to the end of the column. Two packhorses had been allotted for hauling the second special weapon requisitioned by Lofley: muzzle-loading artillery rifles.

Carlson was more familiar with these weapons, having trained with them at West Point. There were three of them, Parrot muzzle-loaders with three-inch bores. Wing nuts held the detachable barrels to portable wooden tripods that folded for packing onto a horse. With a muzzle velocity of 1,000 feet a second, their range was an incredible 3,000 yards. They fired ten-pound charged artillery shells that burst near the ground in a lethal, destructive radius.

Carlson knew that Indians had some knowledge

of Bluecoat canister shot. But Gatling guns and artillery shells were strong bad medicine completely foreign to their experience. When the Cheyennes got a taste of this, they would begin to understand the white man's concept of Hell.

Two hours after sunset, just as they were set to picket for the night, a Ute scout named Scalp Dancer rode back from his forward position.

"Indian camp ahead," he said.

Silver moonlight glimmered like fox fire on the surrounding rocks and pinnacles. Carlson's tow eyebrows knit in confusion.

"Not a Cheyenne camp? According to the map, that's hours from here."

The Ute shook his head. "Piegan. Not a full camp, perhaps a hunt camp. Perhaps twenty braves."

Carlson looked annoyed. Blackfeet Indians were not in the battle plan.

"Can we get around them?"

Scalp Dancer shook his head. "It would be a full day's delay because of cliffs and rubble on both sides of them."

Carlson considered, glancing back once again toward the Gatling and the muzzle-loaders. This might be a perfect opportunity to hone the attack on the Cheyennes.

"Would gunfire be heard by Shoots Left Handed's band?"

The Ute shook his head. "Too many ridges between this camp and theirs."

Carlson turned to his sergeant. "Pass the word back quietly. Rig for battle and prepare to mount."

Quickly, conferring with Scalp Dancer, Carlson formed a plan. Holding their mounts to a walk, enforcing absolute silence, they advanced behind the Ute to within 100 yards of the camp. Every man hobbled his horse and then fanned out in a skirmish line, advancing from rock to rock, tree to tree. As agreed, Ulrich moved into position first, accompanied by a private who had been shown how to feed ammo into the Gatling gun while Ulrich cranked and aimed it.

Carlson supervised as Ulrich set the gun on its tripod atop a flat rock. Below, Carlson could make out the shadowy shapes of the Blackfeet as they moved in and out of the glow of small camp fires. Another two-man crew assembled the muzzle-loaders.

"You two fire first," Carlson ordered, speaking in a hushed whisper. "That'll set up illumination. Then Ulrich opens up."

The rest of the men, armed with carbines, formed a semicircle behind the Gatling and the artillery rifles.

There was a long silence while bullfrogs croaked and cicadas hummed. One of the Blackfeet coughed, another laughed.

"FIRE!" Carlson screamed.

There was a belching roar from one of the Parrots; then below, the night suddenly exploded. A second shell, a third, exploded with deadly accuracy, hurling bits of rock, ground, and Blackfeet to the four directions of the wind. In the incandescent glow of the explosions, Ulrich opened up with the Gatling.

He cranked the revolving barrels once around to check the action. Then bullets were whacking into the camp below as fast as the private could stuff them into the hopper.

Carlson stood there in mute shock, forgetting to even draw his revolver. Nor was it necessary. The destruction below could not have been more complete if a hundred men had opened fire with pistols.

Indians, caught flush in the Gatling fire, seemed to perform a grotesque dance in the moonlight as the slugs jerked and lifted them like rag puppets. Horses nickered piteously and collapsed, bullets stitching snake holes across their flanks. Another artillery shell exploded, obliterating the faces of four Indians. Caught flush in this lightning attack, the Indians did not return even one shot.

Carlson didn't believe it, but his watch wasn't lying. The "battle" was over in less than two minutes. A few Blackfeet still required a slug to the brain to finish them off. But not one had gotten away.

Elated, throat swelling with the effortless victory, Carlson reminded himself: This was a far cry from Orrin Lofley's debacle with the Hunkpapa Sioux. And it was a sweet foretaste of what was in store for Hanchon and the rest of the Cheyennes.

Chapter Ten

"Is this a wise thing, brother, riding out by yourself?" Little Horse said. "One more sleep and I will be strong enough to ride with you. Perhaps I could now."

Touch the Sky was stitching a tear in his moccasins with a bone awl and buffalo-sinew thread. He looked up at his friend. Little Horse was recovering from his wound, though he still moved stiffly and tired easily.

"You shall not ride today, buck, though I would feel easier if you could go," he admitted. "But brother, I must scout on my own. That Ute I killed—or rather, who fell on his own knife—I fear he was only waiting for soldiers. I know that Pawnee Killer has sent out scouts, but I am weary of doing nothing except wait for death to arrive."

Little Horse eyed his friend's many knife

slashes. They were crusted in dried blood. "From the look of you, death has already arrived and been repelled."

"As you say. But count on it, he will return, and soon."

"Brother," Little Horse said, "do you think these pretend Cheyennes might be Bluecoats in disguise? After all, the little eagle chief named Carlson was with them."

"I have wondered this same thing. But soldiers or no, count upon it—they are palefaces. Carlson despises all red men too strongly to ever join with any tribe."

"I have ears for this." Little Horse paused, then added carefully, "I also have eyes to see."

"And what do these eyes see, brother?"

"That you are worried about more than the fate of this camp. That your mind is on our own camp, and how it goes with Honey Eater."

"Those eyes of yours see well. But if you have eyes to see, then you also have eyes to sleep. Close them, brother. I am leaving now."

"Let me ride with you."

"Has Little Horse been visiting the Peyote Soldiers? You must rest."

"*Ya-toh-wa ipewa,*" Little Horse called behind him. "May the Holy Ones ride with you."

Touch the Sky sought out Pawnee Killer and explained to the battle leader that he was riding forward to scout. Pawnee Killer, busy counseling with White Plume and Chief Shoots Left Handed, only nodded, his eyes sliding away from Touch the Sky's.

Again the youth realized: So far, with the exception of killing the Ute, he had done precious little to justify Arrow Keeper's faith in sending him. The others were only politely hiding their scorn.

Holding his face impassive, Touch the Sky grabbed a handful of the bay's mane and swung up onto his pony.

After the massacre at the Blackfoot camp, Seth Carlson ordered his men to make a camp for the night. The horses were still nervous from the sudden commotion of battle, the men still adrenaline-tense from the encounter.

Carlson set up the picket outposts, warning the sentries to keep an eye open for the Ute scout Rough Feather. He was supposed to rendezvous with the main unit, then guide them in to the Cheyenne camp.

By dawn, when Rough Feather still hadn't appeared, Carlson was fretting. Clearly, he told himself, something had gone wrong. Before he had more information, it was dangerous to move his unit further. Yet with Matthew Hanchon to sweeten this kill, this mission was too important to trust to the others. He decided to scout ahead on his own.

He ordered his men to lay low in a canyon sheltered from view overhead by huge limestone outcroppings. Then, after consulting the map Rough Feather had made for him, he broke out his compass. He sighted on a distant pinnacle and shot an azimuth. After he had his bearings firmly fixed, he set out.

*   *   *

Touch the Sky crossed ridge after ridge, sticking to cutbanks, coulees, and other natural shelters as much as possible. As he had been taught to do in dangerous situations, he did not let himself "think"—thinking distracted a brave and got him killed.

Instead, he attended only to the language of his senses. His shadow grew steadily longer behind him as he advanced north across the face of the rugged Bear Paws. Always, he was keenly alert for any sign of soldiers, watching for sudden movements by flocks of sparrow hawks and finches.

The provisions he and Little Horse had brought in their legging sashes were gone, much of it given to the hungry children. Now hunger gnawed steadily at the pit of his belly. It made him recall his vision quest to Medicine Lake and how starvation and murderous Pawnees had tracked him every step of the way. He had also had a brief glimpse of Seth Carlson, though his enemy hadn't spotted him.

He found a handful of chokecherries and ate them, popping them loudly between his strong white teeth. He was still scouring the area for food when he rounded a dogleg bend and encountered a huge deadfall.

It blocked the narrow trail completely. Sheer granite walls rose on either side. He realized there had to be a hidden opening in the deadfall because Shoots Left Handed's band had had to use this trail to reach their camp from this direction.

He approached, cautiously reaching out to separate the obstructing branches. Even as his fingers made first contact, a chill premonition of danger moved up his spine.

Carlson approached the huge deadfall carefully, telling himself the same thing Touch the Sky had: There must be a way through it. Rough Feather had marked some sort of obstruction on his map, but indicated nothing about an opening.

Carlson walked the entire length of the deadfall twice before he spotted it: a little opening, near one granite wall, that grew wider as one penetrated the mass of limbs and debris. Obviously it had been ingeniously designed by local Indians.

Carlson was a big man, with muscles heavily bunched around his back and shoulders. It was a hard struggle at first as he wriggled past the opening. But he quickly wormed his way through the leafy tunnel and stepped out on the other side.

Coming face to face with his enemy Matthew Hanchon!

The Cheyenne had been rattling the deadfall on the other side of the trail at the same time Carlson was emerging from his side. Each man's noise had covered the other's.

"You!" Carlson shouted, blood surging into his face. A moment later he was clawing at the snap on his holster.

Touch the Sky seized the throwing ax in his sash and whirled it even as Carlson's revolver cleared the holster. The officer leaped back just in the nick of time, the ax slicing past his face and missing by only inches. The leap threw him off balance, and he fell awkwardly into the dead brambles and limbs.

Touch the Sky's rifle and lance were back on his pony, well behind him. He raced at Carlson, jerking his knife from its sheath, and leaped on him as the big man struggled to stand back up.

Carlson was a trained wrestler. As soon as the Cheyenne landed on his back, he went forward with the motion, then tucked and rolled clear of his attacker. A moment later he had whirled and connected a solid right fist to Touch the Sky's jaw.

A bright orange light exploded inside the Indian's head. But he knew if he let himself pass out now, he'd never wake up again. Rallying strength he didn't even realize he had, he raced at Carlson full-bore and head-butted him, knocking the soldier back into the deadfall for a second time.

Before he could get clear of Carlson, however, the cavalry officer brought a vicious knee up into the Cheyenne's groin. As the Indian fell forward, pain knocking the breath from him, he latched onto Carlson's neck with both hands and squeezed with all his strength.

Carlson was pinned at an awkward angle, one arm trapped by a dead branch. His face bulged as the young brave squeezed harder and harder, then it turned purple, then black. The whole time, he beat at the Cheyenne's head with his free hand, adding bruises and cuts to the knife slashes already disfiguring him.

Touch the Sky refused to let go, his mouth a grim, determined slit. Finally, moments before Carlson would have passed out, the officer's twitching death agony dislodged a huge limb from the top of the deadfall. It crashed down on top of them, knocking the Cheyenne clear.

Touch the Sky wasn't hurt by the limb. But by the time he made it to his feet again, Carlson had his .44 in his fist.

The Cheyenne knew a moving target was difficult to hit with a short-iron. He immediately burst back down the trail toward his pony and his rifle, zigzagging to make a difficult target.

Shots rang out behind him, bullets whanged past his ears. On the run, he snatched his rifle from its scabbard and then leaped for the side of the trail, even as another slug nipped at his heels.

For now it was a standoff. Carlson was crouched inside the deadfall, Touch the Sky in the bushes beside the trail. His pony was around a slight bend now, having shied back at the first shots. But he would be killed trying to mount and ride out. The Cheyenne had a rifle, which was a slight advantage.

Until he heard it: the sounds of more gunfire as Carlson's men answered his shots, letting him know they were on the way.

Touch the Sky hunkered down, snapping off a round now and then just to keep the soldier honest. But he knew he had to somehow get out of this death trap, and quick.

Concentrating on the sounds as men approached the other side of the deadfall, Touch the Sky failed to glance overhead. A sharpshooter from the unit had arrived ahead of the others and circled around through the rimrock. Now he was moving into position about 50 feet over the Cheyenne's head.

Only when the bolt of the soldier's carbine snicked home did Touch the Sky realize his danger. He glanced up, but too late. The soldier's finger had curled inside the trigger guard and was taking up the slack.

A second later there was a booming report, and the sharpshooter dropped dead from the rimrock, almost crushing Touch the Sky when he landed below.

"Brother!" Little Horse screamed, signaling from the rim of the opposite wall. He raised his shotgun to get his friend's attention. Some sixth sense had warned him to disobey his friend and follow him. "Fly like the wind now! I will cover you!"

With Little Horse's revolving-barrel, four-shot scattergun roaring over and over, forcing the soldiers to hunker down, Touch the Sky raced for his pony.

Chapter Eleven

"I don't get it," Lumpy said. "Wha'd'you mean, we ain't gunna meet up with Carlson after the heist? We always go to the shack and divvy up the swag with him."

Woodrow Denton was busy tucking horsehair braids under his Cheyenne headdress. He looked at Lumpy as if he were something he had just scraped off his boot.

"Is your brain any bigger 'n that bump on your neck? Now why would you *think* we won't be meeting him?"

"Cuz," said a man named Omensetter, "we ain't dealin' him in for this hand?"

All five of the disguised thieves sat their mounts in a little shortgrass clearing near the Milk River Road. Their rifles were balanced at the ready across the withers of their Indian ponies. By now the whites had gotten proficient at riding without saddles. Beaded leather shirts and fur leggings, the style of northern Indians, covered the skin that wasn't darkened with berry juice.

"Right as rain," Denton said. "We'll be going to the shack, but Carlson won't. Soldier Blue set this one up weeks ago. Since then he's got ice in his boots. His C.O. is still farting blood on account of how 'Injuns' aired out his wife. Carlson says no more Cheyenne attacks. But *I* say, he can go piss up a rope! There's going to be one more heist. This haul today will leave all of us in the Land of Milk and Honey."

"We talking gold?" Lumpy said.

"It will be soon enough. It's a freight wagon, and we're heisting the whole damned she-bang. It's loaded with good liquor, tobacco, and coffee, all bound for the sutler at Fort Randall."

"Hell," Lumpy said, "a wagon? Are you soft between your head handles? What need we got for such truck? We already smoke good Virginia 'baccy and drink top-shelf mash liquor. I reckon my coffee ain't fit for the Queen of England, but—"

"Lumpy," Denton cut in sarcastically, "if brains was horseshit, you'd have a clean corral, you know that? Of course *we* don't need the goods. The Blackfoot Indians need it. They need it so bad they're doing the Hurt Dance. Oh, do they want it."

"Blackfeet! *They* ain't got no gold."

"Neither does a beaver, numb-nuts. But what he don't carry in ready cash he's good for. The Blackfeet tribe is rich right now in good beaver plews. They'll give us every damn one of 'em for that wagonload of goods. Then we haul 'em to the trading post at Pike's Fork. The dandies in London are crying for their beaver hats. The price is up to two hundred dollars for a pressed pack of eighty furs."

"Hell, that shines fine by me," Omensetter said. "But the Blackfeet are no tribe to fool with. How do we get them plews without them gettin' our topknots?"

"I know a war chief named Sis-ki-dee. Leads his own band, palavers English real good. He's a crafty son-a-bitch and keeps one hand behind his back. But he's smart nuff to know when the wind's blowing something his way. I've dealt with him before."

"The hell we do with the freight wagon?" Omensetter said. "Where do we store the goods until we can swap 'em?"

"You ever knowed ol' Woody to leave any loose ends? I already checked behind the shack. There's a watershed gully runs right down to the road. She's bumpy, but not so steep a wagon couldn't make 'er. Carlson won't be coming around here for at least a few days. He's off in the field killing Cheyennes. We unload the stuff into the shack, then wait until nightfall and douse the wagon with kerosene. Nobody'll spot the smoke after dark."

"All right," Lumpy said. "But what about when Carlson comes back? Won't he get wind of this raid?"

"Does asparagus make your piss stink?" Denton

said. "Of course he'll get wind of it. He's a soldier, ain't he? But 'zacly what will he do about it? Go to law, for Christ sakes?"

Denton had been wanting to part trails with Carlson anyway. True, it had been useful having a soldier in his camp. But Denton realized this little piece of cake had finally gone stale. The newspapers were full of outraged editorials about the savage aboriginals. It was only a matter of time before the U.S. Army—treaty limitations be damned—sprang a nasty surprise on them.

So why cut the officer in on this last haul? Besides, Carlson wasn't putting all his cards on the table either. He was nursing some private grudge against the Cheyenne tribe. During that last raid, Denton had heard Carlson busting caps behind them, had heard riders. But when he'd asked him about it later, Carlson had lied. Denton had no desire to put his bacon in the fire just to help a man settle a private grudge.

Omensetter had broken cover to ride down and scout the road. Now he came racing back.

"She's a-comin'. I see a dust plume on the horizon."

Denton nodded. "Remember, this is our last strike in these parts. We're taking the entire team and wagon. That means no one can survive this one—they'll get too close a look at us and guess our game. That means we kill the driver and the guards. We'll leave the bodies behind with their hair raised and Cheyenne arrows in them."

War Party

Touch the Sky and Little Horse knew better than to flee south toward Shoots Left Handed's camp. That would be like leading wolves to a warren. Better to escape in the opposite direction, diverting the soldiers. Now that Carlson had recognized his archenemy, they knew he would lock onto their scent.

The two friends joined up while fleeing down the backside of a steep ridge. Arrow Keeper's surefooted ponies managed to find footholds that mules might have missed.

But Carlson's mountain troopers too rode excellent mounts—half-wild mustangs from the high country, broken in by Indian trainers. For some time they stayed right behind the fleeing Cheyennes.

And as they did, the two braves realized they were up against a dangerous new breed of Bluecoat fighter. Paleface soldiers were always dangerous down on the open plains, waging the style of warfare suited to their formations and training. But usually, in this kind of rough terrain, shaking white pursuers was a matter for Indian sport. But not now. Now they were forced to ride full out, barely outrunning the bullets behind them.

Several times they were forced to assume the defensive riding position invented by the Cheyenne tribe: They slid far forward, clinging to their ponies' neck with their legs. The rest of their bodies were tucked down under the horse's head, out of sight. If a pony were shot, this position allowed the Cheyenne to kick off and away from the falling weight.

"Brother!" Little Horse shouted as they raced along a rocky spine, looking for a way to cross to the next swayback ridge. He pointed down into a small valley to their right. "Look!"

Touch the Sky's glance followed his friend's finger. A moment later he tasted the bitter sting of bile rising in his throat.

Dead Blackfeet and horses lay sprawled everywhere, thick with blue-black swarms of flies. Touch the Sky, who had grown up next to Fort Bates, recognized the brass casings of artillery shells. His face went cold and numb when he saw that several of the bodies had literally been blown apart. Carrion birds were everywhere, forming a living, moving carpet of black over everything.

It took him a moment to realize why the birds kept turning their heads to expel something from their beaks. Then he understood. They were spitting out lead slugs—some of the bodies, incredibly, had been shot dozens of times.

The two braves locked glances. Little Horse was clearly dumbfounded—what kind of powerful hair-face magic could open a man up like a dressed-out deer?

But there was no time to wonder. Behind them, a sharpshooter's carbine cracked, and a bullet whizzed past so close to Touch the Sky's ear that it sounded like a bumblebee.

Despite the tenacious mustangs pursuing them, the superior training of Arrow Keeper's ponies eventually began to show. But as the distance between Carlson's men and them opened up, Touch the Sky saw that fatigue was sapping Little Horse.

"Brother!" he said. "Make for the wagon road. These ponies are keen for speed. It is dangerous to ride in the open, but we must open the distance and then you must rest."

His words rallied Little Horse. "I have ears for this. As you said when I lay in the tipi, brother. Today is not a good day to die! *Hi-ya, hii-ya!*"

Touch the Sky's hunch proved right. Arrow Keeper had indeed blessed these ponies with great speed.

Not since his great chase across the plains after Henri Lagace, the white whiskey trader, had Touch the Sky felt a pony fly on the wind as his blood bay did now. Nor did Little Horse's buckskin lack heart for the run. Once they gained the wagon road, both animals tucked their ears back and forced their riders to hang on dearly.

Carlson and his men were nowhere in sight. Touch the Sky's plan was to find a good shelter for Little Horse, then backtrack and find the soldiers. If they planned to resume the ride to Shoots Left Handed's village, Touch the Sky would have to somehow divert them—even if he had to make himself a target again for Carlson.

They flew over a rise, rounded an S-turn, then drew their mounts in when they saw what lay beside the road.

Three white men, riddled with bullets and arrows—flint-tipped Cheyenne arrows. All three had also been scalped. The attack had been recent, for the pungent smell of spent cordite still tainted the air.

"Our make-believe Cheyennes are back," Little Horse said.

"All the merrier for us," Touch the Sky replied, "if we are caught down here. Do not forget a Bluecoat pack is on our heels, buck! Now we ride."

But despite their urgency to escape, they were soon forced to stop once again, amazement starched into their faces.

The two young braves had left the road and were threading their way across a long pine slope. They were slipping across the treeless swath of a watershed when Touch the Sky spotted the danger just in time to halt his friend in the trees.

Well up the slope, the watershed veered hard right and disappeared behind the treeline. Just to the left of this point stood a run-down shack. A huge wooden wagon stood in the watershed nearby, wheels chocked with hunks of wood. Several men worked steadily at hauling goods from the wagon into the shack— men dressed in Cheyenne garb, though most had removed their fake braids and went bareheaded. One was bald as a newborn, another had an odd lump on his neck. All looked like hard-bitten killers. The two Indians could clearly make out where the white men had dyed their skin.

"Finally," Little Horse said, keeping his voice low, "we meet the white dogs who would stain our sacred Arrows. I am for them now, buck! I count five. We have killed more."

"We have, but not so many as are still closing in behind us, brother. And do not forget how close this place is to the soldiertown called Fort Randall. If you want to catch an eagle, you never climb up to its nest. Nor is this any place to be attacking hair-faces when you still lack red blood. Maiyun will be with us enough, buck, if we are alive tomorrow when Sister Sun claims the sky."

Little Horse frowned at these words at first, still keen to send their enemies under. Then, as weariness began to make his limbs feel like stones, he saw the truth of his friend's words.

"It is clear Arrow Keeper had a hand in shaping you," Little Horse said admiringly. "As you say, now we ride."

"As for these," Touch the Sky said, nodding up the slope. "I feel we may lock horns yet. For now, let us remember that Shoots Left Handed's camp is the next place Carlson will hope to find us."

"Then, brother, let us not disappoint so worthy a foe. Let us be there to welcome him!"

Chapter Twelve

While Touch the Sky and Little Horse were fighting for their lives up north in the Bear Paws, their enemies back at the Powder River camp continued to tighten the net of danger around them.

Even as the white thieves were loading stolen goods into the shack, the Headmen were meeting in council. The common pipe had been smoked and laid aside. Now the Headmen and warriors—the only ones permitted to attend at council—sat in a semicircle listening to an important report from the Bull Whips named Stone Jaw and Angry Bull. Though he was the youngest brave present, Two Twists was allowed to attend. This was in recognition of his bold fighting against the Kiowa and Comanche during the last buffalo hunt.

"Fathers and Brothers!" Angry Bull said. "You have heard me recite my coups. Now have ears for these words. Several sleeps ago, Lone Bear, leader of our Bull Whip troop, sent me and Stone Jaw to the Valley of the Greasy Grass. Our mission was to scout the wild pony herds. Our riding out was approved in council."

Black Elk had instructed Angry Bull to include this last sentence. Now Black Elk slyly watched Arrow Keeper. But the old shaman merely held his seamed face impassive, revealing nothing.

"When we arrived, we found paleface soldiers on maneuvers there. They were accompanied by turncoat Pawnee scouts. It was a mighty battle force."

Though this news made many uneasy, it drew few surprised reactions. The Valley of the Greasy Grass offered excellent graze and was a favorite spot for the hair-face war games.

"And we saw two Cheyennes counseling with them. Eating their contaminated food, drinking their strong water."

A shocked silence met this remark. Now Two Twists understood what was on the spit. A tight bubble of anger rose inside him.

"We dared not ride close enough to study them well," Angry Bull continued. "True it is, they might have come from any band. But one was tall, the other short and solid. They rode a blood bay and a ginger buckskin."

Everyone present knew by now that Touch the Sky and Little Horse were missing. Again, Two Twists watched all eyes focus on Arrow Keeper. Everyone present also knew those were his ponies. But his face was still an inscrutable leather mask.

Like Two Twists, Arrow Keeper read the sign clearly enough. Touch the Sky's enemies knew better than to swear they had recognized him—this could be verified by making them take an oath on the Medicine Arrows. Even the most corrupt Cheyenne feared such serious blasphemy. But so long as they fell short of swearing to their claim, they were immune to such a demand.

The council lodge had been buzzing ever since Angry Bull's announcement. Now Chief Gray Thunder folded his arms—the command for silence.

"Stone Jaw," Arrow Keeper said, cleverly directing his question to the more stupid of the two, "you both got close enough to make out a tall and a short Cheyenne?"

"Truly, Father, we did."

"And you also got close enough to make out a ginger buckskin and a blood bay?"

"As Angry Bull said, Father. All this was clear enough."

"Then tell me, Bull Whip, which Cheyenne rode the buckskin?"

Stone Jaw gaped stupidly, glancing toward Angry Bull for a clue.

"The tall one," Stone Jaw said.

"The short one," Angry Bull said at the same moment.

Arrow Keeper smiled, nodded, glanced at Gray Thunder. "Remember what you just heard."

Now Arrow Keeper directed himself toward the leader of the Bull Whips.

"Lone Bear, I have never seen your troop's pony string look finer. Why send scouts out now?"

Lone Bear shrugged, already well rehearsed by Black Elk and Wolf Who Hunts Smiling. When he answered, he used the new tone Wolf Who Hunts Smiling had assumed with Arrow Keeper—not one of respect, but of condescending amusement, as if Arrow Keeper were senile.

"Father, since when can Cheyennes have too many good ponies? This is truly an embarrassment of riches."

Several braves laughed at this. Now Wolf Who Hunts Smiling spoke up.

"Clearly, Arrow Keeper does not believe Angry Bull speaks straight-arrow. Our old shaman can resolve this mystery for us quickly enough. Where did he send Woman Fa—that is, Touch the Sky and Little Horse?"

Again all eyes were trained on Arrow Keeper. He could reveal the mission. But such information would alert Touch the Sky's enemies as to the direction from which he and Little Horse would return—assuming they survived their ordeal up north. Then they would face death as they rode in.

"It is a sorry day," Arrow Keeper announced, his voice solemn as he stared at Wolf Who Hunts Smiling, "when Cheyennes would conspire to stain the sacred Arrows by shedding the blood of their own."

Now he looked at Angry Bull. "You say we

should listen to you here today because you have recited your coups. True it is, you have counted coup. Do you think *he* has not? Who here now saw him count first coup at the Tongue River Battle, which saved our hunting grounds from the white land-grabbers?"

"I did, Father," said Tangle Hair, a Bowstring soldier.

"You and many others, buck! You and many others also saw him savagely beaten when *this* one"—Arrow Keeper nodded toward Wolf Who Hunts Smiling—"lied and accused him of chasing buffalo over a blind jump during the hunt. This same two-tongued Cheyenne who also bribed an old grandmother to lie about a vision, causing Touch the Sky to hang from a pole for hours."

Now Arrow Keeper's accusing stare also took in Black Elk, Swift Canoe, and Lone Bear.

"It is a sorry day," he repeated, "when Cheyennes speak in a wolf bark against their own. Have not the red men enough enemies from without? Do they need to kill each other? Now look here, how this Wolf Who Hunts Smiling pretends to swell up with 'righteous' anger. Do not let him place a lie over your eyes, Headmen—he is a base plotter, and has the putrid stink of the murderer on him!"

Now Arrow Keeper stood up, stiff kneecaps popping, and turned his back on the proceedings. A moment later he did something no brave present had ever seen him do—without conducting the usual prayer and the closing smoke, he clutched the long clay pipe to his chest and simply walked out.

War Party

As Arrow Keeper had wisely foreseen, his abrupt exit from the lodge completely disrupted the careful ritual of tribal law. Chief Gray Thunder was forced to immediately suspend the council without taking further action. Otherwise, the Headmen might have voted with their stones—sentencing Touch the Sky to death or banishment.

Two Twists was in a welter of nervous excitement. For the rest of the day he stayed within sight of Black Elk's tipi, impatiently waiting for the brave to leave. Finally, Black Elk selected his favorite pipe and strolled across the camp clearing to join his brothers at the Bull Whip lodge.

Trying to will himself invisible, Two Twists slipped up to the entrance flap of Black Elk's tipi.

"Honey Eater!" he called out. "I would speak with you!"

The words were barely spoken before the flap was lifted and a slim, pretty arm reached out to tug him inside. Honey Eater had been sick with worry ever since Black Elk returned from council, smiling smugly.

"Two Twists! I know it went hard for Touch the Sky," she greeted the young buck. "Has he been banished or . . . worse?"

"Nothing yet, sister. But it went hard for him indeed, and only Arrow Keeper's playing the fox has delayed a terrible fate. Now the time has come. Touch the Sky's enemies are keen for his vitals. Now I think it is time to approach Arrow Keeper about our Star Chamber plan."

She nodded, realizing it was true. Black Elk should be gone for some time. The greatest risk was getting caught entering or leaving Arrow Keeper's tipi. But by no means could *he* come *here*—not now.

"Let us go then," she said, taking Two Twists' hand for courage. "I am frightened, Two Twists. We must be careful. Black Elk will kill both of us if he finds out."

Thus alerted to Black Elk, they set out. Honey Eater was right that Black Elk would be gone for some time. What she failed to watch for was Swift Canoe's hawk eye. Black Elk, suspecting something, had instructed him to watch his tipi while he was gone. Now Swift Canoe saw Black Elk's wife and Two Twists slip out, hand in hand, and hurry across toward Arrow Keeper's tipi.

Now the bull will roar, Swift Canoe assured himself as he hurried off toward the Bull Whip lodge.

Arrow Keeper listened patiently, as still and quiet as the totems in front of the council lodge, while Two Twists summed up everything he had seen and heard.

"Away from camp, Wolf Who Hunts Smiling is sewing seeds of hatred in the younger warriors, Father. He speaks against you and the other elders, calling you soft-brained fools who play the dogs for hair-faces. He plans to take over the tribe. And because Touch the Sky is your loyal ally, Wolf Who Hunts Smiling is eager to kill him."

Two Twists fell silent. Now Honey Eater told about all she had seen—about Black Elk's plotting with Angry Bull and Stone Jaw before they rode out, as well as his secret meetings with Wolf Who Hunts Smiling and Swift Canoe.

When both had finished speaking, Arrow Keeper pulled his blanket tighter around his shoulders. Finally he spoke.

"Perhaps I may try to approach the Star Chamber. But this thing troubles me: that we have no proof, nothing we may offer them to place in their sashes. Rebellious speeches by Wolf Who Hunts Smiling, furtive meetings between Black Elk and his Bull Whip brothers, to the Star Chamber these are things of smoke.

"Remember, young ones. The Star Chamber is the Cheyenne's court of last resort. These are good men, but they are very reluctant to override the Council of Forty. If only we had some proof we could swear to. But we are up against some influential men in the tribe."

Honey Eater could not fight back the crystal dollops of teardrops running down her eyelashes.

"Father, my own husband is one of the murdering cowards who plans to do him in! I am worried enough about whatever trouble you sent him to face. Now I have to worry what new storm will engulf him when he returns."

"You and I both, little daughter. But the berry will not ripen before its time. For now you and

Two Twists must keep what you know close to your hearts. The three of us must stay silent and watch or listen for the proof we need. One solid word we may swear to on the Arrows. Meantime, give nothing away by word or glance, or I fear it may go hard for more than just Touch the Sky."

Grainy twilight had descended on camp by the time Two Twists and Honey Eater slipped out of Arrow Keeper's tipi.

The flap had no sooner settled behind them when strong arms encircled both of them. Hands were clamped over their mouths, and they were dragged roughly through the bushes and trees until they were well away from the main camp.

The two hapless victims could recognize their tormentors in the twilight: Black Elk, Wolf Who Hunts Smiling, Swift Canoe, Stone Jaw, Angry Bull, a few other Bull Whip soldiers.

Angry Bull held Two Twists against a tree, his mouth still covered, while Stone Jaw thumped his chest and stomach hard with his stone war club. Honey Eater winced, her screams cut off, as Two Twists flinched hard with each blow. Surely some ribs had been broken by now! But Two Twists defiantly kept the pain from rising into his face.

The Bull Whips formed a gauntlet, each trooper in turn passing by the tree and hitting or kicking Two Twists, striking him in the head with their bows, flailing him with their knotted-thong whips. When they had finished with their sport, Angry Bull turned him loose. Two Twists collapsed to the ground, breathing hard, bloody foam bubbling out of his nostrils.

"Report this to anyone," Black Elk declared, "and this is what we Bull Whips will say, to the last man: that we caught my squaw letting this youth bull her! Neither one of you will ever live with the tribe again."

But clearly, the main brunt of Black Elk's wrath was to be Honey Eater. Too late she realized he had overheard every word she spoke to Arrow Keeper.

"Brothers," Black Elk said to the rest, even as he pulled his whip from his sash and unwound it, "return to the lodge now. I have business alone with my woman."

The rest exchanged glances, nodding. This was right. This was Black Elk's business, to be settled privately. Swift Canoe dragging Two Twists, the rest disappeared into the gathering darkness.

"Now, you Cheyenne she-bitch," Black Elk said, drawing his whip back for the first lash, "the husband you called a 'murdering coward' will cool the blood that boils for your randy buck!"

His whip cracked, and Honey Eater felt an incredible pain as white-hot fire licked at her shoulders. Again, again, Black Elk's whip sang its lethal song. But not once, as her blood stained the earth and pain tensed her body like a bow, did the proud Honey Eater cry out or beg for mercy.

Chapter Thirteen

Touch the Sky had guessed correctly. So long as Seth Carlson thought there was the slightest chance of catching him and Little Horse, he would delay his advance toward Shoots Left Handed's camp. Now and then, as they topped a rise, they could glimpse the soldiers still dogging them.

But this game could not go on forever. The two Cheyennes were in unfamiliar country, an area swarming with blue-bloused enemies. And blessed with magic or no, their ponies would soon be played out. Nor did Little Horse possess the stamina for a sustained hard ride so soon after his wound. Already, the constant bouncing and jostling had started fresh bleeding. Eventually Carlson would hunt them down. Then he would return to his original mission of exterminating Shoots Left Handed's band.

"Brother," Touch the Sky said when they stopped briefly to water their ponies in the Milk River, "Arrow Keeper always says you must pop a blister before you can get rid of it. We have been running scared before a stampede. Now let us play turnabout and take the bulls by the horns."

Little Horse looked exhausted. A network of deep lines covered his face, and his normally copper-tinted skin was pale.

"How, brother? You saw that Blackfoot camp. These are some strong bulls on our tail."

Touch the Sky pointed toward a huge rock formation just across the river. Pawnee Killer had explained that it was a familiar landmark known to Indians as Wagon Mound because of its resemblance to the canvas-covered "bone shakers" white settlers traveled in.

"Pawnee Killer has a sentry up there. The same lookout who sent the mirror signals when the whites attacked. We are going to find him. Pawnee Killer said to let him be our mouth if we have messages."

"Find him? But why, brother?"

"Because it is time to play the fox, not the rabbit. Now hurry, while enough sun remains to send our message."

They forded the shallow river and pointed their bridles northeast toward Wagon Mound. While they rode, Touch the Sky explained his plan. The only map Carlson could possibly have, he explained, would be a crude pictograph done by that Ute scout. That meant distances and locations would not be precisely marked. Growing up all of his life next to Fort Bates, Matthew had learned this was one of the chief complaints officers had about their Indian scouts—the red man's vastly different notions of time and space.

Touch the Sky's plan was a strategy he recalled from the recent buffalo hunt in the Southwest. The two Cheyennes would indeed lead the soldiers to camp. But not to the camp of Shoots Left Handed—rather, to a false camp set up further down the trail. Clearly the murdering palefaces always attacked in the night, and with poor visibility it might not take much to fool them. Once the soldiers attacked it, the Cheyenne warriors would close in on them from behind. With luck, the element of surprise would counterbalance those terrifying Bluecoat weapons.

It was a desperate plan, full of risks, and both youths knew it. But at least it *was* a plan. As things stood now, they were simply waiting to die.

They reached the rock formation. After they signaled to him with the familiar owl hoot, the sentry popped up from behind a pile of scree and raised his lance in greeting.

They explained the urgent situation and their plan. Then the sentry, a brave named Eagle on His Journey, scaled up to the top of the rocks and broke out his fragment of mirror. Touch the Sky and Little Horse waited nervously below. If this message was not received, all hope was lost for the camp.

"They are signaling back!" Eagle on His Journey finally called down to them. "They will do as you say. They will meet you at the place you mentioned and bring the things you said."

Now both braves knew that time was their worst enemy. There was no way to double back toward the mountain hideout without Carlson and his unit knowing about it soon enough. They had to get well enough ahead of the soldiers again to leave time for setting up the camp and getting into position.

As they mounted again, Touch the Sky scattered some rich tobacco as an offering to the Four Directions.

Then he offered a brief prayer to Maiyun, the Good Supernatural, asking him to once again turn their ponies' feet into wings.

Their shadows gradually lengthening in the westering sun, the two Cheyennes deliberately rode straight into the teeth of their enemy.

Carlson spotted them as they emerged from a cutbank near the river, aiming due south into the Bear Paws. In classic Cheyenne style, they divided and raced wide around both flanks, also dividing Carlson's force.

And despite the superior training and breeding, these cavalry horses were also burdened with heavy ammunition and other field gear. As the chase once again began to lead upward, they began to tire more rapidly than the Indian ponies.

The sun dropped lower, became a dull orange ball just above the horizon. The trail wound ever upward, crossing steep cliffs and climbing torturously winding pinnacles.

"Brother!" Little Horse cried finally, "I see them ahead!"

The pathetic-looking group of underfed, discouraged braves waiting for them disheartened Touch the Sky and made his plan seem worthless and foolish. They had gathered just past a sharp turn in the trail, in a clearing under a ridge similar to the one further up where camp was located. There were only about 20 of them, only a few clutching rifles—beat-up British trade rifles, many of them held together with patches of buckskin.

"Brother," Little Horse said quietly as they drew close, "the children back in our camp could whip this group using just their toy bows and willow-branch shields."

"You speak the straight word, buck. However, no amount of hoping will turn them into Southern Cheyenne Dog Soldiers. So we had best work quickly and well. You shall soon hear enemy horses snorting behind you."

The braves had already started setting up the false camp. Several tipis were still going up, taking much longer to assemble than to take down. Fires had been built, and even two skinny nags—their ribs showing like barrel staves—had been tethered nearby in a patch of graze. Limbs and bushes had been stuck here and there to approximate human shapes. The size of the camp would not be immediately apparent in the darkness. Masses of bushes well back from the fires already appeared to be more tipis.

Touch the Sky stepped back for a critical

glance. It was a hasty job, but it would have to do.

"You warriors," he said. "The best opportunity for attack will not last long. You must seize it when it comes, and understand, it will not come twice. The moment the soldiers open their attack and move in, we must strike from the rear.

"You braves with rifles! One bullet, one enemy! We will have at most only a few heartbeats in which to act. That quick strike must be devastating enough to send them scattering. If they regroup, count upon it, you will experience a firestorm of bullets like you have never seen."

Down the trail, Little Horse was keeping watch. Now he called up to them. "Here they come, brothers, now the fight comes to us!"

"You know where to go and what to do," Pawnee Killer told his men. "The Arrows have been renewed, you are painted and dressed. If you must die, you are ready."

The Cheyennes knew that all talk had gone as far as talk could go. The rest now was in the doing. Silently, their faces grim, they moved back into the rocks and bushes circling the camp clearing.

Darkness fell, so black it seemed like vengeance. Yet Touch the Sky welcomed that blackness. Now the fake Cheyenne village took on a realistic appearance in the flickering, shadow-mottled light. The limbs and bushes did indeed appear to be vigilant Indians.

The fires burned lower as the night advanced. The soldiers, knowing full well the Indians knew they were coming, would expect the braves to be in rifle pits or behind breastworks in front of the tipis. The women and children would be expected to huddle inside the tipis. So Pawnee Killer had made sure his men built a line of log breastworks too, on which the enemy could concentrate their fire.

The soldiers waited well into the night, letting a damp chill settle over everything. Clearly they hoped to lull the Indians into thinking the attack would not come until tomorrow.

Touch the Sky had taken up a position behind a boulder just to the right of the trail. Little Horse hid to his left, Pawnee Killer to his right. When Little Horse imitated the clicks of a gecko lizard, Touch the Sky knew the sharp-eared brave must have heard signs of an advance. Sure enough, moments later Touch the Sky saw dark shapes massing toward them out of the night.

Touch the Sky had warned the others. Even so, when the first artillery rockets burst down onto the camp, many of the Cheyennes thought they were staring into the face of the Wendigo himself.

A tipi exploded, flaming bits of buffalo hide and wood flying everywhere. The explosion suddenly spilled a ghostly orange light over everything. The horses nickered in fright. Another explosion, another, and the ground seemed to be heaving all around Touch the Sky. Rock fragments rattled through the trees, sounding like a powerful hailstorm.

The Indians stared, fascinated in spite of their

bone-deep fear. What was this thing with a flaming tail so like a fire arrow? But no fire arrow could explode just above the ground like that in deadly bursts of powerful bad medicine.

A Gatling opened up, chattering its mad, lethal message of death. One of the horses was cut down, blood pumping from dozens of holes. Entire trees were fragmented as the bullets raked them.

Through all this, the Cheyennes held their discipline, waiting for the Bluecoat charge. It came only moments after the Gatling opened up.

Screaming their savage kill cry, the riflemen poured into camp to finish off the job.

"Hi-ya!" Touch the Sky screamed, *"Hii-ya!"*

Even before he realized how he had been duped, Seth Carlson had spotted uneasy signs. Why weren't the warriors singing their battle songs to rally their courage? Now, as his surprised men whirled to confront a rear assault, Carlson caught sight of his enemy Matthew Hanchon.

The officer was just in time to watch the Cheyenne squeeze back the trigger of his Sharps. A moment later, the soldier just to Carlson's left crumpled to the ground, his carbine flying from his hands.

Little Horse surged forward, adrenaline-quick despite his weakened state. His four-barreled scattergun roared and roared, dropping a soldier each time. In the precious few seconds before the soldiers could regroup, Pawnee Killer and other warriors also scored lethal shots and blows.

Panic swept through the paleface ranks like a

prairie fire in a windstorm. These were hard men accustomed to killing. But most of them were sharpshooters, experts who killed at a long distance from the safety of secure positions. They were not experienced in close combat, nor eager to confront Indians defending their very homes. After all, the soldiers were only in it for two hot meals a day and a straw mattress full of bedbugs back at Fort Randall.

"They've bamboozled us!" someone shouted. "We're surrounded!"

"Stand and hold, you white livers!" Carlson shouted, even as he drew a bead on Hanchon.

But a moment before Carlson's carbine fired, the Cheyenne leaped forward and used his tomahawk to kill a soldier who was about to plug Pawnee Killer from behind.

The attack had turned into a rout. Soldiers fled back down the trail, some abandoning their weapons. Ulrich was unhurt but unable to fire his Gatling because the private feeding ammo into the hopper had just caught a Cheyenne arrow flush through the eye. Watching the man flop on the ground like a fish out of water and screaming piteously, Ulrich had abruptly joined his comrades who were retreating at breakneck speed.

Suddenly Carlson too realized the danger he was in. Most of his unit was already gone. He was eager enough to confront Hanchon, all right, but only on his own terms. And being taken prisoner in a Cheyenne camp was no fate for a soldier—especially one who had already shed so much Cheyenne blood.

So far Hanchon had failed to spot him. Carlson decided to keep it that way, for now. But this was only a battle, not the war. Carlson knew that if he returned to Fort Randall without destroying these Cheyennes, his Army career was over. Worse, this campaign now was probably the last opportunity he'd ever have to kill Hanchon. And letting that red bastard live would canker at Carlson for the rest of his life, destroying the peace of his old age.

No. This tonight, he told himself again, would not be the end of it.

Clutching his rifle at a high port, he ran back down the trail and joined his panic-stricken unit.

Chapter Fourteen

Woodrow Denton's deal with the Blackfoot war chief Sis-ki-dee went off without a hitch.

Soon after the goods heisted from the freight wagon were stored inside the cabin, Sis-ki-dee and his braves showed up after dark with many travois piled high with beaver plews. The goods were exchanged, and now the shack was crowded with furs.

"Soon's we can lay hands on a wagon," Denton told his men, surveying the tall stacks of plews, "we'll haul the whole shitaree to Pike's Fork. Dragging them damned travois would be harder 'n snappin' snot off a fingernail."

"Hell," complained Lumpy, poking at his goiter, "why'n't we just use the damn freight wagon when we had it? It was plumb stupid to torch it."

Denton shook his bald, fish-belly-white head, clearly disgusted. Today the men wore their usual clothing. The "Cheyenne" raids had been pushed as far as they'd dared push them.

"Lumpy, what have you got inside that skull o' yourn? Rabbit turds? Did you swear-to-Jesus think we was gunna ease up to the trading post in a heisted wagon? One that's got 'Milk River Stage and Freighting Line' writ in big one-foot letters on the sides?"

From outside the shack, Omensetter's voice called, "Look sharp, fellahs! Somebody's comin'!"

"Shit," Denton said, suddenly all business. "You two," he said to Lumpy and the man named Noonan, "stay inside with the plews. Anybody comes through that door, you don't know their face—bust caps. You, Bell, come on out with me."

"It's Carlson!" Omensetter added.

"Worse luck!" Denton said. "The hell's he doing back so soon? He's spozed to be sendin' Injuns to the Happy Hunting Ground. If he's been to the fort and heard about that last raid, we can stand by for a blast."

Despite his bluff talk earlier, Denton feared Carlson's temper and didn't want him to know about that last strike just yet—not while this shack was full of plews. For one thing, Carlson would insist on dividing the profits up six ways himself—whereas Denton had plans to pull stakes and rabbit with the entire amount.

"All right," Denton said, changing his plan. "We'll all get the hell out of the shack now. We were just leaving, is all, after having us a little fun with a Mandan squaw, unnerstand? Let me do the talking."

Carlson had ridden about halfway up the watershed clearing when he spotted Denton and his gang, just now mounting. He hailed them, roweling his mount and riding quickly up to meet them.

"There you are!" he said, clearly impatient from searching for them. "I'm glad I found you, but what're you doing here? I told you not to come around here unless we had a job to pull."

His words secretly reassured Denton. The officer must not have heard about that last raid yet.

"Ahh, you know how it is, Soldier Blue." Denton winked. "Me 'n the boys here, we was just plantin' carrots in a little Mandan gal. She give all five of us a little fofaraw just for a half bottle of liquor. Too bad you wasn't here, coulda drained your snake."

Carlson wrinkled his face in disgust. The notoriously promiscuous Mandan women were known for being venereal-tainted. But obviously he had something more pressing on his mind than the morality of heathen women.

"The hell you doing in these parts?" Denton said. "I thought you was up in the Bear Paws giving grief to the red Arabs."

Irritation sparked in Carlson's eyes as Denton's remark forced him to relive the humiliating debacle of that raid on the false Cheyenne camp. Badly shaken, encumbered by wounded, his unit had deployed back to their field camp at the Milk River. The wounded had been transported back to Fort Randall. But Carlson refused to ride back through those gates himself until that Cheyenne camp—and now, Matthew Hanchon—were reduced to a bad memory.

There was one serious problem: manpower.

The botched assault had resulted in a dozen deaths and as many wounded in the Army ranks. The men were demoralized and nervous about returning to finish the job when the unit wasn't up to strength. But Carlson wasn't about to return to Fort Randall and request replacements. That meant also explaining how he'd ended up with a dozen men dead yet no enemy scalps.

"I want to hire all five of you," Carlson announced bluntly. "To help my unit kill Cheyennes. I'll pay you in good color. You know I'm good for the dust. You helped me earn it."

This took Denton by surprise, as did the sudden urgency of Carlson's tone. He had been about to laugh at the crazy suggestion. Now he thought better of it.

Why not? he thought. Why the hell not? Clearly Carlson had not been back to the fort and didn't want to return yet. The longer he put it off, the better for Denton. At least until that shack was empty again. Besides, this was a chance to make some more money while getting a little target practice in.

"Maybe. We talking rough weather ahead?" Denton asked.

"Only for the Cheyennes. For us, it'll be a turkey shoot."

"Well, if that's so, how's come you need us?"

"The more the merrier. I don't want to take any chances."

Denton studied the officer closely, noting the obsessed glaze to his eyes. This was a man on a personal vendetta. He wanted to kill some poor unlucky sonofabitch with a desire as intense as hell-thirst. He was so eager to kill him, in fact, that he was taking out insurance by adding mercenaries to his regulars.

Carlson pulled a fat chamois pouch out of his tunic. It was heavy with gold dust. "How about it? This one here's got brothers back in my quarters."

Denton stroked his chin, eyeing the gold. "What say, boys? Do we let daylight into some Innuns?"

One by one, they all nodded.

"Captain," Denton said, "'pears to me you just enlisted five more Injun killers!"

The victory over the paleface soldiers was sweet and heartened Shoots Left Handed's people. But the Cheyennes did not boast, as Indians do after a victory.

True, they had captured a few carbines and now had more rifles. But the false-camp ruse was only a way of adding a little length to the tether, not a decisive victory. The soldiers would be back, vengeance on their minds, and they would not fall for that trick again. Touch the Sky and Little Horse knew it as well as everyone else in the tribe. Next time the Bluecoat death company would know right where to attack, and the tipis wouldn't be empty.

Despite this grim truth, Touch the Sky's successful ploy had at least raised his status as a warrior in the eyes of the rest, if not as a shaman. Though they said little openly, Pawnee Killer, White Plume, Chief Shoots Left Handed, and the rest had decided that Arrow Keeper had picked a competent enough brave to send—only, the old man had erred in his judgment that the youth's medicine was strong.

Therefore, intent on preparing for the battle of their lives, most of them ignored Touch the Sky when they realized he was once again invoking magic to protect the tribe.

The decision had come to Touch the Sky while talking with Little Horse in their tipi. They had returned from the raid on the false camp and Touch the Sky had applied a fresh willow-bark dressing to his friend's wound.

"Brother," Little Horse said, "I saw Carlson's face during the attack. I swear by the sun and the earth I live on, it was like beholding the face of the Wendigo! He is crazy-by-thunder and lives to kill Cheyennes. Those guns that spit many bullets, the flaming arrows that explode—this power in the hands of such an insane hair-face frightens me."

"There is no place to run now, buck, and as you say, this Carlson lives and breathes to make sure we do not. This next attack, it will be the last one needed."

"We have renewed the Arrows," Little Horse said. "We have left our sacrifices. There is no more medicine to help us, brother."

But Touch the Sky was silent at this, recalling

something Arrow Keeper had told him once during a sojourn to Medicine Lake. There was a special prayer-offering ceremony which was seldom invoked because it was so grueling for the shaman. It was known as the Iron Shirt Song, and its medicine was said to be the most powerful that a shaman could conjure up. If successful, it could turn enemy bullets to sand or make them fly wide.

Tragically, however, the price of failure was the death of the shaman. And very seldom—almost never, Arrow Keeper insisted—did the ceremony succeed. And even when it did succeed, this could only happen after great suffering on the part of the medicine man.

But it had come down to this, finally, and Touch the Sky realized: *This* was why Arrow Keeper had sent him. It was the ultimate test of his faith in Cheyenne magic, in the Cheyenne High Holy Ones. It was the ultimate test of his belief in himself as a shaman.

As Arrow Keeper had wisely foretold, it would not be just his skills as a warrior which would save them this time—if they were to be saved at all.

"Brother," he said to Little Horse. "There is more medicine. But I tell you now, you will not like it. Do you have faith in me?"

"Will a she-grizzly fight hard for her cubs?"

"Good. You will need faith in me. Will you do what I tell you, no matter how hard your nature rebels against it? Will you swear this thing on your honor?"

Despite his confidence in his friend, Little

Horse hesitated before he finally nodded. This was serious business indeed. "I will, brother," he said. "I have seen the mark on you, and I believe."

"Good. Now hurry. The sentries at Milk River have flashed the warning. Carlson's unit has taken to the Bear Paws again. And this time he is accompanied by the white dogs who ruined our tribe's name."

Little Horse soon deeply regretted his promise to cooperate with Touch the Sky.

First, following Touch the Sky's instructions, they had gone to a remote spot just past camp in a thicket. There, Touch the Sky and Little Horse fashioned two poles out of saplings. The poles were extended between a pair of nearby tree forks, about a foot and a half above the ground.

Little Horse's face grew grim when Touch the Sky stretched himself between the poles, face down, and instructed his friend to lash his wrists and ankles to the poles securely.

His back arched like a bow, Touch the Sky said, "Good work, brother. Now, see that pile of rocks over there?"

Little Horse nodded.

"Start piling them on my back. I will tell you when to stop."

Little Horse hesitated, looking at him askance.

"Did you give your word or not?" Touch the Sky demanded. "Do as I say, buck!"

"Brother, this is—"

"Little Horse! If you love me as your brother,

153

you will not say another word. You will do as I tell you, and know you act for the people."

That settled it. One by one, Little Horse carried the rocks over and placed them on his friend's back. When Touch the Sky's breathing began to be forced, Little Horse stopped.

"More," Touch the Sky told him. "Keep piling them on."

The pain distorting Touch the Sky's face also twisted Little Horse's. Fighting back tears of pity and frustration, the game little warrior added rock after rock, until it seemed there was no place left to pile them.

He could not believe that his friend wasn't crushed by now. Each breath Touch the Sky took cost him an agony of effort. A group of children had spotted the strange spectacle and raced back to tell the adults. They just shook their heads, too worried about the upcoming attack to care about more supernatural foolishness. Secretly, some of the braves resented this young fool for weakening himself this way—he would be useless in the fight.

"Brother," Little Horse finally said, "I fear your back will break. Is that enough?"

Touch the Sky's words seemed to be spoken through several layers of thick cloth, the pain was so intense. "Are there more on that pile?" He could not lift his head now to look.

"There are, brother."

"Then pile them on, buck, pile them on!"

Chapter Fifteen

Carlson dropped back until he was riding abreast of the corporal named Ulrich.

"You've got a replacement on the Gatling? Someone to feed rounds into the hopper?"

"Yes, sir. Hank Jennings from the first squad. He's a mite soft in the brain, I reckon, but he keeps a cool head when it comes down to the nut-cuttin'. It wasn't easy, sir, finding a volunteer after what happened to ol' Smitty. Him catchin' a arrow flush in the eye like that, hell, the men figger it's bad luck on this gun."

"Yes, that was a bad break," Carlson said vaguely, his mind on nothing but the pleasure of killing Matthew Hanchon.

"Hell, like I tell the boys, sir. It wasn't the arrow in his eye what kilt ol' Smitty. It was when the sumbitch poked through into his brain!"

Ulrich slapped at his saddlehorn, laughing

again at his own wit. Carlson, the son of a wealthy Virginia plantation owner, detested the man, knowing he was from hardscrabble trash back in Missouri. But he forced himself to smile anyway.

"Good man. Make that gun hum, and maybe there'll be some sergeant's stripes in it for you. I promise, this next attack will be just like the raid on the Blackfoot camp."

Carlson had been forced to some tricky diplomacy since that defeat the other night. Morale was dangerously low at Fort Randall, due in large part to the poor leadership of Colonel Orrin Lofley. So Carlson had wisely avoided berating his men's cowardice in retreating as they had.

Instead, he'd appealed to their sense of pride as the Indian-killing elite. Every newspaper in the country, he assured them, would soon be singing the praises of the First Mountain Company. Wiping out that Cheyenne camp would restore law and order to these parts—and faith in the U.S. Army.

The addition of the five hard-bitten civilian riders had also heartened the men—especially when Carlson spread the false rumor that they had ridden with the famous Indian fighter "Big Bat" Pourrier. To this rumor the first sergeant added another: that the plug-ugly sonofabitch with the bump on his neck was a famous writer, one writing a book on heroes of the American frontier.

Now Carlson sensed it going through the ranks: a collective, fire-breathing will to give these upstart Cheyennes a comeuppance they'd never forget. Men who had bolted a few nights earlier were now determined to return with Cheyenne ears and skulls as war trophies for their grand children.

Now, symbolizing the tight esprit de corps of the entire unit, the sergeant belted out a training chant familiar to all of them:

> We're marching off for Sitting Bull,
> and *this* is the way we go . . . !

As one the entire unit responded:

> Forty miles a day
> on beans and hay
> in the Regular Army, *oh!*

Like a sinewy, many-headed death machine, the double columns wound their way steadily higher into the Bear Paw Mountains.

Little Horse refused to leave Touch the Sky's side during the grueling sacrifice. He was afraid his friend would suffocate, the heap of rocks finally crushing his lungs.

But staying with him, seeing this unbelievably painful suffering, was as hard as leaving him.

"Brother," he said at one point, "this has gone on long enough! Maiyun is stern, perhaps, but not cruel. He has heard your prayer by now. Now let me remove the rocks."

Touch the Sky only shook his head, too short of

air and strength to say anything. It felt like a huge stallion had plopped down on him. Each breath was a hard struggle and rattled in his throat like pebbles caught in a sluice gate. Otherwise, he might have told Little Horse that it was not a question of Maiyun hearing him—it was a question of deserving such powerful and direct attention from the Great Spirit that ruled infinity, not just Cheyennes. *A shaman must suffer*, Arrow Keeper had told him once, *to be deserving*.

While he waited, Little Horse tended to his battle rig. He cleaned and oiled his shotgun, and wiped every last grain of sand or speck of dirt off the few remaining shells. He pulled a whetstone from his possibles bag and sharpened the single edge of his knife. He used tightly stitched buckskin to reinforce a weak spot in his shield.

Throughout the squalid camp, the remaining braves were doing the same. Women, elders, children old enough to walk—all were armed with some kind of weapon, be it nothing but a pointed stick or a pouch filled with sharp rocks.

Pain was etched deep into Touch the Sky's face, adding ten winters in age. His tautly corded shoulder muscles strained against the incredible weight of the rocks. Surely his back must break at any moment!

But behind it all, Arrow Keeper's voice kept reminding him: The Iron Shirt magic was the most powerful medicine of all. A shaman, in contrast, was a mere speck of humanity. For those very reasons, the sacrifice to invoke the Iron Shirt protection must be almost superhuman.

As badly as he wanted this terrible pain to end, he must endure more for the sake of his people.

The sun was only a blushing afterthought on the western horizon. Carlson halted his men at the site of the first attack. The area was still covered with debris, mocking the soldiers' failure.

"We rest here," Carlson said. "We eat, we make our last equipment check. Then, well after dark, we make our final movement to the camp. Any questions?"

No one had any. Denton and his men stood in a little group to one side, mildly amused at all the attention they were getting. Denton figured it was funny as all hell, how all the soldiers kept making sure Lumpy knew how to spell their names—hell, Lumpy couldn't read or write his own name! But clearly they planned on impressing him with their killing power.

Carlson glanced overhead at the darkening dome of sky.

"Full moon tonight with plenty of stars. Moving in on them will be easy as rolling off a log. This time, count on it—you won't be shooting at sticks and bushes."

Well after dark, Little Horse's voice cut through the wall of red, burning pain. His words were calm, completely devoid of fear.

"Brother, the outlying sentry has sounded the wolf howl. Our enemy is upon us. Soon comes the attack. Now the rocks come off whether you will it or no."

At first Touch the Sky noticed no difference as his friend tossed the rocks away. Then, gradually, cramped muscles began to expand toward their normal shape. Little Horse knelt to untie the rawhide thongs which lashed his friend to the poles.

Touch the Sky's first attempts to rise to his feet were pathetic. Little Horse thought of a new foal trying to struggle up from the ground.

"Brother," Touch the Sky said finally, "I fear you will have to help me."

Little Horse had wanted to help his friend, desperately. But a warrior's pride was a delicate thing, and he knew it was better to let his friend try on his own first. Now, gently, he helped Touch the Sky to his feet. But still the brave could not straighten up completely nor walk except in a drunken shamble.

"Where are your weapons?" Touch the Sky asked him.

"I have given them to a brave who had none."

"But how will you fight?"

"I will not fight," Little Horse said.

Touch the Sky paused to look at him, waiting.

"I have heard," Little Horse said, "that an act of faith can sometimes give wings to a prayer. Sometime earlier, I heard you chanting the bullets-to-sand prayer. I know that you plan to stand where you will draw the first bullets. Brother, unarmed, I will stand beside you. If we are meant to live, we will live together. If we are meant to die, we will cross over together. I have spoken, and will brook no discussion from you. You are too weak to fight me, so accept it."

This was a long speech for Little Horse, and both braves knew it.

"All right, then," Touch the Sky said. "Then help me walk now, brother, for I confess I need your strength."

"You have it, Cheyenne."

Touch the Sky knew he must be a strange and disheartening sight to the others as he limped into camp, Little Horse supporting him. Already he could hear women sobbing from the tipis, many singing the death song and saying good-bye to their children.

Most of the men ignored them as they advanced forward of the breastworks and took up their position at the only approach to camp.

Another wolf howl sounded, this one much closer.

The Bluecoat death company was closing in.

It can't be true, Carlson told himself.

Again he cautiously eased his head around the huge boulder and glanced toward the camp, aglow in moonwash. But it was true.

Matthew Hanchon and his sidekick stood side by side, unarmed, presenting themselves as easy targets!

Carlson estimated the range. They were well out in front of the main camp, maybe only about 100 yards away. With his carbine, they were already dead.

He dropped back and spread the order: Nobody must shoot at the two bucks. Anybody else, but not them. They were his. Commence fire, he added, only when they heard him shoot.

Carlson returned to the boulder and laid his carbine across it to steady his aim. He centered the notched sight on Hanchon's bare chest and slipped his finger inside the trigger guard.

Breathe, he told himself.

Relax.

Aim.

Take up the slack.

Squeeeeze . . .

His carbine cracked loudly, splitting the stillness of the night. Immediately, all hell was unleashed as his entire unit unleashed every bit of firepower they owned.

Even in all the earsplitting din, Carlson frowned.

Hanchon hadn't moved a muscle. But how could he have missed? He had qualified easily on targets up to 500 yards away.

The Gatling was chattering to his left, the artillery rifles belching smoke and fire to his right. Carbines cracked all around him. He could hear Denton's French bolt-action rifle making its solid reports.

Carlson drew another bead on Hanchon, fired, missed again.

He frowned.

A line of braves had surged forward from the tipis, and Ulrich raked the line with a sweeping pass of the Gatling. Behind the braves, tipis shredded, limbs broke, and objects lying about camp rolled and bounced as bullets struck them. But not one brave went down.

"Ulrich!" Carlson screamed. "You idiot, *aim!* You're burning good ammo!"

"Aim?" Ulrich shouted back. "Hell, I'm shootin' right into their bellies!"

Even as Carlson watched, an artillery shell thumped into a tipi. There was a terrible explosion, a shower of fire and sparks. But every occupant of the tipi ran out into the night, screaming and crying but completely unharmed.

Ulrich had seen it too. His eyes met Carlson's. Neither man was quite able yet to grasp exactly what was happening. But the first dull tickle of alarm moved up their spines.

"Keep firing that weapon!" Carlson growled. "Or I'll shoot you on the spot for mutiny!"

The braves of Shoots Left Handed's camp knew about Touch the Sky's special medicine ceremony. But none gave it any credence or even a second thought as the Bluecoats opened fire.

It was Pawnee Killer who first began to wonder why Touch the Sky and Little Horse were still standing.

Then, when he saw a limb exactly behind Touch the Sky suddenly snap as one of Carlson's bullets caught it, he realized—the bullet could not have hit that spot without passing through the Cheyenne. Yet there he stood, the worse for his ordeal, but clearly unwounded.

Screaming the war cry, Pawnee Killer led

his braves forward. Touch the Sky and Little Horse watched, their faces elated in the eerie flickering light of the flames and artillery explosions, as they washed over the first line of soldiers like a raging river obliterating a line of anthills.

Touch the Sky watched Pawnee Killer sink his lance deep into the soldier firing the Gatling. Other Bluecoats raised hideous death cries as Cheyenne blades and bullets found easy targets. Yet they could not score a kill against the Indians even at point-blank range.

One soldier drew his Bowie knife and lunged at White Plume. White Plume made no effort to move, yet a moment later the soldier's knife was embedded in the tree just to White Plume's left. Calmly, White Plume pulled the soldier's own pistol from his holster and killed him with it.

By now the entire camp knew that Touch the Sky's big magic had worked the ultimate miracle. Women and children raced forward from the burning tipis, snatching up guns, knives, hatchets. They rushed at the soldiers with open impunity.

A soldier held his gun to a little boy's head and fired. A moment later the boy smashed the soldier's cheekbone with a rock.

Carlson, his face a frozen mask of unbelieving shock, snatched up the Gatling from the dead Ulrich and set the tripod down so the gun was pointed directly at Touch the Sky and Little Horse. Hank Jennings had been killed, but not before he had stuffed the hopper full of bullets.

Carlson cranked the gun over and over, spraying a nonstop stream of lead at the two Cheyennes. He cut down an entire stand of cypress saplings behind them, but they still stood staring at him, their eyes mocking.

Only then did Carlson truly understand.

At first, like his men, he had been puzzled, then mystified.

Now, as Touch the Sky and Little Horse began to advance toward him, he felt something else: a cold, numbing panic that was building in his limbs and made the hair on the back of his neck stiffen.

He noticed it for the first time: The light in this village, it was unnatural, almost ghostly. A luminous white light, oddly different from moonlight, seemed to glow around Hanchon.

This place wasn't right.

He threw down the gun and bolted at the same time that Denton and his men reached the same conclusion. As those five tore off from the left flank, riding hard toward the trail, Touch the Sky cried to Little Horse, "Turn the gun for me, I can shoot it!"

Little Horse quickly did as told. Wincing at the incredible pain as he knelt, Touch the Sky led the five riders with his barrel, then cranked the Gatling into life. The entire tribe had the satisfaction of watching all five men fly from their mounts like clay targets lined up on a limb.

But even as the soldiers bolted in panic and a resounding cheer rose up from the camp behind him, Touch the Sky realized: Once again Seth Carlson had slinked away under cover of darkness.

Chapter Sixteen

To the vastly outnumbered red men, all victories against soldiers were sweet. But the remarkable triumph of Shoots Left Handed's long-suffering Cheyennes had no comparison in the history of the Shaiyena people. Even before the battlefield had been picked clean, an elder had named this encounter the Ghost Battle, and the name stuck.

Word of Seth Carlson's ignominious defeat was not long in getting to the journalists. This topped Orrin Lofley's debacle with the Hunkpapa Sioux—at least Colonel Lofley's men had killed a few women and children. How, the writers screamed in derision, did a trained officer take such heavy losses without one confirmed kill?

The men's absurd story about Indian magic ruining their aim was only more proof of their drunken lack of discipline. The War Department stepped in quickly, immediately transferring Lofley and Carlson to the Dakota Territory and bringing in a new commander with a reputation for successfully negotiating with the red nations.

All this happened quickly, and Touch the Sky learned of it just as quickly from circular fliers and the newspaper published in Great Falls, copies of which scouts brought back from the trading post at Pike's Fork. The new changes gave Shoots Left Handed and his people the one valuable thing they needed: time. Time to get stronger and time to flee out of the mountains, back down onto the plains where this horse-loving, roaming band belonged.

The mass, panicked exodus of the soldiers had left a windfall of weapons and supplies for the tribe. The soldiers had been provisioned for quite a stay in the field, and most of their rations had been discarded in the rout. Now the tribe had hardtack, dried beans, bacon, coffee, and other goods.

Shoots Left Handed was able to wink at Pawnee Killer and the others. Had they not questioned his loyalty to Arrow Keeper, his steadfast belief that this Cheyenne youth possessed strong medicine indeed in spite of appearances?

"Already the babies have stopped crying and sleep through the night," the old chief told him several sleeps after the Ghost Battle. Even the eye covered by his milky cataract seemed to glimmer with new hope. "Soon the tribe will move south toward the Powder River hunting grounds, where we belong. The day of the red man has reached its final hours, and we must join one more time as a people before we follow the buffalo into the last hiding places."

Touch the Sky and Little Horse would gladly have stayed longer and traveled south with them. But as soon as he had recovered enough strength and movement to ride, Touch the Sky said his farewells. Trying not to worry about Honey Eater was useless. Her image seemed to be painted on the back of his eyelids.

The night before they rode out, they were feted as heroes and saviors of the tribe. But Touch the Sky found it embarrassing when several of the elders timidly approached and reached out cautiously to touch him, as if verifying he were solid flesh and bone. When he was asked to bless several objects with medicine, he politely refused, saying he was not yet a shaman.

"Brother," Pawnee Killer said as the two visitors mounted to ride out, "I confess that, at first, I was skeptical of you. Now I see that it was only unfortunate timing, this thing of finding Goes Ahead's body right after the Renewal. You are both straight-arrow Cheyennes and the finest warriors this battle chief has ever known."

"We will meet again at the annual dances," Touch the Sky told him. "Your ponies will be fat then, your camp full of dogs again as it should be."

Nearby, a group of children were throwing stones at birds. Now they shrieked with excited laughter when one of them nicked a finch and it flew angrily away.

"Brother," Pawnee Killer said, "I have not seen a sight like this for many sleeps. You are both warriors, so I will not embarrass you with too much gratitude. Just know this, and know it forever. It was *you* who gave those children back their lives. For this, I swear my own life to you. You have but to send word, and Pawnee Killer's lance will go up beside yours."

These words, spoken simply and from an impassive face, nonetheless swelled both braves' hearts with pride. But the final tribute came as they were about to round the bend that would cut them off from view of the camp.

"Brother!" Little Horse said, pointing back behind them. "Look!"

Touch the Sky did look. The children were playing another game. Two of them stood side by side while a group of them pretended to be soldiers, trying to shoot them with their stick rifles. The two unarmed children merely smiled smugly back as soldier after soldier threw down his rifle and fled in panic.

"They are refighting the Ghost Battle," Little Horse said. "I have a feeling it is going to be won many times over from this day on."

But despite the elation of this sweet victory, both youths knew they were riding back to an uncertain fate.

Their enemies had been conspiring against them even before they left; their secret departure from camp had only given their enemies more fuel for the fire. So they were not at all surprised by the hostile stares of many as they finally rode in, late one morning, and turned their ponies loose in the common corral.

"At least," Little Horse said as they crossed toward Arrow Keeper's tipi, "we were not arrested as we rode in. This means no decision was reached against us in council."

Touch the Sky barely heard his friend, so nervous was he about spotting Honey Eater again. So far he had seen no activity around Black Elk's tipi. At this time of the morning, she might well be visiting with her clan sisters.

Then he spotted Two Twists, and his face went cold.

The youth had been savagely beaten. He was leading his pony to the corral, obviously favoring his sore midsection. A mass of bruises covered half of his face.

His eyes met Touch the Sky's. Two Twists then glanced hurriedly around before crossing to greet his friend.

"Touch the Sky, I am glad to see you alive! But I fear you will not remain that way long around here. Your enemies are more determined than ever to—"

"Never mind that, little brother," Touch the Sky said grimly, still eyeing the bruises. "I know who did this to you. Tell me I am wrong."

Two Twists glanced at the ground, saying nothing.

"He will pay for hurting you, buck. But now

tell me this, for it is the only thing else I need to know. *Look* at me, Cheyenne!"

Two Twists did.

"Honey Eater?" was all Touch the Sky had to say. And the glint of confirmation in the youth's eyes was all he needed to see.

Vaguely, as if in a thick fog, Touch the Sky was aware of both Little Horse and Two Twists trying to stop him, trying to change his mind as he bore down on Black Elk's tipi. He felt them pulling on his arms, shook them off as easily as flies.

He reached the tipi, grabbed the entrance flap, threw it back.

Black Elk was gone. But Honey Eater was inside, brewing yarrow tea in a clay pot over the firepit.

Her eyes flew up, startled, when the flap was lifted. She expected to see Black Elk, back from his Bull Whip lodge.

Instead, the man she loved with all her heart stood staring at her—staring at the deep whiplash cuts in her face, on her neck and shoulders and back, clearly visible above the neck of her doeskin dress.

Touch the Sky said nothing. He met her eyes with his for several heartbeats. Then he lowered the flap and turned around, his mind bent toward one purpose only: finding Black Elk and killing him.

But it was Arrow Keeper who now stood in front of him, not his enemy.

"Listen to me, little brother, and place my words close to your heart. I know that you are now setting out on the course of murder. If you murder a fellow Cheyenne, the Arrows will be stained forever. You can never be a shaman with the blood of your own on your hands."

Touch the Sky shook his head. "Father, I swore an oath to Black Elk during the buffalo hunt in Comanche country. I told him, after he beat Honey Eater, that I would kill him if he touched her again. I swore this oath on my medicine bundle."

"And do you see *this* bundle?"

Arrow Keeper pulled a coyote-fur pouch out from under his blanket. "These are the sacred Arrows. I have hoped that someday soon, when I am gone to the Land Beyond the Sun, you would be the Keeper. Go kill this dog now, and you kill those hopes too. For you have made an oath on *this* bundle too, Cheyenne. An oath to keep them forever sweet and clean. Now make your choice."

With that the old shaman turned his back and walked to his tipi.

Miserable, Touch the Sky stood there, unsure what to do. Conflicting emotions warred inside his breast.

"Brother," Little Horse said in a low voice, "look behind you."

Touch the Sky did. Honey Eater had lifted the flap of the tipi and was watching him. Despite the cuts, her beauty again took his breath away.

And now, rising steadily louder, they all heard it: the young girls in their sewing lodge. They were singing the song about a Cheyenne girl and the noble brave who loved her—a song about suffering and patience and bravery and goodness triumphing over evil in the Life of the Little Day.

It was a song about *them*. And as Touch the Sky watched her, Honey Eater crossed her wrists over her heart: Cheyenne sign talk for love.

He crossed his too. And he understood what her eyes were begging him to do right now: She was begging him to make sure that satisfying his manly pride was worth being banished forever from the tribe. Because that also meant lifetime banishment from her.

He made up his mind. Speaking loudly enough for Honey Eater, Two Twists, Little Horse, and even old Arrow Keeper to hear him, Touch the Sky said, "Let us turn our ponies out to graze, brother, then bathe and sleep. It is good to be home!"

CHEYENNE

DOUBLE EDITION
JUDD COLE

One man's heroic search for a world he can call his own.

Arrow Keeper. A Cheyenne raised among pioneers, Matthew Hanchon has never known anything but distrust. The settlers brand him a savage, and when Matthew realizes that his adopted parents will suffer for his sake, he flees into the wilderness—where he'll need a warrior's courage if he hopes to survive.

And in the same volume...

Death Chant. When Matthew returns to the Cheyenne, he doesn't find the acceptance he seeks. The Cheyenne can't fully trust any who were raised in the ways of the white man. Forced to prove his loyalty, Matthew faces the greatest challenge he has ever known.

___4280-0 $4.99 US/$5.99 CAN

DOUBLE EDITION
They left him for dead, he'll see them in hell!
Jake McMasters

Hangman's Knot. Taggart is strung up and left out to die by a posse headed by the richest man in the territory. Choking and kicking, he is seconds away from death when he is cut down by a ragtag band of Apaches, not much better off than himself. Before long, the white desperado and the desperate Apaches have formed an unholy alliance that will turn the Arizona desert red with blood.

And in the same action-packed volume....

Warpath. Twelve S.O.B.s left him swinging from a rope, as good as dead. But it isn't Taggart's time to die. Together with his desperate renegade warriors he will hunt the yellowbellies down. One by one, he'll make them wish they'd never drawn a breath. One by one he'll leave their guts and bones scorching under the brutal desert sun.

_4185-5 $4.99 US/$5.99 CAN

Dorchester Publishing Co., Inc.
P.O. Box 6640
Wayne, PA 19087-8640

Please add $1.75 for shipping and handling for the first book and $.50 for each book thereafter. NY, NYC, and PA residents, please add appropriate sales tax. No cash, stamps, or C.O.D.s. All orders shipped within 6 weeks via postal service book rate. Canadian orders require $2.00 extra postage and must be paid in U.S. dollars through a U.S. banking facility.

Name_____
Address_____
City_____State_____Zip_____
I have enclosed $_____ in payment for the checked book(s).
Payment <u>must</u> accompany all orders. ☐ Please send a free catalog.

COMANCHEROS

Touch the Sky heard the loud, fast clicking of a lizard. He thought nothing of it until another lizard answered the signal. What happened only a few heartbeats later shocked all the Cheyenne braves into frightened immobility.

Yipping their battle cries, the Comanches and Kiowas poured up from the canyon and leaped out onto the plains, racing straight at the startled Cheyennes.

"Fly like the wind!" Touch the Sky shouted to his companions.

An arrow flew past Touch the Sky's head so close he felt a hot wire of pain crease his ear. He glimpsed Little Horse on his left and Two Twists and Tangle Hair on his right, all bent low over the necks of their ponies as they drove them on. Behind them, rolling thunder welled closer as their enemy gained on them, bringing the promise of an agonizing death closer and closer...

WAR PARTY

Touch the Sky spotted it first.

A brief glint of military brass, emerging from the opening of that coulee on their left. And even as he spotted it, his newly emerging shaman's sense told him it was too late.

Only a heartbeat after Touch the Sky made the discovery, Little Horse too spotted the officer.

"Brother, leap!"

But it was too late to jump out of the way. Even as Carlson pressured the last fraction of trigger resistance, Little Horse lunged off his pony and into the path of his friend.

Touch the Sky felt his face drain cold when, with a sound like taut rawhide bursting, the bullet struck Little Horse in the chest.